Dedicated by Alex Kendrick and Stephen Kendrick to:

Joshua, Anna, Catherine, Joy, and Caleb Kendrick—This book is evidence that God can do far more than we could ask or imagine. We trusted God for this story, and He amazed us with the results! He is faithful and trustworthy! We love you.

Sherwood Baptist Church—May God continue to give you vision, passion, and fruitfulness beyond your expectations. Your love and support for these movies and novels is priceless! May they continue to reflect your faith in Christ and bring glory to Him!

Dedicated by Eric Wilson to:

Robert and Maxine Mart—from armed service, to seaside car accidents, to beautiful oil paintings, you've been there guarding and inspiring me through the years . . . I'm glad I married into the family.

Neil and Blanche Monaghan—from mechanical knowledge, biblical study, and good old Irish blarney, you've invested in me since my childhood . . . I'm proud to call myself an in-law.

FLYWHEEL

Based on the original movie by
ALEX KENDRICK and STEPHEN KENDRICK

Novelization by ERIC WILSON

THOMAS NELSON
Since 1798

NASHVILLE DALLAS MEXICO CITY RIO DE JANEIRO

Published in Nashville, Tennessee, by Thomas Nelson. Thomas Nelson is a registered trademark of Thomas Nelson, Inc.

Thomas Nelson, Inc. titles may be purchased in bulk for educational, business, fund-raising, or sales promotional use. For information, please e-mail SpecialMarkets@ThomasNelson.com.

Publisher's Note: This novel is a work of fiction. Names, characters, places, and incidents are either products of the author's imagination or used fictitiously. All characters are fictional, and any similarity to people living or dead is purely coincidental.

ISBN 978-1-4016-8525-6 (repak)

Library of Congress Cataloging-in-Publication Data

Wilson, Eric (Eric P.)
Flywheel / novelization by Eric Wilson ; based on the original movie by Stephen Kendrick and Alex Kendrick.
p. cm.
ISBN 978-1-59554-522-0 (softcover)
1. Automobile dealers—Fiction. 2. Used car trade—Fiction. 3. Automobiles—Conservation and restoration—Fiction. I. Kendrick, Stephen, 1973– II. Kendrick, Alex, 1970– III. Title.

PS3623.I583F58 2008
813'.6—dc22 2008005554

Printed in the United States of America
11 12 13 14 15 RRD 6 5 4 3 2 1

Prologue

FIFTEEN YEARS LATER

TODD

My dad's eyes are closed. In the candlelight of his birthday cake, his mouth twitches with a hint of glee, and a lifted eyebrow squeezes the wrinkles on his forehead. His hair is thinning, and his goatee and mustache are streaked with gray. We're here, in mid-May, celebrating his fiftieth.

"Jay, you made a wish yet?" Mom asks him.

He lifts a finger to his lips.

"You only get one," she says.

"C'mon, Dad," I urge. "The smoke alarm'll go off any minute now."

Smiling, he opens his eyes, aims that finger at me, and pulls the trigger. Standing on the other side of the table at the same dining nook where we used to share family meals, I feel like a little boy again, back when his impatient tones were my nightly companions. He could freeze me with a look. He could crush me with his silence.

Things have changed, thank God.

Yeah, well, that would be Dad and Mom's explanation. They raised my sister and me to believe in all that stuff—church on Sundays; Bibles under our arms; tithes dropped into the offering plate. All fine and good. Now that I'm out of college and trying to cover bills at my own art studio, I just don't have time for it. Sure, it's a solid basis for moral standards, but beyond that it seems sort of stodgy for my tastes.

Of course, Dad won't let it rest there, and I remind myself to avoid the subject at all costs. If it weren't for the changes I've seen in him, I would never even consider it.

"Todd," my mom calls. "You wanna help divvy out the plates?"

"Okay."

I spend the next few minutes distributing slabs of chocolate fudge cake. I haven't seen some of these relatives in ages, and I'm tempted to also pass out my studio business cards. The whole crew's here to watch Jay Austin tuck another year under his belt. Soon he'll be opening presents, and already I feel ashamed.

I brought no gift. I have no idea what to get the man.

Everyone else seems cheerful. My sister sits cross-legged on the carpet in front of the TV, chatting with a group of her teen friends. It's the same spot where my buddy Jeff and I used to play Battleship.

I head upstairs to my old bedroom. I think back on the life that was mine, before college, and debt, and my latest breakup.

I stand in the doorway, staring at the globe on the nightstand, at the same comforter I used to sleep under, and my old soccer trophies—for participation, but never for the coveted Most Valuable Player. It's not that I was bad at sports. They just weren't my forte.

Sometimes I wonder if that disappointed Dad. Faith was only a freshman when she became point guard for the high school varsity basketball team, and I hear that he goes to every one of her games.

"Hey, Todd."

I turn at my sister's voice. "Hey, how're you?"

"Dad says you're in town till Sunday."

"Yeah. Then it's back to Atlanta."

We stand in awkward silence. Faith's fifteen and I'm twenty-four. I was nine years old when she came along. She was a little chatterbox. From that time on, I let her have the spotlight while I focused on my writing and artwork.

"I'm glad you came for Dad's party," Faith tells me.

"Thanks."

"There's something I wanted to ask you."

I've seen that *trust me* look before. She's up to something. I raise an eyebrow and fold my arms, the same way our dad does.

"Can I move into your room?" she says.

"What? All my stuff's in there."

"I'll put it away carefully. Box it up. You know, label everything."

"What's wrong with your room?"

"I'm right above Mom and Dad's. My music's always too loud for them."

"Fine," I say.

"Really?" she squeals.

"Not like it matters."

"You sound upset."

"I'm fine. My room's not a shrine or anything. It's all yours."

"Only if you don't mind."

"I don't mind," I say again, a little annoyed.

"Thanks." She gives me a hug and skips back downstairs to her friends.

At the top of the landing, against the wall, an antique mahogany dresser is topped with a lamp, a stack of classic cloth-bound books, and an opened family Bible. As Faith rushes past, something flutters from the gilded pages to the carpet. A laminated, homemade bookmark.

For some reason it looks familiar. Those colors spark a memory.

As I bend to pick it up, I hear footsteps on the staircase. They're heavier than Mom's, less bouncy than Faith's. I say, "Hey, Dad."

"Be careful with that." He points at the object in my hand. "You know where it came from?"

I nod.

"Those're special memories. I'm hoping to write them down one day, but I'm just not creative like you. I wouldn't even know where to start."

"Mom could do it, couldn't she? Or Faith."

"Faith? She wasn't even born then."

"Oh, yeah."

Though Dad's been talking about this for years, he's never gotten around to it. I know it'll take hours for him to tell me his side of things, and I'm too overloaded at work to even think about helping him. True, though: I *am* here for the weekend. And now that I think about it, all I brought for his birthday is a cheesy—and I mean cheesy—greeting card.

"I didn't know you still had this," I say, contemplating the bookmark.

"You kidding, Todd? It means the world to me."

I shrug, thinking back to a time when Dad surprised our entire town. Maybe there's a story here after all, a tale of a father and son.

PART ONE

"The flywheel's outer ring gear has gotta mesh with
the starter's driving gear, or the engine
just ain't gonna crank over."

—MAX KENDALL, MECHANIC

Chapter 1

OLD TRIUMPHS

JAY

Jay Austin kept his expectations low.

A 1958 Triumph TR3A, with all original parts? What were the odds? The thing was nearly five decades old, and only a few thousand remained in existence. Jay could hardly believe one would be hiding here in the rich farmlands that surrounded Albany, Georgia.

He coasted along Newton Road, checked the scribbled directions in his left hand against a numbered mailbox on a red post, then turned onto the white-fenced property. Sturdy live oaks and pecan trees shaded his approach to a country home and free-standing workshop.

"Must be in there," he mumbled, peering through the windshield.

This wasn't the smartest idea. He knew that. He already

owed money to the bank, both personally and professionally, and he had a feeling his wife would be upset if she knew what he was up to.

Something about this particular vehicle, though . . .

His life revolved around cars. He owned Jay Austin Motors, a used-car lot, and he'd been captivated since boyhood by the growl of automobile engines and the smooth lines of a well-designed chassis. He still dreamed of the day he could ride in style, showing off his success without having to say a thing.

Success. Such an elusive word.

One man's pride could be another man's folly, and a fortune in the eyes of one might be play money to another.

The late-November sun illuminated a wide patch of sparkling emerald grass that skirted the workshop. A black dog slumbered in the warm rays. Jay saw an older gentleman descending the steps from the home, and he climbed out of the SUV.

"Good morning, Mr. Austin," the man said.

Jay strode past the dog and shook the extended hand. "Mr. Herr?"

"That's me."

"Good to meet you, sir."

"You ready to see the car?"

"You bet."

Jay scolded himself for sounding too eager. He knew that the moment a buyer revealed excitement, he lost negotiating leverage. Delayed gratification was the seam that held a buyer together. Once the seller located that thread of desire, once he gave it a tug, the buyer started to unravel.

"I'll meet you right there at the garage doors," Mr. Herr said. "I've gotta open the doors from inside."

Jay placed his hands on his hips and cooled his expression as he watched the old man stroll toward the building's side entry. He had to stay in the game. Stay focused. When it came to negotiations, he liked to be in the driver's seat.

TODD

Todd Austin knelt beside his bed, an open box of colored pencils by his pillow. It was cold up here in his second-story, corner room, and he had pulled on a turtleneck sweater with long sleeves. His dad wanted them to keep the heat down as low as possible because of rising electric bills.

"Got cold feet?" Dad liked to say. "Why do you think God made slippers?"

Todd always grinned at that. His mom always frowned.

Ignoring the chill in his fingertips, Todd focused his light-brown eyes on the drawing in front of him and filled in an area with orange pencil. He wanted this to be just right.

It was Saturday. A little later he and his mom would be stopping by the car lot, and Todd would give the picture to his dad. Already he could see his father patting him on the back, congratulating him on a job well done.

Wasn't that what every kid hoped for?

JAY

Jay stood outside the workshop and heard the sounds of Mr. Herr disengaging the locks. What would he find behind these tall, corrugated aluminum doors? Although he tried to conceal any facial expressions of excitement, his heart thumped against his ribs.

He thought back to his father's purchase of a '57 Chevy. The car had become a long-term restoration project for the senior Mr. Austin and Jay's older brother, Joey. As for Jay, he was a fifth grader at the time, a busybody, fumbling nuts and bolts and getting in the way.

Joey went on to dental school and became a stinkin' dentist, of all things.

Jay, meanwhile, was still trying to impress his father with cars and machinery. When Jay had moved his wife and son down from Atlanta to Albany, he'd even talked his father into investing the initial twenty grand, the down payment to get the used-car lot up and running.

"I'll do it, Jay," Mr. Austin had agreed. "On one condition. You don't quit on this project, you hear me? And you pay me back, in full, within three years. No interest, that's the good part. No excuses. That part'll be a little tougher."

Jay had nodded. "No excuses, Dad. You'll get your money, no problem."

Nearly two years later, Jay had yet to repay his father a dime.

From within the workshop, Mr. Herr pushed, and the large doors began to creak open. Jay helped swing the right door out, while Mr. Herr attended to the other. Inside, a white Triumph crouched in shadowed glory.

"That's it," Mr. Herr said. "The real deal."

The farm dog came alongside, wagging his tail in approval

of this antiquated mechanical wonder. The car's wide oval grille seemed to flash its teeth.

Jay found himself walking onto the oil-stained concrete pad, running his fingers along the British convertible's smooth front quarter panel. The TR3 was the first production car to come with standard disc brakes, and its fuel economy was excellent. To this day, these sports cars saw action in vintage auto races.

"You wanna see it out in the light?" Mr. Herr offered.

Jay made a show of looking at his watch.

"Won't take long, Mr. Austin."

"Uh. All right."

"Just slip it into neutral and we can push it together."

"The car doesn't run?" Jay acted surprised.

"I believe I told you that on the phone."

"Hmm. Maybe."

Mr. Herr adjusted his glasses. "That's why the price is so low."

"But, sir, I'm looking for a running vehicle."

"Let's just bring it out here where you can give it a good lookin'-over. I don't think you'll be disappointed. Little work, it'll be purring like a kitten. Body's in great shape. Interior's all original."

Jay shrugged, then pushed in the clutch and wiggled the gearshift. He saw that the black bucket seats had white piping. He liked the low dip of the door and the curvaceous lines from front to back. Chrome panels guarded the wheel wells.

Nice. Very nice.

Once he and Mr. Herr had rolled the sleek roadster out onto the grass, the entire vehicle seemed to come alive in the sunlight. Jay spent some time examining it and asking questions. He stood back and looked for flaws in the body. He saw none. The silver-spoked wheels glistened, and round headlights stared straight ahead as though confident of, almost impervious to, his final judgment.

"I like it," he told Mr. Herr.

"I knew you would."

"The price, though. It's too much."

"Actually, it's within the normal range for—"

"It doesn't run," Jay cut in.

"I don't know exactly what's wrong with it, Mr. Austin, but I drove it this summer with barely a hiccup. I'm sure it's something simple. I just don't have any—what do you younger people call it?—disposable income for the repairs."

"Any quotes on what it'll cost?"

"Haven't got that far."

Jay put his hands on his hips. "Your asking price is a thousand dollars too high. Maybe more. Who knows what kinda mess I'll be getting into?"

"So you do want it?"

"I don't wanna get ripped off."

"I'll knock off a thousand, best I can do."

"Thank you for your time, Mr. Herr. I've gotta get going."

"Okay, listen. Hold on. We'll go with twelve hundred off." The gentleman looked defeated, even desperate. "I've got prescriptions eatin' away at my Social Security, and I need to do something to cover my costs. It's nothing wrong with the car. It's *this* old engine"—he tapped his chest—"that's taken a beating."

"Well, you're still looking strong," Jay said. "And the car's beautiful, no argument there."

"It's yours, if you want it."

"Mr. Herr, I think you've got yourself a deal."

The older man reached out to shake on it. His eyes were watery with relief behind his glasses.

Jay wondered for a moment if those were actually tears of sorrow, but he pushed that thought away. He whipped out his company checkbook, glad to be helping the fellow out. This was a win-win situation.

Especially for Jay Austin.

TODD

Todd was finishing up his drawing. He added the last pencil strokes to the race car on the paper, outlining the number 71. That was the year his mother had been born, and Todd thought it was a nice touch.

Not that Mom was into roadsters or anything, but Dad loved cars, and Dad loved Mom, so it all made sense.

At least, that's what Todd hoped.

He lifted the picture, surveyed his work, and grinned in satisfaction. A few weeks ago, he had given his parents a colored sketch of a magnolia blossom. His dad had cracked jokes about this son of his drawing flowers, then ribbed his wife about the boy needing to be toughened up instead of pampered.

This picture wouldn't get that reaction, Todd decided. Earlier, he'd overheard his dad talking on the phone about a sports car he might buy today. Well, this artwork would be the perfect gift for the occasion. Todd couldn't wait to see the look on Dad's face.

Chapter 2

IMPRESSING THE LADIES

JAY

Jay eased along North Slappey Boulevard, checking his side-view mirror to verify the tow truck's presence behind him. The title had been signed, and the Triumph TR3 was now his. He would have his tune-up guy take a look, and with a little luck, they might have the thing running in no time.

Either way, at the price Jay had paid, the car was a steal.

Ahead, across from a CITGO gas station, he saw the sign for JAY AUSTIN MOTORS: "SUPER WHEELS . . . SUPER DEALS."

He still reveled in the sight of his name up there, a declaration of his plans to make his mark in this world—and beware the man who stood in his way.

Red, white, and blue pennants were strung from the corners of the lot to the top of a flagpole, where klieg lights perched.

Pickups, sedans, SUVs, and the typical clunkers were on display. Beneath an American flag that snapped in the breeze, the modular sales building bore large red letters that read WE FINANCE.

Jay led the tow-truck driver down a side street that gave access to the lot's garage and carport. A battery box and a bucket for washing cars sat at the mouth of the open service bay.

He parked his own vehicle, then directed the driver as the truck backed the TR3 into the service driveway. "All right, c'mon back. C'mon back."

Max Kendall, the on-site mechanic, left the vehicle he was working on. From the corner of his eye, Jay saw him lean a hand against the garage. Bespectacled Max was in a blue-collared shirt that bore his name in stitched lettering. His face was a map of wrinkles, each line leading to another story. He was shaking his head as though unsure what to think of Jay's latest project.

"Okay, whoa." Jay held up a hand for the driver. "Yeah, that's good."

The tow truck lurched to a stop. Max came forward to help, setting the hand brake on the convertible while the bearded driver hopped down to make sure all was in order.

"What do I owe you?" Jay asked the man.

"Forty's fine."

Jay had lived in south Georgia only two years, but he was still amazed at how different things were here. In Atlanta, a towing service would've doused him for three times this amount. Jay pulled a wad of bills from his pants pocket. He peeled off two twenties and relinquished them.

"There you go." He shook hands with the driver. "Appreciate it."

"No problem."

"Thank you."

The driver departed, and Jay circled to the back of the car. He admired the TR3's shimmering curves, then clapped his hands once in satisfaction.

Today was a new day. No more hanging of heads and dragging of feet around here. It was time to sell some cars, reel in some hefty profits, and head into a new year with some momentum.

This classic car would be his side project, an investment. His wife, Judy, would know nothing about it until the thing was in working order, and then she would be unable to resist the Triumph's allure.

Anyway, wasn't that how they'd first met? Looking at cars?

Judy had been handing out event flyers on the display floor of the Atlanta Auto Show at the World Congress Center. She was trying to earn some extra money to help with expenses at Georgia State University. Jay was cruising the rows of cars and spotted her Panthers sweatshirt. He was in his sophomore year at the same institution, which was all the excuse he needed to strike up a conversation.

They'd never crossed paths before that day, but the romance budded quickly. Jay was attracted by her soft caramel eyes, her bright smile, and the way she looked in jeans and that school sweatshirt. She told him later that she was charmed by his easygoing personality and the fact that he was comfortable to talk to.

Here, ten years later, the flames had cooled to mere embers.

Jay wasn't even sure he still deserved her.

Deep down, he longed to reignite the spark in Judy's eyes,

but life had a way of snuffing that out. Household expenses were piling, their spiritual lives were on different tracks, and in a few months Judy would be giving birth to their second child. Now that she was on maternity leave, her thoughts were centered on doctor visits, baby showers, and decorating the nursery for their new arrival.

Maybe, Jay figured, he could regain her attention with the TR3. She'd always loved convertibles.

He would wait until the car was up and running. Then one evening he would arrive in front of the house and sweep her away for a night on the town—dinner at the Plantation Grill, maybe a movie after a drive with the top down. She would be impressed by this deal he had finagled and its long-term investment value.

Jay smiled at the plan. How could a woman not respond to that?

"Now, what is *this*?"

The voice stabbed through his thoughts. He looked up and found his lead salesman, Bernie Myers, standing in the drive with a mocking stare. Bernie's stomach stretched his knitted vest in all directions. His name tag was pinned to the material, ready to spring free at any moment.

"This?" Jay put his hands on the hips of his pleated slacks and walked over to Max the mechanic. "It's a 1958 Triumph TR3, two-door coupe, four on the floor, twin carburetor, electric overdrive."

"How's it run?" Bernie asked.

"It don't. Least not yet."

"Figures."

"That's what this man is for." Jay clamped a hand over Max's shoulder and squeezed. Max's arms were folded against his chest, matching the firm line of his mouth. "He's gonna fix it up for me."

"Jay, I'm your tune-up man. I don't restore classic cars."

"Sure you do."

"I wouldn't bet on it."

"You hear that, Bernie? Sounds like our resident army vet is afraid."

With his eyes on the Triumph, Bernie gave no response. The roadster was a cat coiled on its haunches, ready to spring, soothed only by the brush of Bernie's hand along its door panel.

"I ain't afraid," Max said to Jay. "I just don't bend to your every whim."

"Hey now, I sign your paychecks."

"Is that whatcha call those?"

Jay smiled and slapped his mechanic's back. He knew Max was a kindhearted man beneath the sometimes-prickly exterior.

Max Kendall had seen combat in Korea, nearly overdosed on heroin, and outlived two wives. Just when he thought life was mellowing, he had been robbed at gunpoint downtown by the riverfront. The close-quarters shot to his stomach had missed his vital organs but left him with some permanent medical complications. His doctors said he was fortunate to have survived, and around the hospital he was known as Miracle Max, the name of Billy Crystal's cantankerous character in the movie *The Princess Bride*.

"Let Bernie fix the car for you," Max said.

"What?" Bernie exclaimed. "Whoa. I *sell* cars, and that's it."

"Nah," Jay said. "Don't try getting out of this, Max. You've worked miracles before. I know you can do it."

The mechanic grimaced. "And he says that every time he wants something he can't have."

BERNIE

Back in the office, Bernie settled his weight into the corner chair near the front door. He parted the venetian blinds with his fingers, saw Jay out on the lot, talking to a young buyer in a leather jacket.

Bernie was on the point, meaning that the next customer was his.

"C'mon," he mumbled. "I need a good one."

He was hoping to slam-dunk one more deal before November's books closed—no ifs, ands, or buts. Though he'd had a decent sales month, he could definitely use the extra cash before Christmas. If things went right, he and his wife would be basking in the Bahamas for New Year's.

Did anything yell *rich and successful* louder than tan skin in January?

The back door opened, and Max trudged into the office's kitchen area. He started making a cup of hot cider.

"Hey," Bernie said. "Whaddya think about Jay's new project?"

Max shrugged, stirring in the powdered mix. "What good's a car that don't run?"

"Typical Jay Austin, huh? Lotsa hot air, and not much to show for it."

"Whoa there." Max lifted an eyebrow. "I don't see the man here to defend hisself, so I suggest you keep those comments to yourself."

"You're standing up for him?"

"He's my boss. Yours, too."

Bernie huffed.

"Anyhow," Max said. "You got me all wrong. I'm not standing up for him so much as for treating others the way they oughta be treated."

"Yeah? Well, you might wanna remind Jay of that." Bernie peeked through the blinds again. Jay and the kid in leather had just returned in the black Honda Accord. "In fact, there he is now—with another victim."

Max propped himself in the doorway, sipping cider and staring at Bernie over the rim of the cup. Bernie shifted in his seat. Scanned the lot for customers. He propped a leg on the wooden desk and flipped open a magazine.

He didn't look up again until Max had gone out to the garage.

JAY

The sun was high in the sky, and the noise of passing cars on North Slappey couldn't mute the chattering of birds in the nearby Georgia pines.

On the sales lot, Jay stood beside the Accord and gave the young buyer a few seconds to think over the car's smooth ride and powerful speaker system. Scott wore spiked hair and a leather jacket. He looked to be a man who hoped to impress the ladies.

Which meant he was presently unattached. Jay would bet money on it.

"It's a good car, Scott," Jay said.

"Seems like it."

"Clean interior. Good stereo. Low mileage for an '88 Honda."

"Mm-hmm."

Jay put his hands on his hips. He spotted his porter, Sam Jones, off to the right, cleaning up a trade-in that had arrived this morning. That was always a good selling tool, a free car wash and detail. Sam never moaned about it, though some days such deals kept him at work later than expected.

"What about the back end here?" Scott said. "Has it ever been wrecked?"

"Uh, no. I don't think so." Jay measured his words. "I think that was, uh, repainted from scratches in the bumper paint. I see that done pretty often. Actually, this here was a one-family car passed down between three brothers, so I don't think you have anything to worry about."

Scott pushed his hands into the pockets of his jacket and ran a look of concern down the length of the car.

"You said you like the way it drives?" Jay asked.

"Yeah."

"Tell you what, Scott." Jay rested his hands on the roof and gazed across, as though they were just two guys chatting about the afternoon's football game. "If you want the car today, I'll give you a free tune-up and oil change down the road, and a free car wash from my porter anytime you want it."

"All right," Scott said. "You know, I think I'll take it."

"That's my *man*." Jay met the kid at the front of the car and shook his hand. Another sale, another conquest. He placed a hand on his buyer's back, steering him toward the sales building. "We can do the paperwork real quick, and you can be showing it off to your girlfriend inside of half an hour."

"Uh. I don't have a girlfriend."

"Really? No kidding."

Chapter 3

KING OF CHEESE

JAY

The door chimed as Jay and Scott entered the office. Bernie Myers was seated at the corner desk, and Jay greeted him in a warm voice, presenting the image that it was all buddy-buddy here—good friends passing on good deals to good people.

"Hi, Bernie."

"Jay."

"We finally got a smart buyer for that beautiful Accord."

Bernie set down his magazine and stood to shake Scott's hand. "Congratulations. I didn't think that car would stay out here as long as it did."

Jay plopped into the black swivel chair at the sales desk. "Bernie, this is Scott. Scott, Bernie Myers, one of our sales associates."

"Wow," Bernie recited on cue. "That's a great car."

"Thanks," Scott responded.

"Scott, if I could get you to have a seat right there. And I need to see your driver's license." Jay slipped a contract and a pen across the desk. Beneath his elbows, a desktop calendar marked upcoming appointments. Manila folders were piled next to the multiline phone.

Setting his checkbook on the desk, Scott eased into his seat.

Checkbook first, Jay noted. The hook was set deep. This was one fish that wouldn't be wiggling free.

"If you'll fill this form out. Just sign there. Fill that out." Jay indicated each spot with the point of his pen. "Initial there. And there."

Scott surrendered his driver's license.

"Thank you. I'll be right back, while you do that."

Jay made a photocopy in the adjacent room, then came back in to file it away. He heard the scratching of Scott's pen come to a stop, and Jay glanced toward the desk.

Scott lifted his head. "I don't mean to be rude, but what is this?" He had his leg crossed, the pen poised in his hand.

From behind the buyer, Bernie shot Jay a look.

"Well," Jay said, "that's a retail installment contract that says what you purchased the car for. You've also got a warranty disclaimer there, and a mileage statement. You know, most people don't ask. They just sign away. You're pretty smart to check it out before you sign."

Bernie rolled his eyes.

"Thanks," Scott said.

Bernie shook his head.

Through the doorway into the kitchen area, Jay spotted Sam the porter in his ball cap, washing up at the sink. Sam had his lips pressed together as though holding back words that begged to be said.

Scott was oblivious. "You know, Mr. Austin, this is really the first big purchase I've ever made."

"It's a good one. You'll love it, and your friends'll love you in it."

Bernie was a bobblehead doll, shaking his chin at every line out of Jay's mouth. Jay narrowed his eyes, warning his salesman to keep quiet while Scott finished initialing.

Next came the check-signing stage.

After last-minute questions about finance options, Scott applied himself to his task with diligence. Jay watched the string of figures parade across the *amount* line, listened to the satisfying tear of perforated paper.

Jay handed back the license he'd been holding hostage. "There's your driver's license." He took the check. "Thank you, Scott. Congratulations. And here are your keys."

"Thanks."

"You're now the owner of a beautiful car." Jay stood, signaling his buyer to do the same. He clapped Scott on the back. "Time to go take that girl of yours for a ride."

"Uh. I don't—"

"Oh, that's right. No girlfriend." Jay double-clapped the back of the leather jacket and prodded the kid toward the exit. "At least not yet. But a handsome guy like you and a hot car like this . . . Not gonna be *long*."

The door chimed. Birds chirped. Scott beamed.

BERNIE

From his seat, Bernie watched Jay lead the buyer across the lot to the Honda coupe. He turned his attention to the African-American man in the kitchen area. "I don't believe it, Sam. Did you see that kid's face? He's convinced he just bought his dream car."

Sam sighed. He peered through the window over the sink.

Bernie chuckled. "Poor Scott's gonna wonder what went wrong when the girls don't come running."

"I know that's what *my* woman always wanted," Sam said. "A 1988 wrecked Honda."

"Wonder how much Jay got outta him."

"I already know how much."

"What? How could you—?"

"Too much."

"Aww, Sam. Think you're funny, don'tcha?"

Sam mumbled, "Not as funny as *some* of the guys working in this place."

Bernie went to the sales desk, ran his eyes over the contract. He scooted back to the blinds and glanced again over the car lot. He heard Sam depart through the side door, then felt the floor quaver beneath each step of his approaching sales partner. Not many men could match Bernie's girth. Vince Berkley was an exception.

Short and wide, Vince filled the kitchen doorway. His hair was gelled, his shirt tucked into his slacks, a cell phone clipped to his belt. His pleasant face was an asset in the sales process—if, and when, Vince worked up the courage to approach buyers.

Vince was *too* nice, though. Bernie knew that nice didn't go far in this cutthroat business.

"Get this," Bernie said. "Jay just sold the Accord."

"The wrecked one?" Vince popped a chip into his mouth.

"Yep. Just cleared three on it."

"He did not."

"Yeah, he did." Bernie nodded toward the sales desk. "See for yourself."

Vince leaned down to check the paperwork. "No way. How does he do that?"

The front door pushed open. Bernie and Vince stared as Jay walked around to the desk. Jay slapped Vince on the arm, a self-congratulatory gesture that turned Bernie's stomach.

"Man," Bernie told his boss. "You are the *king* of cheese."

"What does that mean?" Jay said.

Vince leaned against the wall. "Jay, you just made three thousand dollars off that car?"

The boss man organized the documents on the desk. "That's why the sign says Jay Austin Motors, not Vince Berkley Motors."

"I didn't think we'd make a thousand off that Honda." Bernie cocked an eyebrow. "You tell him it was wrecked?"

Jay looked up. Gave no answer.

"No?" Bernie chortled. "Man, you are slicker than snot on an ice rink."

"You're just jealous 'cause you wouldn't have cleared two."

Bernie shook his head. "You amaze me."

Vince hitched up his pants. "Remind me to tell my friends to never buy a car from this place."

"All right," Jay snapped. "Shut up and go sell a car."

TODD

Judy Austin slipped into a parking space next to the sales building. In the passenger seat, Todd held his new masterpiece facedown on his lap. He watched his mom fiddle with her brown, shoulder-length hair in the rearview mirror, watched her dab lipstick at her mouth. She was wearing a black sweater with large buttons over a green shirt.

"You look pretty, Mom."

"Thank you, honey. You're looking sharp in your bomber jacket."

"Thanks for putting the patch on for me." Earlier, Todd had watched her sew on the latest emblem, a birthday gift last month from his uncle Joey.

She rubbed the back of his neck. "What've you got in your lap?"

"Something for Dad."

"Okay. Well, let's go see what he's up to."

Todd was glad his mother didn't push for more information. She and he shared their own special hobbies, including word games such as Scrabble and Boggle. Some things, though, were to be shared between a father and his son. The picture Todd had drawn for his dad was one of them.

He clutched the paper to his chest, the race car hidden from view. He wondered if Dad would realize the significance of the number 71. Maybe it wasn't as obvious as Todd thought.

In fact, maybe the entire picture needed more work.

"You coming, Todd?"

"Yeah."

Todd followed his mom through a side door into the office, appearing behind the sales desk where his dad was leaned back in the black chair. Todd liked to spin in that chair, when his dad wasn't looking—faster, faster. It always made Bernie laugh.

"Hey, Judy. Hey, Todd," Bernie greeted from across the room. "How y'all doing?"

"Hi, Bernie and Vince." Todd's mom was holding her belly. She did that a lot nowadays, like she was already trying to cuddle the new baby. "We're doing good. How are you?"

Todd was about to reach forward and show his dad the picture, when the phone jangled on the desk.

His dad picked up. "Jay Austin Motors."

Todd moved back into place beside his mom.

"So," said Bernie to Judy. "What're y'all up to today?"

"Oh, we're just out running some errands. We thought we'd stop by and see if Jay needed something to eat. Have y'all eaten yet?"

"I just ate," Vince said. "And Bernie? He's always eating."

Judy laughed. Bernie shot Vince a wide-eyed look that made Todd grin.

Todd never knew what to say around these guys. They were like a comedy team, and he was always afraid he'd be the one to break their rhythm with a lame joke. He'd tried once or twice before and discovered there was nothing worse than having a roomful of adults fall silent while you were trying to blurt out something funny.

Jay was still on the phone. "No, no, no," he was saying. "Don't do that."

Todd wondered if he should just slip the drawing onto the desk.

"Okay," his mom said to the two salesmen. "Well, if you want us to pick you up something, we will."

"Aww, no. Thanks for the offer, Judy, but I think Jay's the only one who hasn't eaten. Actually, me and Vince were about to go back outside."

Todd couldn't wait any longer. He stepped up beside his dad's chair.

"No, you can't do that," Jay spoke into the receiver.

"Dad?" Todd gripped the drawing.

His dad held up a finger as if to say *wait a minute*, swiveled toward the wall, and kept talking. "You just do what you did last time. What's the problem?"

On the mantel over the decorative fireplace, framed certificates and bronze plaques extolled the sales team. A number of them bore Jay Austin's name. That used to make Todd proud, but now he just wanted his dad to recognize him standing here.

Bernie and Vince headed for the front door.

Vince fired off a farewell. "See ya, Judy. See ya, Todd."

Judy waved. "It was good to see you guys. Have a good day." She came up and put a hand on Todd's shoulder while Jay continued on the phone.

"I've already spent too much," Jay was insisting.

"Jay, what do you want for lunch?" Judy asked.

"I don't care. Just grab something." He spoke back into the handset, "No, do not do that. I'm not spending any more than my average."

Judy said, "How 'bout a burger?"

Jay fired back, "I *don't* care."

"All right." She threw her hands in the air.

Todd's mom headed out to the car, but Todd was rooted in place. He'd imagined his dad's pleasure at this homemade gift, and now he couldn't even get his attention long enough to hand it over. Maybe he should just take the picture back to the house and wait for dinnertime. Of course, Dad would be cranky after the long workweek, so that wasn't a great idea either.

Please, Dad, he pleaded silently. *Just look over at me.*

"No, don't you let them do that to you," Jay rambled on. "You tell them you've already gotten permission. That it . . . It doesn't matter. Just make up something. If he . . . No, if he gives you a hard time, you tell him to call me."

Todd moved a step closer. He could see that his dad was busy and the timing for this was all wrong. Without a word, he set the drawing in the center of the desk and backed away.

Jay barked into the phone, "He can't deny you access to the lot. What? No, he did it last year . . . It doesn't matter." Jay reclined in the chair, almost bumping into his son.

Todd flinched, then slipped back outside.

Chapter 4

THE SLIVER

JAY

Still on the phone, Jay heard the door close behind him. Oops. Judy was probably upset with him. And it was too bad, because he had wanted to spend a few minutes chatting with Todd.

On the other hand, it was a distraction to have the family here at work, and now—finally—he had the office to himself. Judy was trying to be thoughtful, picking up lunch for him while he was on the job, but her timing always seemed to clash with an important call or potential sale. To add insult to injury, she was sure to rant at him about it when he got home.

Didn't she realize he was trying to put food on the table?

Really, was that such a crime?

Jay said to his broker, "How many are you bringing back?"

He started organizing the desk, still holding the phone between his shoulder and ear. "What year?" He aimed some old messages at the garbage can. "Yeah. It *is* in good condition?" He straightened a stack of folders, filed some papers. "Fine."

A drawing sat in the middle of the desk. Where had that come from?

Jay was about to give it a more thorough inspection, when the man on the phone launched into a new tirade about trucking regulations and traffic.

"Look," Jay snapped, cutting him short. "Just don't get pulled over this time, all right?"

Mindlessly he snatched up the drawing, crumpled it with both hands, and dropped it into the wastebasket. Kids sometimes scribbled while waiting for their parents to negotiate and sign papers. Probably one of Bernie's deals. Did that man ever clean up after his customers?

"Yes. Good," Jay said. "Bye."

He ended the call and headed for the main door.

Overhead, the winter sky was bleached out by the sun, while here on the sales lot, strands of pennants fluttered in a cool breeze. Bernie was showing a Chevy truck to a middle-aged couple. Sam was crouched next to a vehicle on the front line, buffing the paint job with a chamois cloth.

Jay angled toward him. "Sam, you seen Max or Vince?"

"I think Max went to pick up his new fishing pole."

"That's right. He got off early, didn't he?"

Sam looked up from beneath his cap, dark eyes twinkling. "So what's Vince's excuse?"

"What, did he take off, too?"

"Over there." Sam jerked his chin to the left.

Vince was propped against a car, feeding M&Ms into his mouth.

"Vince Berkley." Jay strode toward his underachieving salesman. "Are you eating on the clock again?"

"We're on salary."

"That's just so you have pocket change. The real money's in selling cars."

"Hey, I don't do well under pressure."

"The only pressure on this lot is in the tires," Jay retorted, playing off an old sales joke.

Vince popped another M&M. He still hadn't met Jay's eyes.

"Listen, Vince, this lot is your pond. The fish are here, but if you don't drop a line, you won't get any bites. They're not gonna just hop into your lap, you know? You gotta go get them. That's why Bernie outsells you every month."

"I'm just honing my craft."

"Really."

"You'll see." Another morsel. "I'll be the main man soon."

"Not by just standing around."

"I'm not just standing here, Jay. I'm watching the customers. That way I learn how to make the best approach." He nodded, enamored by his own brilliance. "That's right. Every move I make is calculated."

"Well, don't calculate too much. All right?"

"All right."

Jay punched the man in the shoulder and left him to his

dubious plan. As he strolled up the wooden steps to the office building, he caught a whiff of KFC from up the street. Where were Judy and Todd? He was getting hungry.

Ten minutes later, Jay's stomach was grumbling. He was in the copy room, searching customer files. If he made a selective list of previous buyers, it might enable Vince to make some calls and drum up new business. More money toward the bottom line.

The side door opened, the one only Judy and Todd used.

About time.

"Here's your lunch, Dad."

Jay threw a glance back over his shoulder, saw Todd standing in his bomber jacket by the desk in the outer office. He held a brown paper sack in one hand, a large soft drink in the other.

"Is that a new patch?" Jay inquired.

"Mom sewed it on for me."

"Is it the one from Joey?"

"Yes, sir."

The thought of his brother edging in on his relationship with Todd rankled Jay. As if Joey wasn't *already* the family favorite.

"I like it," Todd said.

"I'm sure you do."

TODD

Todd had entered the office with high hopes. He'd let himself imagine his artwork on the mantel beside the framed certificates. And if not that, at least he would get a smile or a thanks.

Instead, he detected bitterness in his father's voice.

Why should Dad be upset about a gift from Uncle Joey? Todd

didn't have a brother, so maybe he just didn't understand. Of course, with Mom being pregnant and all, he might be getting a brother soon enough.

Jay flipped through more files. "So'd you get me a burger?"

"We got you a chicken sandwich," Todd said.

"I thought you were getting me a burger. Just put it on the desk."

Todd obeyed. As he set down the sack, his eyes searched the dark wooden surface for any evidence of the drawing. Found nothing. Maybe his dad had tacked it up in the other room, or hung it with a magnet on the small refrigerator in the kitchen area.

Suddenly, Todd knew.

He peeked over the edge, and sure enough, there it was at the bottom of the garbage can. A sharp-edged paper ball. A piece of junk.

His picture.

Whenever Todd got a sliver, he had a habit of picking at the thing. He would run his fingernail across its invisible edge, or scrape at it with his pocketknife—which Joey had also given him, a gift his Mom had protested. He could never explain why he did this, since it only intensified the pain.

Now, in the same way, he knew he had to retrieve the picture from the trash. He had to see it for himself, had to scrape at it until it hurt.

He bent over. Picked out the paper. Uncrumpled it.

His pulse pounded in his throat, making it hard to breathe. Tears of resentment burned at the corners of his eyes, but he refused to let them out. He was *not* a pampered boy, and he *definitely* didn't need any toughening up.

He stared at the colorful number 71 race car. He looked at Dad's back, then let the picture tumble back into the receptacle.

At last, his father closed the file cabinet and turned. "Todd. You're still here? Hey, tell your mom I'll be home at five."

Todd stood with his hands at his sides.

Jay exited the building through the front door, leaving Todd on his own in the middle of the sales office. The door chime was shrill in his ears. The sheepskin collar of his jacket felt warm, almost hot. He looked down into the garbage again, then blinked as he eyed the door through which his father had disappeared.

Chapter 5

IN KNOTS

JAY

Another week was over, and sales had been mediocre. Jay drove home in silence, wanting nothing more than to kick off his shoes and stretch out on the bed with the TV remote all to himself.

Judy was sure to still be smoldering from this afternoon.

His sales staff was grating on his nerves.

As for customers . . . Well, everyone in this industry knew that buyers were liars. They'd make up excuses, claim to have seen the same car cheaper somewhere else, and test-drive vehicles for the weekend that they never intended to purchase. Knowledge was power, and with the power of the Internet at their fingertips, more and more people were armed to haggle prices.

"Lord," Jay spoke into the ether, "what've I gotten myself into?"

He shoved away any thought of the money he still owed his father.

Jay followed the twining gravel drive between the pine trees to his two-story, three-dormered home. White posts girded a front porch that ran the length of the house, and trimmed hedges squatted on either side of the front steps.

Inside, Jay picked up the mail from the mahogany stand in the hall.

"I thought you were coming home at five."

Jay stepped into the dining area and saw Judy drying a glass at the counter. "I guess I'm late," he said.

"Does it not bother you that you don't keep your word?"

"Don't start, Judy." He slapped the mail down on the counter and turned down the hall.

Behind him, she sighed. "Guess not."

He paused, his stomach knotting, then decided to let it go.

Jay didn't have the energy for a knock-down-drag-out. Not tonight.

Upstairs he found Todd on the bed, with schoolbooks propped against the pillow and fanned across the blanket. Soccer and softball trophies stood on the nightstand beside a medium-sized globe.

"Todd, why aren't you helping your mom set the table?"

Todd turned on his side, pencil in hand, toes wiggling in his socks. "She asked me to do my homework."

"You can do your homework later. Go help your mother."

"But Jeff's coming over. He's spending the night."

Jay should've known there would be no solitude in his own

home this evening. Judy knew how tired he got by Saturdays, yet she'd made arrangements without consulting him. These days, that was no surprise.

He turned to go.

"Dad?"

"What?"

"You wanna play a game with us, when Jeff gets here?"

"Uh, I don't know."

"Checkers? Or, I know you like Monopoly."

"Been a long week, Todd. Maybe another time. Finish up what you're doing," Jay said, "then wash your hands and come to the table."

Todd rolled back onto his stomach and stabbed his pencil at his paper.

"Did you hear me, Son?"

"Yes, sir."

JUDY

Frustrated, Judy slid plastic plates onto the polished hardwood dining table. She had been set on holding her tongue when Jay arrived home from work, yet within seconds she had snapped at him, slipping back into their now-familiar patterns of communication.

Why did she do that? Why did he?

She braced a hand on the dining bar and closed her eyes. "I'm so tired, Lord. I just want Jay to be a man who follows after You. I'm trying my best, but it seems like it's never enough."

Her emotions had been on a roller-coaster ride throughout

this pregnancy. Although she'd never expected to be carrying another child in her early thirties, she was relishing the idea of a precious baby in her arms again.

Todd was at the age where he shrugged off her hugs, especially in public.

As for Jay, he had been more distant of late. He'd been an attentive father when Todd was an infant, but he now avoided family interaction as though it were an obstacle in his race toward success.

No wonder she found herself transferring her affections to this new life within. She wanted to be a good mother to Todd, a good wife to Jay, but both of her men seemed to be slipping from her fingers.

She took a long, slow breath. With ten weeks to go until the due date, the baby was already pressing up under her ribs. The occasional pangs were poignant reminders of the child growing inside. Why was it that growth never happened without stretching, without pain?

"Lord, please give me strength to embrace this."

She rested her arms on her belly, then called Jay and Todd for dinner.

MAX

The evening sun was melting down into a burnt-orange smear, streaked with pink and light purple. Max Kendall stood on the banks of the Lower Flint River, new fishing pole in hand, line played out into the current, where insects were hovering in the dusk and largemouth bass were perking up.

Max loved this time of day, just before darkness fell, when the pine trees stood in rigid silhouette as though getting orders for the night watch.

He had done his own share of sentry duty, along the DMZ between North and South Korea. That'd been years ago, back when he was nothing but a boy in army boots, back when he knew it all. When he thought heroin was his friend. He'd ended his tour of duty, but the internal war he'd carried home with him had destroyed his first marriage.

His second wife was the one who had brought grace into his life. Although she was a tough old bird, she had loved him unconditionally—the way Christ loved, that's what she'd always reminded him. "Those who deserve love the least often need it the most," she used to say to him.

Max had loved her unconditionally, too. Right to the end.

Frail and weak, Shirley Kendall had looked him in the eye the day before she died and said something that meant the world to him, meant he had not lived in vain. "Max," she said, "you know I love you." He had nodded. "More important," she added, "I know you love *me*. I know it deep down, so far down that this cancer can't get to it."

For the first time in decades, he had cried.

Not only to know you are loved, but to know that you *have* loved . . . Wasn't that one of life's truest gifts?

Max was using suspended jerkbait, and he gave the line a few tugs to entice any lurking fish. He already had a decent-sized catfish in his ice chest and was now angling for a largemouth-bass dinner, breaded and panfried with butter and herbs.

Funny thing, how he drew sustenance from this very river, where three years earlier he had almost lost his life at the business end of a mugger's gun.

That incident didn't keep him from coming back here.

If anything, it made him more determined to prove that evil did not have to win, no matter how hard it tried.

Of course, that didn't change the fact there were consequences to pay. The doctors told him he would be wearing this colostomy bag for the rest of his days, a pouching system secured with latex-free tape to his lower left abdomen, meant to capture what could no longer process through his bullet-damaged intestines.

Thankfully, with regular changes during the day, it remained odor-free and discreet. He lived alone now, had for years, so it was his inconvenience alone. He'd told Jay Austin about it, and only because it limited his speed and mobility while working under vehicles.

Jay was a decent guy, understanding and all that. He'd been fair to Max, even a friend of sorts.

But he was tied up in knots. That was plain to see.

Max sent up a prayer, a spiritual flare, right there from the riverbank. He asked God to show Himself in Jay's life, to give him a wake-up call, if need be. Max had needed the same thing a time or two—or ten.

Without grace, he thought, *we'd all be up a creek*.

The pole quivered in his hand, its tip dipping toward the water.

"Oh, here we go. Here we go."

He let out the line, then set the hook. With patience born of experience, he started reeling in his catch.

TODD

In the windowed dining nook, Todd dangled his feet beneath the table and pushed against the wood support with his toes. They were using plastic dining ware and disposable cups for dinner. He couldn't even remember the last time the china had come out of the cabinet, but he sure didn't mind.

Why did adults like all that fancy stuff anyway? You had to be so careful that it took all the fun out of things.

Todd's parents sat on opposite ends of the table, mouths set into grim lines. They'd said nothing since the blessing.

Which was fine with Todd.

He still ached at the thought of his discarded artwork, and he hoped no one asked how his day had been. He'd have to gloss over the truth. Either that, or risk a long lecture about some lesson he needed to learn, or some attitude that needed to change. No, it was best just to keep quiet. He would eat his food, wait for Jeff to show up, then try to forget about all that.

Mom was the first to speak. She looked up from her plate. "Did you sell any cars today?"

"One." Dad pushed food around his plate.

"Which one?"

"The black '88 Honda."

"The one that was wrecked?"

"Yep," he said through a bite.

"How much?"

Dad looked up. "Does it matter?"

Todd dropped his focus to his bowl of Froot Loops. The cereal was by his request. Since Mom's pregnancy, she'd loosened up about dinner options. She said she was too warm, too tired to be standing over the stove—especially for guys who didn't know the difference between canned ravioli and the real thing.

Strange. Todd thought the ones in the can *were* the real thing.

"Jay, I'm just asking," Mom said. "Can't we at least talk?"

"There's not much to say."

"So? How much?"

Todd sneaked a peak and saw his dad pushing at the inside of his cheek with his tongue.

Mom frowned. "You don't wanna tell me, do you?"

"Six."

"Six *thousand*? You said that car wasn't worth three, Jay."

Todd waited for his dad's reaction.

"Why do you care?" Dad hissed. "It was worth six thousand to the buyer."

"Did the buyer know it was wrecked?"

"Judy." Jay gripped a dinner roll in one hand, his fork in the other. "I've had my mind on work all day. I don't wanna talk about it now."

"No? You didn't tell him, did you?"

Todd knew his mom had guessed right. He recognized that look on Dad's face, the way he froze in his seat when he didn't want to talk.

"Why're you interrogating me? I'm a used-car salesman. I sell cars."

"At dishonest prices," Mom mouthed.

"That's enough." Dad glared across the table until she lowered her eyes to her plate. "It shouldn't bother you, anyway. I make more money when I sell more cars. *You* benefit from it."

Todd tried to down the cereal in his mouth without making that swallowing noise that annoyed his father. He didn't understand his father's words. Was Dad saying it was okay to overcharge people if it benefited you personally? Something didn't feel right about that at all. He hoped Jeff would get here soon. For a few moments, no one spoke. His dad went back to stabbing at his food with his fork, while his mom let shiny brown bangs conceal her face.

Once again, she was the one to break the silence. She slid her gaze from her son to her husband. "Are we going to church tomorrow?"

Sometimes, it seemed that his mom pushed this on his dad, like a pill he was supposed to gulp down to make all the problems disappear.

"Did we go last week?" Dad questioned.

"No."

He mulled it over. "I guess we'll go tomorrow." He took another bite.

Todd could imagine a list of things his father had left unsaid: *If it'll keep you off my back . . . If it'll help me find more customers . . . If it doesn't cut into the kickoff time of the Falcons game.*

Strained silence returned to the dining table. This time even Mom let it linger, until the crunch of tires on gravel signaled Jeff's arrival.

Todd scooted from the table and dashed to answer the door.

Chapter 6

SUNDAY BEST

JAY

Jay was making a play for his wife's favor. He rolled his neck, then padded down the stairs in his slippers to fetch her a cup of hot tea. It would help her relax before bed, and he knew no one was happy if Momma wasn't happy.

He wanted some happiness. Or at least some peace.

Though she'd ragged on him at the dinner table, he had to admit that he had been curt with her. She tried to be involved in his life, and he kept slamming the door on her interest.

Then, too, he had tomorrow's worship service to think about.

How could he parade through the hallowed halls if he was still peeved with Judy and Todd? That sort of tension was a cloud overhead, and it tended to drench any enthusiasm others might have about dropping by his sales lot during the week.

And—just being honest here—the church crowd was one of his best customer pools.

He slipped through the dining room and spotted Todd and Jeff facing each other on the living room floor, stomachs on the carpet, feet up in the air. The television was on. They hadn't heard him come in. Their attentions were focused on a game of Battleship.

"E5," Jeff said.

"Nope." Todd fidgeted. "Uh, C3."

Jeff made a soft explosion sound with his mouth. "Got him."

Jay thought of creeping up behind Jeff, mouthing the coordinates of his aircraft carrier to Todd. Not exactly cheating. Just a little family help, right?

Nah. He'd better see to Judy's tea first. He turned on the stove, where a water kettle waited, then headed for the cupboard.

From the TV, a commercial blared louder than the scheduled programming: "Don't miss it! Jay Austin Motors . . . Blowout Blitz!" The words flew across the screen, with cars glimmering in the background. "It's *crrrrazy*," said Bernie Myers, jumping into view with his sunglasses on. Jay was next, waving his hands toward a vehicle. "A '99 Chevy Blazer, $11,995." He pointed toward the camera and rattled off more bargains. "'99 Ford F-150 King Cab, $14,995; 2002 Avalanche C-71, $25,995."

Jay peered around the edge of the cupboard door. There was something embarrassing about the over-the-top hype, but it still tickled him to see his lot featured on the air. It smelled of success. It said to others that things were hopping for that savvy sales crew at Jay Austin Motors.

From the living room, Jeff perked up. "Hey, look, Todd. Your dad's on TV again."

"Yeah, I've seen it." Todd studied his battle grid.

On the screen, Jay was barking out more descriptions and prices. Bernie came back on, staring down through his shades into the camera. "We're out of our *minds*." A voice-over said, "Got bad credit? Still come and get it!" Jay gestured toward a car on the lot's front line. "Pick out your wheels," he said. "I'll give you a deal." The voice-over wrapped it all up in a final barrage of excitement: "Jay Austin Motors . . . Blowout Blitz!"

Todd aimed the remote from the floor and shut off the TV.

"Is it weird seeing him on TV?" Jeff asked.

"Not anymore," Todd said. "It *used* to be cool."

Jay set Judy's mug on the counter, her alumni memento from Georgia State. Jay had dropped out to pursue a business idea, one of many that fell by the wayside.

But here he was. Back on his feet. On TV.

He listened in on the boys, thinking how proud he would've been to see his own father on television. That wasn't something every boy got to experience. Instead, Jay's dad had started a Southern Gospel traveling group. Now, *that* was embarrassing.

"So," Jeff said to Todd, "do you wanna sell cars, too?"

"I don't know. It seems like it's hard."

Jay was amused. His son was no dummy, obviously attentive to the things that went on behind the scenes at the lot.

Todd continued. "And I don't really wanna be like my dad."

Jay's fingers tightened around the mug.

"Why not?" Jeff asked.

"Well, sometimes he lies to people."

"Whaddya mean?"

"Sometimes he doesn't tell them if something's wrong with the car and stuff."

"Like if the engine doesn't work?"

"No, the engine works. But it might've been wrecked or have bad parts."

"And he sells it to them anyway?"

"Yeah." Todd sounded ashamed.

Ashamed? Jay threw a tea bag into Judy's cup. Didn't his son realize that he was just doing his job, doing what he could to put food on their plates and clothes on their backs?

"Well," Jeff said, "they're used cars."

"I know. But he makes people pay too much. I wanna do something different."

"Yeah, I guess I would, too."

Jay slopped hot water into the mug and headed back upstairs. The drink burned in his hands. His son's words burned in his ears.

JUDY

The lobby of the large Baptist church milled with ushers and churchgoers. Judy blinked as her eyes adjusted from the sun's glare through the outside clouds to the fluorescent illumination inside. She'd had some trouble getting Todd and his friend out of bed this morning, but otherwise Sunday preparations had gone smoother than usual. Jay had even risen earlier than normal for a Sunday.

"Who are you trying to impress?" she'd wanted to ask.

But it was this cynicism she was trying to avoid. It was so hard not to try to fix him, even though she knew her badgering would only push him away.

The happy family . . .

Here they were, in their Sunday best, and Bibles under their arms.

"Good morning." A greeter met them with a smile. "How're y'all this morning?"

"Good morning," Jay said.

Jeff was wandering off, having seen his parents across the lobby.

"Hey, Jeff," Judy called. "Tell your mom I'll pick you up after soccer practice on Thursday, okay?"

"Yes, ma'am."

A white-haired man in a suit and glasses held out a hand as the Austin family headed toward the main sanctuary. It was Reverend Michaels, one of the associate ministers. He was soft-spoken, with intelligent eyes. Judy was glad he would be the one, in a few months, to dedicate their baby before the Lord.

"Jay Austin, it's good to see you this morning."

Jay shook his hand. "Good morning, Reverend. How are you doing?"

"Well," he answered. He turned his head. "Judy, it's good to see you, too."

"You too."

"Todd, you're growing up. You're going to be as tall as your dad. It's good to have all of you here."

Todd glanced down, readjusting his Bible under his arm.

"Thank you," Judy said.

"Jay." The reverend stopped and took Jay's hand again. "I'm getting ready to try to look for a car for my daughter. She's going off to college, and I wonder if I can come by and see you this week."

"I've got some sharp cars on the lot right now. You come anytime you want to."

Judy tried not to roll her eyes as her husband launched into sales mode.

"In fact," Jay said, "you come talk to me directly, and I'll be sure to take care of you. I can only imagine what it's gonna be like to send my own kid to—"

"Kids," Judy cut in, touching her belly.

"To send my own kids to college. Must be kinda scary."

"Oh, we're excited for Lindsay," said Reverend Michaels. "She's got a good head on her shoulders."

"Well, I'll see to it that she has a reliable vehicle."

"Thank you very much."

"Be glad to have you."

"Thank you," Reverend Michaels said again.

Judy started off to find their seats, afraid of the words that might slip from her lips. She could only hope and pray her husband would be a man of his word. She wanted to believe the best about him. She really did. Surely he wouldn't take advantage of a minister.

JAY

Jay sneaked a peek at his watch. Though his tie felt like a noose around his neck, he refrained from loosening it. Appearances,

appearances. Left to him, they would've been seated near the back, but Judy had picked a row in the sanctuary's lower section that was visible to scores of people behind them.

Thanks, he thought. *Thanks a lot.*

After a brief greeting and an introduction of the choir in the loft, a worship minister took the curved platform and led the congregation in song.

Jay was not a singer. He didn't know many men who were. This part of the service seemed geared toward torturing the males in attendance, while giving the females a chance to soar into the atmosphere with operatic grandeur.

Sure, Jay knew that God was a spirit. God wasn't listening with physical ears, judging him on his vocal quality. Still, Jay would rather be anywhere but here. He and the Big Guy hadn't been on the best of terms since, well, since before the turn of the millennium.

Originally, Jay had made church attendance a fixture in his life for one reason: to win Judy's approval and her hand in marriage. Along the way, he had experienced a spiritual awakening. He even started tithing, giving to God from the firstfruits of his labors.

Talk about putting your money where your mouth was. That'd been a real test for him.

Speaking of tests . . .

The ushers were moving up the rows of seats, passing the offering plates.

Jay shifted in place. He found a blank tithe envelope inside the front cover of his Bible. He lowered it to his side, thumbed it open. Nope. Nothing in there. Empty as could be. He reasoned that he had other priorities right now and far too much debt.

He felt Judy's gaze slide down to what he was doing, and he pinched the envelope shut. He sensed her disapproval, oppressive and uncomfortable, like a propane heater radiating warmth in the middle of August.

The usher was upon him.

Jay pressed his lips together and gave the man a nod. He dropped in the envelope, then passed the plate along. He put an elbow on the armrest and ignored Judy's censoring expression. He stared straight ahead, pretending to give his attention to the lady performing a solo number.

Later, through the fog of his discomfort, he caught the head minister's concluding statements: ". . . God searches. He sees. He knows. But now the psalmist is taking that fact and he's turning it into a petition, a prayer before God. And I want us to see what he's doing here. He's asking God to investigate his conduct, to search his mind, to put him under the microscope. He says first of all, 'Search me.' Why? Because I can be deluded and deceived about where I stand in my walk with God. I can think I've dealt with something when I haven't."

Jay tried to remember who the Atlanta Falcons were playing this afternoon, but even that failed to quiet the minister's words in his ears.

"I can think that I've confessed," the man stated, "but I've dealt with the symptom and not with the problem. And so David is saying, 'God, go deep inside of me, in the hidden parts of my life, in the parts that nobody else knows about . . . and search me out.'"

TODD

After the service, Todd followed his parents to the car. It was parked beneath a tree that looked like it was on fire with gold and red leaves. If Todd had things his way, he'd be climbing these trees with his friends or playing tag in the back lot. His dad, however, was in a rush to evacuate the premises.

"Todd, have you got your Bible?" his mom checked.

"Yes, ma'am." He ducked into the backseat.

His dad was shedding his suit jacket. "What're we doing for lunch?"

"I've got a frozen pizza at home," Mom said. "Or we could grab something on the way."

"I'd rather do something else."

"Sonic, Sonic. Please, Dad."

"That work for you, Judy?"

"Sure." She was still standing at her door. "Jay, I wanna come back tonight for the evening service."

"I'm not coming back. I've got some things to do at the lot."

"On a Sunday? *Jay.*"

"I've already tithed my time to church this week."

"Dad, what's a tithe?"

His father hesitated, then loosened his tie. "It's when you give money to help the church."

Judy leaned over the roof. "Or in our case, an empty envelope so people *think* we give money to help the church."

"Is that supposed to be funny?"

"You know, Jay, I never really thought it was very funny."

"We've given money before."

"Oh." She waved a hand. "Then I guess we're okay."

Jay stiffened before folding himself into the driver's seat. Todd looked down at the Bible on his lap, where his name was etched in gold, a gift from his grandparents. He wondered why they didn't come to visit more often.

Chapter 7

PAR FOR THE COURSE

BERNIE

"Aww, c'mon." Vince Berkley stabbed his 3-iron back into his golf bag.

"What was that?" Bernie said. "You sure you know which hole we're shooting at?"

"All part of my plan. You'll see."

Bernie made a show of stifling a laugh.

Vince shielded his eyes, tried to see where his ball had come to rest after its hop onto the neighboring fairway.

"Have you even hit one in regulation yet?" Bernie asked.

"Man, we've only played seven holes."

"Well, there you go."

"Look who's talking, John Daly."

"Hey."

"Just kidding." Vince shouldered his bag and started walking away.

Bernie slouched into the driver's seat of their golf cart and rolled up alongside his golf and sales partner. He nudged closer, feigned a sharp left turn.

Vince dodged left. Kept moving.

"C'mon, Vince. Hop on."

"I'm fine. I'm walking."

"I'm afraid you're gonna keel over, carrying all that weight."

"You watch. By this time next year, I'll be seventy pounds lighter."

"Ha."

"You know, Bernie—you're just rude sometimes."

Bernie grabbed a handful of his own flab. "Hey, I'm right there with you, buddy. Don't think I'm pointing fingers."

Vince selected his 7-iron, dropped his bag to the ground, and set up over his wayward ball. He swung once, expending such force that he almost tipped over on the follow-through.

"Missed," Bernie pointed out.

"That was my practice swing."

"Mm-hmm."

The second attempt was a thing of beauty. The ball arced over a stand of trees, past a sand trap, and rolled onto the green. Grinning ear to ear, Vince hefted his golf bag onto the back of the cart.

"Now, *that* was a nice shot, Vince."

"Thanks, man."

"See? I'm not above admiring a good shot—when I actually see one."

"I might even par this hole."

"First time for everything." Bernie edged the cart forward in lurches. "You getting on now? Or do I have to run over your big white backside?"

"Like you could catch me."

Vince took off running, swinging those stubby legs in rapid rhythm, gliding over the grass, conquering a small hill with remarkable ease.

"Hey. Get back here."

Bernie stomped the pedal to the floor. The electric motor gave all it had, propelling small, fat tires over winter-hardened turf. The white top swayed and creaked as Bernie crested the grassy mound. Vince had a lead of twenty yards and was almost guaranteed—unless he collapsed of exhaustion—to reach the green before Bernie.

This called for desperate measures.

Bernie Myers saw that if he cut up the steep bank to the right of the sand trap, he would shorten his trek by a couple of seconds. Meanwhile, Vince would have to circle around the longer, flatter way or try slogging through the sand.

"I gotcha now." Bernie cackled with glee.

His foot was crushed against the floorboards. The cart charged forward, an intrepid warrior assaulting the emerald bastions of this Scottish-inspired, big boy's playground. The nose dipped, shuddered, then rose to meet the nearly vertical challenge.

For a moment, Bernie was convinced he had it made. He was going to beat Vince to the target—at the risk of a few skid marks along the green's outer edge. Nothing that couldn't be patted down with the end of his putter.

The first flutter of doubt came as the cart's front wheels skipped sideways over a bump in the slope.

The second flutter . . .

Well, all Bernie could do was hold on.

The cart lost traction, lost speed, and in a final attempt to mount the upper lip of the incline, seemed to point straight up into overcast skies. Bernie's weight was leaned back, countering the vehicle's momentum. In an ill-advised panic, he switched his foot to the brake.

It happened in slow motion.

The cart stopped. The front tires said farewell to their good friend the earth, and the entire contraption began to tumble in a skewed, backward free fall. Then the hard-plastic canopy collided with the ground, snapping free of its fittings and collapsing atop Bernie's splayed position in the soft sand.

Everything turned dark.

Had he passed out? Snapped his neck?

Momma . . .

"Bernie?" It was Vince's voice. "Bernie, you okay?"

Bernie watched the hard canopy peel away, revealing his partner's concerned face. He wiggled his toes. Groaned. Realized the darkness had been nothing more than the physical blockage of daylight.

"Man," Vince said. "What happened? Where does it hurt?"

Bernie started giggling.

"Tell me you're okay."

Bernie giggled harder, dropping his head back into the sand and letting relief wash over him. He closed his eyes against the glare. Though a little sore, he was no worse for the wear.

"Oh, please." Vince was still standing over him, his words heavy with despair. "Don't let it be brain damage."

Bernie's eyes snapped open. "Hey."

"Bernie?"

"I'm fine, you hear?" He clambered to his feet, dusted off his plaid golf pants. "Nothing broken. And"—he pointed a finger—"no brain damage."

"Too bad," Vince said, switching back to their normal banter.

"Ha-ha."

"Just take a look at this mess."

"Hmm." Bernie had to admit that it did appear pretty bad.

"Man, they're gonna ban you from this course for life. I bet they'll have to get another cart, too. How much you think one of these things costs?"

"What's it matter? They've got coverage for this sorta stuff. Let's just tell them the steering failed on us. We can make it their fault, not ours."

Vince wore a stunned expression. "Are you really gonna say that?"

"You *amaze* me, you know that. Would you just go with the plan? And lower your voice while you're at it. I don't need their insurance adjusters trying to pin these expenses on me."

Vince Berkley shook his head, then scanned the environs. "If I didn't know any better, I'd think you worked for Jay Austin."

"Learned from the best," Bernie said.

"Just so you know . . ."

"What?"

"I sank the putt. I made par."

"You mean to tell me that you finished your putt before coming to check on me?"

Vince dropped his head and shuffled his feet.

Bernie glared at him. "You are such a goober."

"I know. But I still made par."

Chapter 8

QUESTIONS

TODD

On his way through the dining room, Todd snatched a cookie from the bowl on the bar. He dropped onto the couch and started chewing before his mom could come in and cut short his unauthorized snacking.

He heard her enter behind him, heard her Bible land on the table. The evening service had gone longer than usual, and even Mom had seemed ready to get home. She wasn't one to complain much, but he'd seen her wincing and rubbing her tummy. She looked ready to pop.

Todd wondered what it would be like to have another kid around.

And would he be a good big brother?

It already seemed hard enough to get Dad's undivided attention. A second child would only complicate matters. That was the part that worried him.

"Todd, honey, isn't your volcano project due in a couple of weeks?"

"Yes, ma'am."

"Well then, we better get started on it. We'll go get some supplies tomorrow after school. Why don't you ask your dad to help you with it?"

"I don't think he will."

"Well, you don't know that, honey. Why don't you just ask him and see?"

Todd shrugged.

Behind him, his mom's footsteps moved away, and then the phone rang.

"Hello?" Mom said. "Hey, Papa, how are you? Mm-hmm. Good. Well, Todd and I just got back from church, and Jay's at the car lot doing some work."

Todd saw her step down into the living room, circling around the lamp stand and settling into the cushions beside him. She wrapped an arm around him, which he allowed since there were no witnesses to the event.

Truth be told, he liked it when she did that.

"Yeah, I know," Mom spoke into the phone. She crossed her legs. "Well, he went with us this morning. Mmm, I'd kind of like for you to ask him that yourself. It's hard to say. Sometimes I think we're doing okay, and then other times—well, I just don't know. Jay's just the type of person that does his own thing. But you already knew that, didn't you?"

Todd crammed the last cookie morsel into his mouth.

Mom raised an eyebrow, but voiced no objection. "Thank you, Papa. I cherish your prayers. I'll tell him you called. Yes, sure. He's sitting right here. Hold on." She handed over the phone and whispered, "Say, 'Hello, Papa.'"

"Hello, Papa."

"Well, if it isn't my favorite nine-year-old. How're you doing?"

"The same," Todd said.

"Grams and I miss having you here in Atlanta. You're changing faster than we can keep up with."

"I guess."

"Your mom sent pictures from your last soccer game. I hear y'all are at the top of your division."

"Yeah, I even scored a goal."

"Now, why doesn't that surprise me?"

Todd grinned into the phone.

His grandfather said, "How'd you like to come spend a few days with us after Christmas? Grams has been doing some oil painting, and she thinks you'd make a good student. If you're interested, that is."

"That sounds cool."

"Good. I've already got permission for you to visit, from your mom."

Todd shifted the phone to his other ear. "What about Dad?"

"You know, that's mighty responsible of you to be thinking of his wishes. He's been extra busy, from what I hear. Especially with the holidays and all."

"Yeah."

"I hope you know how much he loves you, Todd."

"Yeah, okay." He brushed crumbs from his pants. "I'm supposed to be getting ready for bed. Talk to you later, Papa."

JAY

Jay headed into the master bedroom after a long afternoon of solitary paperwork, scheduling, and payroll duties in the sales office. The financial crater was growing larger than ever. If something didn't change soon, it would swallow his entire business whole. Not to mention the Austin household's finances.

Although there were legal—and illegal—loopholes that might make things easier, Jay hadn't lowered himself to those levels.

At least not yet.

He untucked his dark gray T-shirt and took a seat on the bench at the foot of the four-poster bed. He removed his watch and rubbed his wrist, while watching a man on the TV juggle a golf ball with the face of his club. He shifted the club between his legs, then behind his back, accompanied by the lively and strangely fitting sounds of the rumba.

Jay rested an arm back over the bed and saw Judy propped against her pillows—always, more pillows—with an open copy of *What to Expect When You're Expecting* atop her belly. A bedside lamp bathed her in a rosy glow.

"Your dad called tonight," she told him.

Jay waited for her to say more. He knew she meant well, but she seemed intent on trying to change him under her own power. It only made him stiffen his spine, sensing a subtle lack of respect for his role as her husband.

He decided to give her the benefit of the doubt. "What'd he say?" he asked, tapping the remote's Mute button.

"He wanted to know how we were."

"What'd you tell him?"

"I didn't know what to tell him, to be honest, Jay."

"Why didn't you just tell him we're fine?"

"Are we?"

He took a deep breath.

"Jay, your dad cares about you very much. He's never wanted anything but the best for you. Just look what he did to get you started with the car lot. That was very generous of him, especially considering we were moving their grandson farther away and—"

"Listen. They were smothering me there."

"I'm not questioning you. I'm just stating the facts."

"I mean, doesn't the Bible say that a husband and wife are supposed to leave their father and mother?"

"And cleave together as one," Judy added quietly.

Jay stared at the television screen.

"You just need to talk to him," she said.

"And what am I supposed to say? He's gonna bring up the money I still owe him, and there's nothing I can do about that. Not right now. It's just . . . It's too overwhelming, okay?"

"If you talk to him, I'm sure he'd work something out."

"Just what I need. More favors. More guilt." Jay turned and pointed across the comforter. "You know, Judy, my dad's still disappointed in me and has been since I was eighteen years old."

"Well, maybe that's because you were stubborn, rebellious—"

"You weren't even *there*."

"And you never listened to him, Jay."

"If he gave me half the encouragement and support he gives Joey, things would be different."

"But your brother's *honored* your father. He's at least shown him enough respect to listen to him."

Jay bolted to his feet. "Okay, we're gonna talk about something else."

He escaped into the bathroom, ran water over his toothbrush, and twisted the cap from the toothpaste. Minty gel spurted onto the counter. He smeared it with his wrist, fumbled the toothbrush into the sink, then stared into the mirror in frustration. Dark eyes and furrowed brows shot anger at him, which he internalized. He scratched at his chin, watched green goop coat his thick goatee.

"Okay," Judy was saying from the bedroom. "When's the last time you did something with Todd?"

Jay rinsed his face and reapplied the paste to his toothbrush. Through bristles against his teeth, he said, "What do you mean?"

"I mean spending quality father-son time with him."

"I *spend* time with him."

"I'm not talking about when you're sitting with him at the dinner table, Jay. I'm talking about investing time with him, doing something worthwhile."

Jay talked around his mouthful of toothpaste. "Okay, why do you do that?"

"Why do I do what?"

See, she was doing it even there. A little respect was all he wanted, and instead she devalued him with sarcasm and subtle jabs. He considered dropping the entire conversation, clamping down on his own thoughts and hoping for some peace in a good night's sleep. If that was possible, after this.

"Do what?" she insisted.

"Why do you put me down and try to embarrass me?"

"I'm just asking a question."

"Well, I have a question." He pointed the foamy end of the toothbrush at her. "You enjoy trying to embarrass me."

"Is that a question? Or a statement?"

"It's a . . . It's a . . . *Do* you enjoy trying to embarrass me?"

"Now, see"—she aimed her finger his way—"*that* was a question."

"Okay, just forget it."

"No, I'll answer the question."

"I don't want you to answer the question."

"Then how 'bout the statement?"

"Forget it, Judy."

"Jay, I'm just saying you should make time for your son. He may not have the same interests. He may like some things that you don't understand—"

"Yeah. I mean, when did he get into this art thing?"

"Thing? It's a talent. You should encourage it."

"He didn't get it from either one of us, though. Not that I can tell."

"Well, your mom's artistic."

"Hmm. Yeah, maybe it skips a generation."

"Jay, the point is that Todd looks up to you."

He ducked into the bathroom, spit, and rinsed. He wiped his hands on a towel and returned to the bed. "No, he doesn't."

"Why would you say that?"

"He said he doesn't." Jay pulled off his socks.

"When?"

"Don't worry about it."

"Jay."

"What?" He tossed the pillows on the floor. Why this female preoccupation with all things soft and fluffy? Maybe it was part of the nesting instinct.

"You're acting like you don't even care about your own son."

Jay sat on the edge of the mattress, his back to his wife. "He told Jeff he did not want to be like me. He did not want to sell cars, and he did not think I was truthful." Jay pulled back the covers and eased into bed, his back still turned.

Judy clicked off her lamp.

Good. This conversation had come to an end. He closed his eyes.

His wife said, "Should he think you're truthful?"

Jay's eyes snapped open again, and he stared at the wall. "I'm not answering that question."

Chapter 9

THE FEEL OF THE WHEEL

BERNIE

Late Monday morning at Jay Austin Motors. Bernie was leaned against a car on the front line, watching traffic flow along the boulevard and hoping for an influx of customers. Already, the smell of KFC was calling to him from across the way.

An early lunch might just work, he decided. Or a late breakfast, depending on how you wanted to look at it.

Down the row, Sam was cleaning the windshield of a Jeep Cherokee that had been egged by late-night vandals, possibly bored teenagers who found some empowerment in the destruction of others' property. More probably, a buyer who had realized the amount he'd been overcharged.

Welcome to the world of used cars.

Bernie pulled the cell phone from his belt and started a

game of Frogger on the display. Beside him, Vince arrived from the warmth of the office building.

"Hey."

"Hey, man," Bernie greeted. "When Max gets done with that Miata, you and me are gonna take it for a test drive. The owners, they wanna know what kind of trade-in value we'll give them."

"A Miata?" Vince crossed his arms. "Cool. I'm in."

"We'll see about that."

"I've never even ridden in one," Vince added.

"Can you fit in one?"

"Oh, I guess *you're* Mr. Universe." Vince shoved his hands into his pockets. His expression turned inquisitive. "All right, man, Jay's on my back about not selling as much as you. Where'd you rip off your selling techniques?"

"Hey." Bernie looked up. "I get my deceit and manipulation honestly."

"Tell that to the Grand Island golf pros."

"No, don't tell them. That's the whole point."

"Right. I forgot."

Bernie gazed off, affecting a look of maturity and wisdom. "Vince," he said. "You just don't have the Touch yet."

"What?"

"Hey, look. When I first got here, I didn't know squat about working people over. I tried reading all that Zig Ziglar stuff, but it was too—oh, I don't know—honorable. So instead, I watched Jay. He's the master manipulator."

"And?"

"Now I've got the Touch."

"The Touch?"

Bernie raised a hand and squinted, as though peering into mysteries unknown. "It's just like the Force, except totally different."

"If you say so, Obi-Wan."

Bernie pressed on. "You've got the Touch when you start taking charge of your car-selling. When you've got the Touch, you'll do anything it takes—and I mean anything—to sell that car."

"Like what?"

"If it's a man, I boost his ego. If it's a woman, I appeal to her emotions. And if it's a teenager, I tell him that his dyed hair and baggy pants look cool, and that I'm thinking about getting a belly-button ring too."

"You wanna know something?" Vince looked around, like he was about to divulge a secret. "I can't even see my belly button."

"Better that way."

"Now, why do you say stuff like that?"

"It's no piece of art, that's all I'm saying."

The corners of Vince's mouth turned down.

"Look," Bernie said, getting back on topic. "When I'm selling a car to a woman, I go after her self-esteem. I make her think she is better for having bought the car and better looking when she's sitting in it."

"Dude."

"Have you ever had one on the line, then lost them when you went to look up the paperwork or answer a phone call?"

"All the time," Vince admitted.

"It's basic psychology. Just open the driver's door, then promise you'll be right back. That one simple action tells them to wait there, don't move, you're on your way back, and they better stay close."

"No way."

"Hey. You try it and then tell me whatcha think. Here's another one for you," Bernie offered. "Say you have a lady who's really interested, but she's teetering over the price. If you want her to keep the car overnight, act like you can't find her own set of keys after she test-drives it. She ends up taking it home, falling in love, and from there she's committed for life."

"The feel of the wheel will seal the deal."

"Yeah. See, Vince. You *have* been listening."

"Jay taught me that one."

"Just don't forget, you always ask the Golden Question: 'What is it going to take for me to get you in this car today?'"

"Sure," Vince said. "I already do that. But what about those guys who won't budge until they talk you down?"

"Oh, no. You have to play that differently. Men wanna feel like they're getting a good deal. So what if they talk you down on the front end? You just dial in the hidden fees on the back end."

"Like what?"

"Well, an administrative fee. A car-preparation fee. Sometimes, I charge an advertising fee."

"An *ad*vertising fee? Man, that's beautiful."

"All in the Touch, my young padawan."

MAX

Max grunted, tightening an engine fitting with a socket wrench. He leaned back from the Triumph TR3 and straightened.

With the typical downtime of a Monday morning, this was a good time for attending to side projects. Either way, he was on the clock. The sales guys, they could have the headaches of working commission. No, thank you.

While fishing the previous day, Max had tossed up a few prayers down by the riverside, and he'd come to see this convertible's condition as a parallel to Jay Austin's spiritual state—clean and polished on the outside, but with problems under the hood. Max was more determined than ever to get it running again.

The car, anyway.

The rest was in the good Lord's hands.

Max Kendall knew, from his sordid past, that he was the chief of sinners. He'd done his share of just about all the sins this world had to offer, with mostly disastrous results. He wasn't one to point fingers. That'd never done anyone any good.

But he had no doubt there was something eating at Jay.

Max had worked for the man since day one, giving two years of his life to this lot. He went out of his way to get vehicles in tiptop shape, and to back up the salesmen's often-bloated promises. As much as was within his mechanical power, he tried to make sure buyers left here satisfied.

Just seemed like the right thing. Do unto others and all that. Now he had the opportunity to do the same for his friend and employer.

As if on cue, Jay walked out from the garage area and joined him under the carport.

"Good morning, Max."

"Jay."

"You seen Bernie and Vince?"

"Uh, they went to test-drive the Miata. They'll be back in a few minutes."

"You're still working on this thing, huh?"

Max gazed over the TR3. "You gave me quite a challenge on this one." He adjusted his glasses on his face and turned his attention back to the task at hand.

"I'm wondering if I made a mistake." Jay put his hands on his hips. "It just looked so good. Price was right. I was just hoping we could get it going."

"Gimme a little longer. Lemme see what I can find."

"So it's not a lost cause?"

"We may have it running yet."

"You really think so?"

"Sure," Max said. "It's in capable hands."

"Well, that much I believe. All right then." Jay patted the convertible's side panel and headed back to the lot.

SAM

Chamois cloth in hand, Sam Jones wiped at another vehicle that had endured splatters from the egging incident.

It amazed him to no end the depths to which people would stoop these days. His own kids were still playing with Legos and Polly Pockets, but he wondered how he would handle things as they grew older. His wife worried herself silly over that sorta stuff, whereas he just gave a shrug and a laugh. What else could you do? His dad had always told him, "Life is best understood and enjoyed when you realize people are imperfect and will let you down. But don't you let that get you down." It was good advice then, and it still worked today.

Sam looked up as the green Miata pulled back into the center of the lot.

Oh, now this would be interesting.

Bernie and Vince were wedged side by side into the compact sports car. If the thing was a stick shift, it was a genuine mystery how Bernie had managed to change gears. The vehicle was hunched down, its chassis scraping the asphalt.

Sam shook his head. How those boys had got into the car was a puzzle. How they got out would be a sight to behold.

He slapped the chamois over his shoulder, tilted back his ball cap, and faced the victimized car. The show was about to begin.

It started with the bursting open of doors.

Then came the squirming of hands and feet, like tentacles seeking some sort of purchase as they emerged from a tight, dark crevice.

"Just . . . uggh . . . move," Bernie said to Vince.

"I'm . . . trying."

"Man," Sam muttered. "I'm gonna have to pry them out."

Vince Berkley's hand stroked the roof. Was he trying to coax the car into releasing him? His fingers found the thin channel designed for wind flow and water runoff. He gripped, pulled, grunted, groaned, tugged . . .

And popped free at last.

"I got it," he said. He stood and looked around, clearly hoping no one had seen this act of humiliation.

Sam shook his head, chuckling.

Bernie was working his way loose as well. He scooted his backside onto the ground beside the Miata, extracted his legs from the cockpit, then bounced up onto his feet. He straightened his knitted vest and pulled back his shoulders, the poster child for smooth.

Sam couldn't stop the laughter that bubbled up from his throat.

"What?" Vince said.

"Hey." Bernie scowled.

"You . . ." Sam got ahold of himself. "You look like two marshmallows trying to get out of a Hot Wheel."

Bernie pointed as he led Vince back toward the office. "That's not funny, Sam."

"Yes it is, too."

What could you do but laugh? No, really. What else could you do? This should be a scene in a movie.

Chapter 10

THE WAGER

JAY

Jay walked the lot's perimeter and verified that things were in order. Overhead, the ascending strings of red, white, and blue pennants formed a big-top circus effect, with the flagpole at its center. Some days, that description fit this place.

He paused beside a gleaming red Ford pickup, a weekend trade-in that had cleaned up nicely. It was sure to turn a decent profit.

His gaze trailed down the row of cars and came to rest upon the familiar face of Reverend Michaels. The minister was no doubt here to take up Jay on his offer. He was in brown pants, a tan vest, and his white hair formed a halolike glow in the daylight. The image seemed a bit far-fetched, but Jay couldn't deny what he saw.

Well, here was an easy sale, at least. Was the Big Guy already kicking in some divine help for Jay's attendance at yesterday's worship service?

Jay strode toward the man. "Well, the good reverend came after all."

"Jay." They shook hands. "How's the car business today?"

"Making ends meet. It's good to see you. Tell me what I can do for you."

"Well, like I mentioned earlier, I'm looking for a car for our daughter. Lindsay's our last one, and I wish she were here, but she's out clothes-shopping with her mother. I'm just trying to find a good buy for her."

"Reverend, let me commit to giving you a good deal."

"I appreciate that, Jay. It's why I came."

"Keeping the money in the flock," Jay said. He'd heard the phrase batted around before, and it seemed religious if not downright churchy.

Probably right up the minister's alley. Or aisle. Whatever.

"Hmm." Reverend Michaels tilted his head. "That's not quite how I see it. In fact, I love to bless those who don't yet know God's grace. Don't you think they need to see Christ's love expressed to them in all areas of life?"

"Uh. Sure."

"Not just if they show up on a Sunday morning."

"Yeah," Jay said. "I agree."

And he did. He'd just never thought about it that way before.

"You know, Jay, I'd really like to surprise Lindsay today, if at all possible. Are there any suggestions you can give me?"

"Sure thing, Reverend." Jay snapped back into sales mode. "Follow me."

BERNIE

Bernie was turned sideways in his chair and butted up to the window. He peered out over the lonely lot. He hated Monday mornings. And, of all things, he was supposed to go down to the police station later to give an official statement of yesterday's accident in the motorized vehicle. Apparently, the golf course was thinking of pressing charges due to his destruction of private property.

What a waste of time. Didn't the cops have better stuff to worry about?

On the other side of the table, Vince was perusing the newspaper while munching on corn chips. "You believe this?" he said. "Bowers is having another sale."

"So?"

"So, I'm just sayin'."

"Gimme that last chip," Bernie ordered.

Vince held it up and then ate it slowly, while taunting him with a stare.

"You fat, lazy, last-chip-eatin' punk," Bernie said.

"Oh, like *I* gotta get on the ball."

"You *need* to get on a treadmill."

"What?" Vince slapped down the paper. "Listen, you better not forget what I did for you."

"Ooooh. Is that a threat?"

Vince hung his head like a guy whose bluff had been called. "No."

"Hey, look. Who's this guy? I'm sure I've seen him before."

Vince moved to the window, peeking between the blinds. "He's a minister, isn't he?"

"Ahh, that's right. He did Keith and Cindy's wedding."

From the corner of his eye, Bernie detected movement. He swiveled his head, watched Vince's arm wrap through the doorway into the kitchen, then retract with another bag of Doritos. The wannabe-golf-pro-turned-chip-thief pulled apart the top of the bag and plucked a tidbit for his enjoyment.

"Hey," Bernie said.

Vince froze, the chip an inch from his lips.

"That would be *my* bag."

Vince gestured to the empty one on the table. "No, *that's* your bag."

Bernie eyed his sales partner, then shifted his attention to the lot. He refused to enter into such juvenile banter. He was too smart for this.

"Jay'll probably give him a deal," Vince said.

"Twenty bucks says he doesn't."

"They *should've* checked you for brain damage. C'mon, you really think he's gonna stiff a minister?"

Smirking, Bernie repeated his wager. "Twenty bucks says he will."

"You're on."

JAY

Jay walked with the reverend down the inner row of cars. Thirty minutes had passed, and he'd struck out with every one of his front-row recommendations. It seemed Lindsay had preferences that could only be pinpointed once her father had spent five minutes in a vehicle.

A common customer was one who, like an ice cube, melted under a little heat. Rarer were the ones like the reverend here, who seemed fluid to start, yet turned rigid as the temperature rose and the time frame expanded.

Passive-aggressives. Tough cookies.

"Right here." Jay's tone had turned lackluster. "These are pretty cars."

The minister nodded. "You've got a lotta nice cars today. Jay, tell me about this Camry."

Jay was losing his mojo, his manipulative car-selling powers. He was no longer directing this purchasing experience; he was tagging along. Now, in a last-ditch effort, he tried to inject an ounce of enthusiasm into his voice. "The Camry's a good car," he said. "It's one of the most reliable on the road."

"You know, Lindsay has a friend that has one. I know she's even driven it."

"What'd she think?"

"She loved it. Maybe we oughta take a look at it."

"It's open. Let's look then."

Reverend Michaels climbed in on the driver's side—a good sign—and Jay felt the first rekindling of hope.

BERNIE

Bernie was still at the window, still on point. Aside from the minister's meandering, the lot had remained clear for the past hour.

Vince was visible in the copy room, putting away files.

"They're looking at the Camry," Bernie reported.

"I say he sells it to him."

"What'd we get it for?"

Vince extracted a manila folder and thumbed through its contents. His jaws were working on another handful of chips. "Sixty-five hundred," he mumbled. "It's got eighty-nine thousand miles on it."

"Jay'll sell it for eight."

"Seven. It is a minister, after all."

JAY

Reverend Michaels was running his hands over the sun cracks in the dash, flipping the visor up and down, pressing the power lock button. Another ten minutes had passed. Though the reverend had yet to declare his verdict, it seemed too late to introduce any more evidence.

Was the man testing Jay?

"I've always liked the storage space in the Camry." Jay was on autopilot again, speaking in monotone. He could do this in his sleep. He pointed at the steering wheel and glove box. "It's got dual air bags. It's done real well in safety tests."

"Well, I know it's a really good car. I'm just wondering if I should try to find one with a few lower miles."

"I don't know. Camrys do real well. The early nineties' models are doing a quarter million miles easily."

"Is that right?"

"Yeah. Great retail value, too."

"What kind of price are we looking at?"

FLYWHEEL

"I've got eighty-five hundred dollars in this car. If you want it, I'll give it to you for nine."

Jay didn't have to go in and check the price. He was lying, and he knew it. Well, after all this fluttering about, didn't he deserve a little profit for his troubles?

"Would you let me take it out for a drive?"

"Reverend, you can drive it all day if you want."

BERNIE

Jay's head popped up from the passenger side of the Camry.

"Aha." Bernie called the play from his window seat. "Looks like he's taking it for a drive. This is where Jay comes in and gets the papers ready."

Jay strolled through the main door, a fresh spring in his step. "Vince," he said. "Get me the forms for the gold Camry."

"Yes, sir."

Jay was all business as he took his seat at the sales desk.

"Is he buying it?" Bernie said.

Jay looked up, a gleam in his eye. "He might."

"You think he will."

Jay took the papers from Vince. "I do."

"How do you know?"

"I sell cars for a living."

"Ha." Bernie coughed out a laugh. "At what price?"

"We'll see," Jay said. "We'll see."

Twenty-four minutes later, according to Bernie's titanium watch, Reverend Michaels was signing a check and handing it over to Mr. Jay Austin.

"Reverend, you've bought a good car," Jay said.

"Thank you. I'm sure I have. I know Lindsay will enjoy driving it."

Jay stood. "I know she will. I appreciate you coming to see me."

"Thank you very much."

"Thank you, sir," Jay said. "Lemme walk out with you."

In passing, the man nodded to Bernie and Max. "Gentlemen."

Bernie sat up straight. "Reverend."

"Good to meet you."

"You too."

Chatting, both buyer and seller marched back outside to the Camry.

Bernie and Vince gave each other knowing glances, then hurried to the desk for a look at the contract. Bernie got there first and snatched up the paperwork. He ran his eyes down the page, double-checked, triple-checked.

"Good *night.*" He started hooting.

Vince grabbed the sheet away. "No way."

"Pay up, baby. I won."

"You didn't say he'd sell it for nine. You said eight."

"Which is closer than you were," Bernie pointed out.

"No, we didn't say whoever was closest. You said he'd sell it for eight."

"I said he would stiff him, and he *did.*"

"I'm not paying you a dime."

"Well then," Bernie compromised, "you're buying lunch tomorrow."

"I'm not buying lunch either. We both lost."

Bernie sniveled in imitation of Vince's objections. He should've known their deal wouldn't hold up. That sort of thing seemed epidemic around this place.

"Listen." Vince softened. "If I'm feeling up to it, I might just bring you a biscuit in the morning."

"Oh, well there's something to look forward to."

Vince pointed out the window. "Jay's still out there working it. What do you think they're talking about now?"

Chapter 11

PUTTING IN REQUESTS

JAY

Jay didn't see it coming.

Reflecting back, he wondered how he could not only miss the inevitable but stumble into it. Not that he could've avoided it. Spiritual pitfalls had a way of sneaking up on you.

He was leading Reverend Michaels around the front of the newly purchased car. The Camry shimmered from its car wash and sat a bit lower beneath a full tank of gas—all thanks to Sam. Even as the driver's door swept open, the scent of carpet deodorizer and ArmorAll wafted into the brisk Monday afternoon air.

Jay laid a hand on his buyer's back. "Listen, Reverend, if Lindsay has any trouble with this car, you give me a call. Okay?"

"I appreciate all your help today. And, if it's okay, I'm going to go pick up Lindsay now, because she's gonna be excited to see this."

"Ohh, yeah," Jay agreed.

"She'll just drop me off, and I'll get my car a little bit later."

"That's fine."

"Jay, I thank you so much." The man's white hair was glowing again in the sunlight. "You've treated me so well today, and I'd like to do something for you."

"What's that?"

"I'd like to pray and ask God to bless you and your business."

Something jolted in Jay's chest. He could use a little help, true. Maybe even a miracle. He wasn't above receiving a blessing, yet in light of the things that went on here at the lot it seemed like it might be misplaced, maybe even inappropriate. Did God have some limit to His blessings, only one or two hundred a week to pass out? If so, the prayer might be better directed elsewhere.

What about the orphans and widows?

Or the poor starving children in . . . in . . . ? Well, wherever they were.

Jay's chin nodded. He heard himself say, "I'd appreciate that."

And why not? Now that he thought about it, having the reverend on his side meant God would be obligated to give heed to this request. You know, bump it up to the top of the list.

"Let's pray."

The man set a hand on Jay's shoulder. There, in the middle of the car lot, he launched into a heavenly petition. Jay followed his lead, lowering his head. Good thing the foot traffic was slow today. This was sure to look awkward.

"Lord," the reverend said, "I come before You and thank You for this day. I thank You for Jay and his business. I thank You for this car for Lindsay. And I ask that You'll protect her and give her grace as she drives this car, and traveling mercies."

Traveling mercies? Yes. Jay was still tracking with the man.

"I pray that You'd give Jay wisdom in his business dealings."

Wisdom? Sure, always a good thing.

"And Lord, I ask that You'd treat Jay just like he treated me today in this deal."

What? Jay's eyelids leaped open. That nine-thousand-dollar check wavered through his thoughts.

Reverend Michaels concluded. "It's in Your name I pray, Lord. Amen."

"Amen."

"Thank you, Jay, for your help."

Jay smiled. "Appreciate it, Reverend. Glad you came by. Take care." He lifted his chin, bracing himself for something—he wasn't sure what. He put his hands in his pockets and watched the minister drive slowly away.

Jay's conscience began speaking to him: *Call him back and fix what you've done.*

What?

Call him back now.

Reverend Michaels pulled into the street and merged into traffic.

I can't. He's beyond earshot now.

His cell phone number is on that contract in the office.

No, what's done is done. It'd only complicate matters to try to undo things now.

So be it.

MAX

Max had located the problem in the '58 Triumph TR3. He pulled himself from under the chassis. Mindful of his medical condition, he climbed to his feet and clapped his palms against his jeans. At times, it was so easy to get caught up in the engine's intricacies—cooling system, fuel distribution, belts, fans, and whatnot—that he forgot to start at the beginning.

Oh, it'd taken a while, but he'd finally arrived at the heart of the matter.

Time to go wash up. Time to let Jay know.

Max grabbed a shop towel and wiped his hands as he headed through the garage into the office building. He felt the blast of heat at the entry. The sales boys had probably been holed up in here, chomping on goodies instead of beating the pavement to get their circulation flowing.

Aww, well. Not his place to say anything.

Head down, he moved through the front office on his way to the washroom. He detected the sales guys in the corner—snacking, as suspected.

"*Max*imus!" Bernie called out. He sounded like a Caesar announcing his champion, yet there was something condescending, even mocking, in the tone.

Max stopped. Shot the big man a look. "Bernie."

"Max the *mar*velous." Bernie snickered. "The mag*nif*icent."

In his earlier years, in the days before Christ had ushered forgiveness into his life, Max would've met this challenge nose to nose. Fist to fist. He had won most of those encounters, and he was sorely tempted to try his hand at another.

He proceeded on his mission to get washed up, turning his back on the continued jests.

"Max-a-*roni*." It was Vince this time. "You get it, Bernie? Max-a-roni."

"That was stupid."

"What? Like yours were any better?"

Max ducked into the washroom, where he worked powdered soap into the creases of his hands, between his fingers, over his fingernails and knuckles. He heard the chime of the main entry and, from around the door frame, watched Jay Austin step into the heat-box.

Bernie pointed at Jay. "Now, there's the man." He bit into a Dorito.

"Why're you guys always eating? When's the last time you sold a car?"

"Sold two last week," Bernie said.

Vince shrugged. "I got a guy coming in today on the Jeep."

"Looking or buying?" Jay asked.

"He might buy."

Jay marched to the sales desk. He seemed irritated.

"I didn't think you had it in you, Jay," said Bernie.

Jay sat and faced him. "What's that?"

"The ability to stiff a minister."

"Oh, excuse *me*, Saint Bernard. I guess you think I'm interested in making the least amount of money we can."

"Hey, I'm all for making money."

Max rinsed his hands and reached for a fresh towel. From the doorway, he watched the goings-on.

"I just thought you would cut the reverend a deal," Bernie went on.

"And you would have?" Jay said.

"I'd try to."

"*Bull.* Vince, would you trust Bernie to sell a car to your mother?"

Vince wrinkled his nose. "Hmm. To *my* mother?"

"To your mother."

Vince chuckled. "No way."

"Oh, c'mon," Bernie exclaimed.

"What's worse, Bernie?" Jay asked. "Overcharging the reverend for the Camry, which is a good car? Or squeezing that old lady for the Marquis last week?"

"She wasn't that old."

"She was in her seventies."

"Late fifties."

"Oh, *please,*" Vince interjected.

"Okay," Bernie said. "Maybe early sixties."

Glaring, Jay jabbed a finger at Bernie. "Don't wag your tongue at me over the Camry. You've ripped off more naive ladies than anyone else in Albany. And stop judging me for something you do yourself. That old lady last week was probably an honorable woman. Her husband probably served in the military."

"Or"—Bernie lifted an accusatory eyebrow—"the ministry."

Vince's expression said *ouch*. As did Jay's.

Max knew Bernie had landed a haymaker, a knock-'em-to-the-canvas blow to the head. In his time working with Jay Austin, Max had noted his boss's inherent respect for older women. He spoke highly of his own mother, and that no doubt played a part in his desire to treat fairly the sweet, silver-haired, elderly ladies that came in—if no one else. Regardless, double standards abounded under Jay's conflicted leadership. And everyone knew it.

Well, if Jay wanted things to change around here, he would have to lead the charge. He was the one heading up this operation, after all.

C'mon, Max thought. *This here's your chance. I've gotcha covered.*

Jay was motionless, his eyes locked with Bernie's.

A ringing phone cut through the office tension. At last, Jay picked up. He motioned for Bernie and Vince to scram, which they did willingly.

Max left as well. He could pass along news of the TR3 later. Jay was suffering under troubles of his own, and Max didn't see it as his place to go meddling. He knew his way around a flywheel and camshaft. Human hearts, now, there was a whole different matter. He'd leave that to a better Mechanic.

The best Max could do was go put in his request for the needed part.

Chapter 12

BOYS TO MEN

JAY

"Jay Austin Motors, this is Jay."

There was hesitation on the other end of the phone, and he considered disconnecting. He didn't have energy right now for prank callers, automated bill collectors, or disgruntled customers.

"Hello?" he prodded.

"Mr. Austin, this is George MacDonald, from Franklin Bank and Trust. I need to talk with you, if you've got a minute."

Perfect. First the reverend's prayer and now this.

"Yes, sir. What can I do for you?"

"You might remember, I used to own a lot myself. I'm not catching you at a bad time, am I? If you're with a customer, you just say so."

Jay almost opted for the escape route. He'd been in Mr.

MacDonald's office before, and he could envision the man at his expensive desk, propped back in his ergonomically designed chair. He would be dressed business-casual, probably in a golf shirt so that he was ready to hit the links. In Jay's experience, he'd always been fair yet firm.

Jay swallowed. "Now's fine, sir. What can I do for you?"

"Mr. Austin, I'm showing that you're over a month behind on the mortgage payment for your lot, as well as for your credit line. And if I remember correctly, this is not the first time this has happened."

"Sir, we've had a pretty slow month."

"That can happen this time of year. I'm sure things'll pick up a bit when people start figuring their tax returns."

Jay clung to this strand of understanding. Maybe he could squirm out of the position he'd gotten himself into. "Mr. MacDonald, we also had some extra expenses we don't normally have. But I think we'll be back where we need to be in a week or two." He wondered, even as he said it, if this conversation was being recorded.

Nah. They had to tell you that sorta thing, didn't they?

"I hope so," the banker said. "It's not my intention to be cruel, but if you don't catch up your payments by the end of next month, we'll come get your cars and close you down."

"I understand, sir."

"To prolong the process only digs a deeper hole for both of us. We're looking at"—the sound of rustling papers came through the phone—"a payment of thirty-two thousand, four hundred dollars."

Jay felt like he'd been struck with a baseball bat. To the knees.

"Do you need me to repeat the figure, Mr. Austin?"

"Uh, I got it. Well, no, I don't have it, and that's the problem. You're sure there's no way we could work out a second mortgage, or—"

"Bottom line is, we need to get our money. That's where we're at."

Jay drew in air. Between his ears, a phrase bounced back and forth: *"Treat Jay just like he treated me today in this deal . . ."*

Mr. MacDonald said, "I don't mean to sound tough, but this is part of my job—and yours—to see to our obligations, even if they require some discomfort."

"Yes, sir. Thank you for your call."

"You have a good day."

Jay wanted to slam down the phone. He held it in his hand a moment, then laid it to rest back in its cradle. There was no reason to punish an inanimate object for the decisions he himself had made, for the consequences he had reaped. For cryin' out loud, these were lessons every child was supposed to learn, and he was a man who could take responsibility for his actions.

Right?

JUDY

Despite the dark outside, and the chill gnawing through the dining-nook windows, Judy felt toasty. Her hormones were wreaking havoc on her internal thermostat, and she was down to a simple aquamarine maternity shirt over stretch pants and a pair of socks.

"Todd," she called. "Come to the table, please."

A slice of store-bought cheese pizza slid from her spatula onto Jay's plate. He'd been in a surly mood since his return from work. He peered over his newspaper at the limp, pasty triangle, looked ready to comment, then—wisely—decided to take what she had served. She had to confess that she'd stopped putting much effort into preparing meals. This was due to her exhaustion, in part, but it was really more a symptom of the tedium that had pervaded their marriage.

She was creating a baby within, wasn't she? *Their* baby. Surely her husband could put aside his troubles long enough to be pleasant with the family. For one meal, at least. Was that so hard?

"Todd."

"What is he doing?" Jay asked.

"He's building a volcano."

Jay paused in his reading. "A what?"

"It's for his science project, he has to—"

"Todd!" Jay shouted. "Come to the table right now."

"Jay, he's coming. He's probably washing his hands. We've got glue and paint all over the place."

"Glue and paint?" Jay shook out the newspaper.

"Yeah, you know. You add baking soda, pour a little vinegar, and get an eruption."

Her husband looked ready to erupt.

No. Judy was not going to allow his negativity to dominate this meal. She felt something rise within, a mother bear's determination to protect her loved ones. She and Todd had been working on the project as a team, and she had no intention of sitting by while he undermined his son's efforts.

As Todd hurried in, Jay gave him a cold stare. "You're not getting any on the carpet, are you?"

"No, sir."

Judy bellied up to the dining table's far end. "Jay, we've got newspapers and towels down. He's being very careful."

"We just finished paying for that carpet. I wanna do whatever it takes to keep it clean."

"Jay, will you stop worrying about your precious carpet? Nothing's going to happen to it."

"What's with the attitude?"

Judy rolled her eyes. "I don't have an attitude."

"You *do* have an attitude." He lifted both hands. "Should I not be concerned about a four-thousand-dollar investment?"

"Jay." She lowered her voice, then tried to communicate with widened eyes that this was not an argument to be carried out in front of their son. Already, Todd's shoulders were slouched, his eyes down. "Just say the blessing."

Jay paused. "Why don't you say the blessing?"

"Okay." Judy lifted her chin and closed her eyes. "Dear God, thank You for this food, Your blessings . . . and the precious carpet we're allowed to walk on."

Jay fidgeted, but she rattled on.

"May it serve us well in the years to come, and be a beacon of hope to all those who live in the house after we're gone." She ended the prayer and met the expected stare from the other end. "Amen."

"That was lame."

"You're welcome to pray anytime you like."

"Thank you for reminding me, Judy."

She lifted the pizza to her mouth.

Todd shifted in his seat, as though mustering the courage to speak. He was wearing a red sweatshirt with designs that he had hand-painted in school. To Judy, he looked warm and cuddly, an imaginative boy full of ideas. To Jay, however, he looked girlish in this sweatshirt. Jay had mentioned it to Judy before, failing to see the beauty in young creativity, finding only flaws in a son with no desire to be a grease monkey or star quarterback.

"Dad," Todd ventured, "would you help me with my project?"

"You know, Judy . . . ," Jay began, giving no heed to his son's request. "I'm getting kinda tired of this holier-than-thou attitude you've been dishing out."

What was she supposed to say to that? How could he be so callous?

"Mom."

"Yes, honey?"

"Can I have cereal instead?"

"Cereal?" Jay said.

Judy touched her son's arm. "Todd, I thought you liked pizza."

"You want *cereal* over pizza?" Jay said.

"Yes, sir."

Jay's gaze panned over the decorated sweatshirt, then cut back to Judy. "What boy doesn't want pizza?"

She lifted one shoulder.

"I don't care." Jay sounded resigned. "Go ahead."

Todd looked to her for confirmation.

"Okay." Judy watched him shuffle into the kitchen. She returned her attention to her husband, who was taking a bite of pizza. She was confused and peeved by his inability to relate to their nine-year-old son. Who was going to be the man here?

"So." She chose another subject for now. "Did Reverend Michaels come by to see you today?"

Jay took a drink. Nodded. "He did."

"And?"

"And he bought a car."

"He did?"

"He did."

Judy watched Todd return with a bowl and a box of Coney Bombs cereal. In a flash, she realized this was his way of making a quiet stand, choosing a meal on his own terms and disrupting the conversation. He'd been ignored, so he had found other means of gaining attention.

Wrong or right, at least he was trying to cope.

Judy had to know, though, what had happened with the minister. "So," she said to Jay, "he came, and you gave him a good deal. Right?"

"It's a good deal."

"A good deal for him?" Judy persisted.

"I see it's time for my nightly interrogation."

"Oh, come on, Jay. You've never kept this stuff from me before. What did you charge him?"

"Nine thousand dollars."

"And what'd you get it for?"

Jay swallowed another bite. He glanced Todd's way, then back to Judy. "Sixty-five hundred."

"That doesn't sound like a deal."

"It was a deal for me."

"Oh, great." She threw her hands up. "Now you're ripping off ministers."

Jay's hand came down so hard against the table that plates jumped and drinks sloshed. Judy flinched in her chair.

"I want you to shut up *now*," he seethed. "The next time you open your mouth, you only open it to *eat*. Do you understand me?"

Judy pressed her lips closed and stared back.

He didn't move. His eyes were hard, burning with rage.

Salty tears clouded Judy's vision. She knew her husband had been fuming for months, yet he'd never lashed out physically. She looked to Todd and saw he had stopped eating, his gaze fixed upon his bowl. In the moment, yes, Jay's action had scared her. More so, though, it worried her for the sakes of her son and baby.

Lord, what's happening here? Where'd we go off track?

Jay gulped down his lukewarm pizza. Judy stood and rushed around the corner, then up the stairs to the master bedroom.

Chapter Thirteen

A DOSE OF LIFE

MAX

Tracking down the needed part was going to be harder than Max thought. He'd called his usual vendors earlier in the afternoon, checked the local wrecking yards, and come up with nothing. Seemed a Triumph flywheel was not in high demand these days.

There was always the Internet. He'd heard people talk about finding parts online, but that sounded strange to his aging ears. If he couldn't touch and feel the thing he was buying, he just plain ol' wasn't interested. The exception being when he got something on the recommendation of a friend, and . . .

Well, most of them were dead and gone. Or in a home, on meds.

Nope, not for him. Max wasn't opposed to a few vitamins

and some pills to help his condition, but he wanted nothing to do with any of them addictive painkillers. He figured it wasn't his place to go playing God. If he was alive and kicking, then he should stay that way. And the day he keeled over—which was sure to come, make no bones about it—he didn't want money-grubbing doctors plugging him into a machine.

Max stretched out on the old sofa. A knitted shawl still covered the arched back—a reminder of a remarkable woman. He missed Shirley. He also knew she was happy where she was, and that was good enough for him.

He tucked a glass of iced tea between his legs, then cracked open a Louis L'Amour paperback. He'd seen to the cleaning of his pouch, and he was ready to settle down for a quiet evening. He'd wake up in the morning with the book dangling from his fingertips or sprawled on the carpet. These days, he could scarcely bring himself to sleep in the bed he'd once shared with his wife. Just wasn't the same.

What was it the Bible said? Something about it not being good for a man to be alone?

Max knew just what that meant.

Of course, at his age he wasn't exactly on the playing field. A crusty ol' guy, cobbled together with fishing line and duct tape . . .

Nope, he'd already had his share of love, and now it was a matter of passing it along to God's children here in Albany—the lost, the found, the red, white, and black. By his way of thinking, there was no better way of saying thanks.

He smiled at the thought. See, he was making headway, still

learning, still growing. Yes, sir, he was a man ready to be used by the Lord.

Lost in these thoughts, Max forgot about the iced tea. The sudden surge of cold liquid between his legs caused him to shoot up from the sofa with a yell. He shook his head in self-admonishment.

Nothing like a dose of life to keep a man in his place.

JAY

Jay kicked off his shoes and leaned back against the couch. Todd had scurried off to his room, and Judy was upstairs, too. It was all because of him, he knew that—because of his explosion at the dinner table.

Well, he'd had it up to here. Couldn't Judy see the pressure he was under? Didn't she understand how much he needed her, of all people?

And still he'd pushed her away.

On the TV, images flashed as Jay scrolled through the channels: a man sprayed by a fire hose's powerful blast; a camouflaged hunter stalking through the woods, rifle in hand; a saluting veteran; a hair-growth infomercial; and a . . .

Was that his own senior pastor on the screen?

Jay turned up the volume. He had to admit this man seemed to have a handle on the struggles of everyday life. Wouldn't hurt to hear what he had to say, especially from the safety of Jay's own living room. If necessary, a click of the remote could end it in a second.

"Listen, folks. Listen." The minister moved from behind his

podium. "You're in the shape you're in today because of the choices you've made. Your marriage is in the shape it's in today because of the choices you've made. Your relationship with your wife and with your children is in the shape it's in because of the choices you've made. You're in financial bondage today because of the choices you've made."

Great. It's all my fault, Jay thought. *Like I didn't know that already.*

"God's Word would set you free if you would read it, but you're in bondage, and you're trapped under all the dirt, and you feel like you're a slave to your debt and to a relationship . . ."

Shoot, if that ain't the truth.

". . . because you've not listened to the Word of God."

Jay let out a breath.

"And until you listen to the Word of God," the minister said, punctuating his points with hand gestures, "you will make the wrong choices, go down the wrong road, lose your family, lose your home, lose your security, lose your investments, because God has a way to live life."

Jay wasn't sure what to think of all that. He knew people who drove expensive cars and lived in fancy homes while skirting all sorts of legal and moral issues. They'd gone down wrong roads and done just fine. Better than fine.

He thought also of the Bakers, a loving family who had served God faithfully only to have their three-year-old son struck down by a drunk driver.

On the television: "I'm not here to say life will be without its struggles. That would not be honest, and even David asked God why it was that the wicked prospered and the righteous suffered." It was as though the minister were listening in on Jay's silent objections. "But you and I cannot live life on our terms and ask God to bless it. The reason that many people I'm talking to today are in bondage, and in frustration, and in defeat, is because . . ."

Let's hear it.

". . . because you don't really want to know what God says. And you don't want to live it God's way."

Jay clicked off the set and stared at the blank screen. Pressure grew in his temples, and warmth burned along the back of his neck. He chewed on the inside of his cheek, not sure what to think or where to go from here.

He tossed the remote back over his shoulder onto the couch.

Landing just right, it snapped the TV back on.

"If any man is in Christ," the minister was saying, "he is a new creation. Old things have passed away. *All* of those old things, not just some things. *All* things. All things have become new."

Jay turned off the TV—again—and pondered that statement.

Becoming new . . .

In his mid-thirties, in debt up to his neck, and in over his head as a father and a husband, he had to admit that becoming new sounded awfully appealing. Who wouldn't want the chance to start over? To start fresh? To have their debts wiped clean?

He rose to his feet and headed upstairs to check on his son. Maybe he could lend some assistance with the volcano project, as a peace offering.

Todd, however, was already asleep in his bed.

Jay watched the rise and fall of his nine-year-old's chest,

then took in the trophies near the lamp and the artwork on the wall. He knew he was not the father he was supposed to be, but he had reasons. Good reasons. He would improve one day. He just needed to focus on some other things first.

He stared at the images on the wall, each lovingly painted by Todd. He wasn't that bad, really. He just needed some time and direction. Maybe one day he would paint Jay a picture.

Then it hit him. His son already had.

The day Todd had brought him lunch was the day he'd thrown away that hand-drawn picture of a race car. Todd's picture, meant for him.

JUDY

Curled beneath the comforter, Judy Austin was shaking. She had never felt more despair in their decade of marriage. Old issues had been simmering for some time, but the heat had been turned up in recent months. Physically, she and Jay had been faithful to each other, but their financial state was a mistress that slipped into the bed between them most evenings, demanding attention—*Look at me . . . Think of me . . . Do you think I'm pretty?*

Jay was trying to provide security. She knew that.

He was trying also to earn his father's favor, to win the respect he felt had gone the way of his older brother, Joey.

Judy thought of her grandparents, who had endured a loveless marriage, nagging and nit-picking at each other on a daily basis. While she admired her grandmother for staying in the marriage for the kids' sakes, Judy didn't want to become another walking martyr. She didn't want to wear her gloom for all the world to see. Wasn't that, in its own way, a form of selfishness?

"Lord," she whispered, "I don't know what to do. Forgive me, but if Jay ever lifts a hand at me or Todd in anger, I don't think I'll be able to stay under the same roof. I know I've been nagging at him, but I just feel so . . . so helpless."

Judy heard her husband's heavy steps on the stairway. She rolled over in the bed, her back to the door, and tried to calm her sniffles. She felt his weight press down on the other side of the mattress, sensed his gaze on her.

There was so much she wanted to say. She felt like sitting up and unloading on him, giving him a piece of her mind.

Instead, she closed her eyes and pressed her head into the pillow.

I give up, Lord. You're going to have to say it for me.

PART TWO

"The flywheel's been around for a coupla thousand years, going all the way back to the potter's wheel."

—MAX KENDALL, MECHANIC

Chapter 14

SLOW DRIP

JAY

In his desire to reach the sales lot early, Jay braved the season's first morning of deep frost. He knew Sam would be close behind, and so he stopped en route and bought a de-icer canister made for dealing with the frozen door locks. It'd save Sam some hassles and numb fingers while opening the vehicles on the front line.

Jay tested out the stuff on the building's main door. Worked beautifully.

He hurried inside, removed his gloves, and disarmed the security system. He hit the lights, turned up the heater—just enough to take the chill off—then moved into the copy room, where he let his hands sift through the recycling bin.

This was his real reason for arriving early. Each evening, he dumped his paper trash here, and he could only hope to find what he was looking for before the truck came by today for the week's scheduled pickup.

Here it was. Todd's picture.

Jay coughed out a laugh of relief, then admired the orange race car and the amount of work that'd gone into it. The number 71 was drawn in large numerals on the vehicle's door.

The year Judy was born. Not that Todd would think of that.

His wife liked to remind him it was also the year Starbucks was started. One of her favorite hangouts. Recently, she'd been laying off the caffeine, in consideration of their baby. Who needed kids to be any more wired than they were already, right?

Jay smoothed the picture on the copy room desk. He wondered if Todd knew what his father had done with the drawing.

The poor kid. He'd probably been waiting days to hear his dad mention it.

Jay dialed his home number. "Hey, Judy. Todd there?"

"Just got on the school bus."

"Oh."

"What's wrong?" Her tone was tentative.

"Aw, it's nothing. I'll catch him later."

"Okay."

"Judy?"

She waited on the other end.

"Listen," he said. "I . . . Well, it can wait, if you're not in the mood to talk."

"It's not that, Jay. I just don't know what to say anymore."

He snorted. "Makes two of us, then."

"What's happening?"

"With what?"

"With us."

"Nothing," he said.

"That's what I mean. That's what's worrying me."

"Judy, there's a customer coming in. I've gotta go."

It wasn't a lie. Not exactly. Bernie was coming up the steps with a brunette at his heels, and in the larger sense weren't Bernie's customers Jay's customers? Anyway, it was rude to argue on the phone in front of other people. Jay's mother had taught him that.

He set down the receiver, glanced again at the paper in his hands.

A blast of cold air ushered in Bernie and the young lady. He must've arranged to meet her before she went to work—or, in her case, maybe college courses at Darton or Albany State. She had long, curly, dark hair, and a strand of puka shells adorned her neck.

From the rotating black seat, Bernie began feeding her payment options, utilizing a worksheet the way Jay had taught him.

A simple trick, really. The salesman started with four squares, one for sticker price, one for the buyer's trade-in value, one for down payment, and one for the monthly payments. If the buyer dickered down the amount in one box, the salesman fluctuated figures in another. And always, always, he tried to bump them up in each box. Okay, so the buyer was willing to pay three-fifty a month? Would they be able to swing three-seventy-four?

Odd numbers made it sound more legit. And, of course, it all added up over time. More money in the seller's pocket.

Jay threw surreptitious glances through the doorway and listened in.

"Oh, yeah," Bernie was telling his gum-smacking female customer. "Believe me, Misty, when these things first came out, they were so popular no one could keep them on the lot."

"Wow."

"I'm just telling you, they're great cars. Obviously, you know that, or you wouldn't be interested in it. I just know that when I test-drove it, it handled great."

"I just *love* them. They're *so* cute." Misty was fiddling with her necklace. "When we graduated two years ago, my friend got one, and she just loves it."

"Well, I've been amazed that it's stayed out here as long as it has. I keep thinking that someone's gonna realize that we've got it and take it outta here."

"Really?"

"Oh, yeah." Bernie chuckled. "If I were able to get it myself, you wouldn't have even had a shot at it. You're getting a corner on an amazing vehicle."

"Well, uh, I'd like to get it. I just don't know about the monthly payments."

"Hey, if you tell me you want this car, I will bend over *backwards* to make it happen for you."

Jay had heard Bernie sell dozens of cars like this, but he winced at how manipulative, how self-serving, those same tactics now sounded.

"You're so *sweet*," Misty responded to Bernie.

"Hey," he said, "I just wanna see you get the best car you can.

Now, if I told you I could get the payments under two-fifty a month, would you be able to do that?"

Misty hesitated. "Uh, actually I was thinking more like *one*-fifty a month."

"I know it seems like a lot, but I don't wanna see you miss out on a good deal like this. It's rare to find one in this good of condition."

Jay listened in disgust. He knew the car's history of transmission trouble—and so did Bernie. Over the sales desk, a sign read HONESTY IS OUR BEST POLICY! He glanced up at it, then back at Bernie.

"Mmm, I don't know," Misty said.

Bernie never eased up. "Well, lemme see if I can get it under two-thirty a month. We'll throw in a free detail, fill it up with gas. We could be done with the papers, and you could be showing it off to your boyfriend inside of half an hour."

"Uh, okay. I guess I should take advantage of this great sale."

"Hey, that's right. You've made a great decision. I would've hated to see you walk away from such a good deal." Bernie slipped the paperwork across the desk to her, ready to seal this thing with signatures and a check.

Jay's stomach churned. Bernie's tactics were effective but somehow disgusted him in a way he had never felt before. He got up and headed toward the washroom, listening to the white lies Bernie continued to dish out about the vehicle. Part of him wanted to interject himself in the proceedings, but he knew the deal was all but done.

Over the sink, he stared at a spot beside the drain, formed by the faucet's slow drip. Each drop . . .

Staining, chipping away, little by little by little.

He looked up and found himself staring at a man he no longer knew. Although the face was familiar, the character was mired in a haze of uncertainty and frustration. There was no peace there. No safety remained.

Bernie and Misty headed outside to her bargain-mobile. Once the door was closed, Jay marched into the sales office and tore the *Honesty* sign from the wall. He dismantled the foam-backed board piece by piece and shoved it into the garbage can.

BERNIE

Despite the icy breeze, Bernie was feeling warm and fuzzy inside. He waved farewell to Misty, and as she steered the car out of the lot, her adorable smile only warmed him further. Heck, in her mind they were pals.

"So long as you're paying for my vacation," he muttered.

Talk about starting the month off right. He could almost smell the Bermuda sea salt now, could almost taste the piña coladas.

Vince Berkley strolled up beside him. "Man, I can't believe you sold her that car. She told me she was just looking."

"You're too nice to them, Vince."

"I'm too nice?"

"Yeah. You've gotta be more aggressive. Flatter the snot out of them, then just reel them in." Bernie sniggered at how easy it seemed sometimes.

"Hey. What'd you clear?"

"You wouldn't believe me."

"Bernie." Vince threw his hands up. "C'mon."

Bernie sauntered away. "Five," he said over his shoulder.

"No you didn't. Bernie, tell me you didn't do that."

"I did. And it felt good."

"I could never do that."

"You could. You just won't." Bernie led the way up the stairs into the office. "I told you, you're too nice."

"You made *five* thousand dollars off that car?"

"I'm bringing it in today, baby." Bernie plopped into the chair behind the sales desk, forcing Vince to choose the customer's hot seat. "Five big ones."

"I think it's time for you to treat me to a round of golf."

"And watch you cheat again? I know you didn't sink that last putt, Vince."

"Yeah, I did too."

"Did not."

"Well, if you weren't so busy wrecking the golf cart . . ."

"Hey." Bernie held a finger to his lips. He'd made his official statement to the cops, and he didn't need his sales partner blabbering any details—even in jest—that might stir suspicions. "Vince, I think you need to start selling some cars like a big dog and buy your own round."

"It'll happen. Maybe even today."

"Maybe." Bernie's eyebrows pushed together. "Hey, what's different about that wall up there? There was a clock there or something."

Vince turned just as the boss man appeared in the copy room doorway. "Jay, did you take anything off that wall?"

Jay said, "You shouldn't have done that, Bernie."

"Shouldn't have done what?"

"One thousand dollars was fine, but someone's gonna figure out Misty got overcharged four thousand on this deal and make an issue out of it."

"*What?*" Bernie was incredulous.

"Would you not wanna kick the guy in the teeth that overcharged your wife several thousand on a car?" Jay said.

"She's not married."

"That's not the point. She's got a boyfriend, parents, or friends that're gonna figure out she got sloshed on this deal."

"Whoa. Who are you talking to? I just made a week's profit—and I'm getting *slammed* for it?"

"Bernie, it's not the profit. It's the way you got it."

Vince sat motionless, his mouth zipped tight.

"Since when did *you* become a Boy Scout?" Bernie shot back at Jay.

"You don't think you did anything wrong?"

"Oh, so if Jay Austin pulls in a few thousand dollars, it's good business. But when Bernie Myers does it to help the team out, it's ripping people off?"

"You *gross*ly manipulated her."

"You taught me *how*!" Bernie yelled.

Jay stared at him, obviously stunned by this comeback.

Bernie knew he was right, and it angered him that the man who'd taught him the plays was now calling him a cheater. He continued, "I don't know what kinda game this is, but you've got different rules for yourself."

"All right, that's it. I don't wanna talk about this right now."

Bernie watched Jay stomp out the door, then swiveled toward Vince. "What the heck was that?"

Vince shrugged. "I don't know."

"Nah." Bernie scowled, rocking back in the seat. "I'm not doing this. If he starts unloading trash on me, I'm *outta* here. He's no saint."

Chapter 15

GLITTER AND FLASH

JUDY

Her husband was no saint. Judy knew it in the same way she knew she shouldn't be standing in line at Starbucks. Sure, she could order decaf as a safe alternative for her child. But that wasn't going to happen. She was here for a morning jolt, and there was no use pretending otherwise. Her son was at school, her husband at work, and this was Momma time.

Her need was only intensified by the gossip being swapped in the line just ahead. Two women were talking about *her* husband.

As if they had any right.

"Oh, sweetie, I'm not here to judge," said the spindly blonde.

"Of course not," the one with heavy rouge responded.

"But with the things I've been hearin' . . . Well, if you want my opinion, Jay Austin Motors oughta be investigated. Poor Miss Marlowe. I mean, it's just awful."

"To take advantage of a single mother."

"'T'ain't right."

The women spoke in the sort of hushed tones that only drew more attention and could be heard by all. Judy had to hold herself back. She knew they were speaking the truth—though certainly not in love—and anything she said would only add fuel to their fire.

"Big-city folks." Spindly's long arms folded into a pretzel shape. "They come swoopin' down on a sleepy town like Albany, and they got nothin' but dollar signs in their eyes."

"*Pheww*. Atlanta. Now, that's like a *whole* other county."

"It *is* another county."

"Country. Country's what I meant."

"Of course you did, sweetie."

Judy thought of that old Norman Rockwell painting, with the town's rumormongers seated in a line at the hairdresser's as they fluffed their beehive hairdos. Seemed the Starbucks line had taken its place.

She watched Spindly Blonde and Heavy Rouge order their drinks, and felt an odd mixture of indignation and embarrassment churn inside.

Or maybe it was her baby. In fact . . .

Yes. She tracked the tiny foot or elbow that slid across her belly.

"What can we get for you today?" inquired the kid in the green apron at the register.

"Uh." Judy stared up at the menu. "I'm sorry, my mind went blank."

"Happens all the time around here."

"I . . . I'm pregnant."

The kid nodded. Clearly he didn't need her to tell him that. Already he was looking past her at the others in line.

"I, uh . . . How 'bout I try—"

"A chai? Coming right up."

Though she hadn't said *chai*, the misunderstanding seemed to be for the best. She was digging for change at the bottom of her purse, when she remembered that chai was made from tea, and tea had caffeine, and—

"Decaf," she blurted. "Make it decaf."

"Sure thing."

"For my baby."

"Okay."

"Ohhh, and lots of whipped cream." She turned aside to wait.

"Ma'am? I'm sorry, but . . ."

"What?"

"You still haven't paid."

Judy hoped Jay was faring better today than she. Between the pregnancy, the lack of caffeine, and last night's tears in her pillow, she was a mess.

JAY

The sun was poking holes in the cold, and cars were whizzing past on the main thoroughfare.

With hands on his hips, Jay paced beside an Isuzu Trooper

in the lot. Here behind the tall vehicle, he was mostly hidden from the spying eyes of Bernie and Vince in the front office. He took a deep breath. Things seemed to be unraveling around him.

He clasped and dragged his hands over his hair, then planted them on his sides again. How had he ended up in this place?

He found himself wandering toward the carport, in need of someone to talk to. As he turned the corner, he spotted Max stretched out in mechanic's overalls beneath the TR3. The convertible's top was down, the hood up.

At Jay's arrival, the older man sat upright on the concrete while still wiping a wrench with a shop rag. Jay took his usual place in a plastic deck chair, leaning his head back against the white siding of the garage.

Max said, "You look like you just got out of a fight where everybody had a stick but you."

Jay gave a half laugh. "How's it going, Max?"

"I don't know yet." The man peered up through his glasses. "I keep thinking I've got it figured out, but I keep being wrong."

"That's true for both of us."

"You got something you can't fix either?"

Jay sighed. "Several things. Least, I think I know how to fix them, but I keep being wrong."

"We both sound pretty pathetic." Max laid down the wrench, then stood and went around to the side panel. He leaned over the engine.

"Is that car worth the time you're putting in it, Max?"

"Well, I can tell you this . . . The flywheel's stripped."

Jay crossed his arms and gave a questioning look.

"Don't tell me you don't know what a flywheel is," Max said.

"I don't."

"How long've you been selling cars?"

"Nowhere near as long as you've been alive."

Max wagged a finger at him.

"Okay, fine." Jay left his seat and faced the mechanic over the exposed machinery. "Tell me what a flywheel is."

"See here, when you put the key into the ignition, that sends power to the starter, the starter engages your flywheel, your flywheel turns your crankshaft, and your crankshaft starts your engine. Without your flywheel, you're not going anywhere."

"So, can we get a new one?" Jay said.

"Already working on it. I just hoped it would be something easier to get to. The flywheel's sandwiched between the engine and the transmission. I'll have to drop the transmission to get to it."

"Sounds like a lotta work."

"No one said it would be easy."

"Well, if there's anybody that can do that, it's you, Max. Then at least one of us'll have our problems fixed."

"You ready to talk cost?"

"What, for the flywheel?"

"Looking at close to four hundred in parts alone."

Jay slouched back into the deck chair. "Figures."

"I'm shopping around, though. We'll see what we can come up with." Max shifted around the front end's gleaming silver grille. "You seem to be carrying a heavy load lately. You okay?"

"Not really. To be honest."

The older man remained quiet.

"I cannot remember," Jay said, "the last time I felt like my life was going right."

"So, I should pray for you."

Jay gave a weary smile.

"Or maybe," Max said, "*you* should pray for you."

Jay looked off. "I don't know about that."

"Why not?"

"I don't think God will listen to me right now."

"Whaddya mean?" Max pushed.

Jay set both elbows on his knees. Like most men, he didn't tend to open up about personal problems—especially to other men. For reasons beyond his own understanding, though, the words spilled out: "I mean, He knows I'm not an honest man. He knows I'm a lousy husband and father. He knows how selfish and prideful I am." Jay hesitated. "I don't even like myself, Max. I've got friction with almost every person in my life. I owe money to the bank that I don't have."

A gust of wind shook the trees along the carport, and a lone limb scratched at the roofing.

"I'll tell you this, Jay. I'm an old man, and there's some things I wish I'd have gotten right decades ago, but my pride was in the way. If I hadn't been so doggone stubborn, I woulda saved myself a good deal of grief and spared my wife a whole lotta pain."

Jay's mind jumped to last night's dinner table.

"Thing is, when I learned to let the Lord run my life, it got a whole lot better. You know me, Jay. You know the things I've done, things I've walked through. I don't mean to preach at you, but I just know I need Him. Frankly, I'd say that we all need Him."

Jay needed *some*thing. On that, he could agree.

"You know, this here's a beautiful car," Max said, patting the side of the Triumph. "Still got a good engine. But until we get that piece that fixes the engine, it's not going anywhere."

Max left it at that. He headed back into the garage.

Jay Austin let his gaze move over the TR3's smooth, waxed finish. He thought about what his friend had said. This vehicle was a classic, a head-turner, yet it was useless at serving its true purpose as long as it remained in its present condition. Without that one essential part, the glitter and flash meant nothing.

Chapter 16

SET IN MOTION

JAY

He was in his usual place on the carpet, his back pressed against the couch. His conversation with Max had stirred something within him. He'd come home early to find a place to think. Judy would be picking up Todd from soccer practice about now, and she'd most likely run a few errands before heading home. The house was so still that the ticking of the clock near the bookcase seemed to reverberate between the walls and the sliding glass doors that led onto the deck.

Jay folded his hands in his lap. He felt small. Insignificant.

His pulse thumped at the contact point between his two wrists, adding a counterpoint to the clock's second hand. He felt drawn into a rhythm that he usually overlooked, though it was beating all the time.

On the lamp stand, a framed wedding photo showed Judy in her dress and flowing veil, holding a bouquet. Her head was turned toward the camera. Toward him. He caressed the ring on his finger, remembering that day. She had been resplendent, taking away his breath as she glided up the aisle. He'd never before felt like his heart could swell to the point of bursting. It had been a cliché to him—until that moment.

Love her, as Christ loves the church.

And what had Jesus done but laid down His very life?

Jay remembered their vows, but they seemed so distant, as if their validity had somehow lessened over the years. At least, he had felt that way. Now, as he recalled the desires he'd had on their wedding day—to love her, to have God's blessing on their lives, and to be a good husband—something in him snapped.

He had failed. He had become someone completely different. Someone so wrapped up in himself that he had hardly noticed the downward slide.

Jay's pulse was pounding. He could hardly hear the clock due to the rush of blood in his head. He had done so much to undermine their marriage, given Judy so many reasons to doubt his decisions about their money and livelihood. The Scriptures instructed her to submit to his leadership, yet he'd squandered that authority in so many ways.

As the head of the church, Christ's authority was rooted in sacrificial love.

Why, Jay wondered, did he think he should have it any easier?

He studied the toddler photos of his son, nearby. Such a handsome little guy. A boy who'd always looked up to his father, even if he had interests of his own. And Jay had overlooked him day after day, year after year. Soon, Todd would have a little brother or sister looking up to him. What kind of model had Jay been for his son? For anybody?

For the first time in his life, Jay truly acknowledged who he was. He was someone who'd fallen short of the mark—in his wife's eyes, his son's, and even God's. He had become callous to his own selfishness and pride, and he knew a day of reckoning would come. A day for which he was not ready.

He needed someone else to take the reins. To show him the way.

"Oh, Lord." Jay got on his knees down on the floor, where the late-afternoon light was playing across the carpet. Any intentions of sounding pious gave way to the need of the moment. "I don't want Your face against me. I need You. I'm sorry. Help me, Lord. Help me get back in Your will. I want to be a good man."

As the words poured from his mouth, he felt his heartbeat falling into step with a greater purpose, like a precision timepiece set in motion by the watchmaker.

"Help me, Jesus," he said. "You're in charge now. You're the boss."

For the first time in ages, Jay felt tears well in his eyes and begin to pour out. As he cried, he felt a release and a peace like he'd never before experienced. He fell silent after that, listening instead. He'd released the reins, handing them over to one who knew the way, and lay on the floor with a new resolve growing in him.

When Judy and Todd arrived twenty minutes later, Jay was seated on the couch, his throat still tight and his eyes heavy. Todd dashed up to his room, following his mother's instructions to get going on his homework.

Judy moved into view in the dining room, where she rested her purse on the table. "I didn't expect to see you home so early," she said.

Jay's gaze met hers. "Can we talk?"

"Sure."

"Would you come sit with me?"

She stepped down into the living room and took her place on the far end of the couch. She propped a pillow behind her back. Her expression was a mixture of suspicion and worry.

"I know I hurt you terribly last night," Jay said. "I was wrong to do that, and I'm sorry."

"You're apologizing to me?"

"I am."

She examined his expression. "Is something wrong with you?"

"There is."

"Jay, are you . . . ?" Her caramel-colored eyes widened. "Are you dying?"

"No. No. I, uh . . ." Jay moved the ottoman in front of Judy, then sat facing her. "What's wrong with me is that I have been living for myself. I have not been the husband I need to be. I have not been the father I need to be. I have not been the spiritual leader I need to be. Today I asked God to forgive me. I have gotten myself in a mess in almost every area of my life, and I can't fix it. I admit that I have not been worthy of honor, or respect, or the love of my family." His voice started to crack. "But I want to be."

"Jay." Her eyes softened, connecting with his.

"Judy, I'm asking you to pray for me. I need you. I need you terribly. I am resolving to let Jesus be Lord of my life. Every day."

"You're serious."

"I *am* serious. I will be honest in my business. I will take responsibility as the spiritual leader of my home. I will love you. I will love Todd."

Judy's lips quivered.

"And I will love our baby," Jay said. "So help me God, I will."

She closed her eyes, and moisture squeezed out along her dark lashes. He leaned forward, wrapping his arms around her, and she let the tears fall. She was so warm. He recalled how wonderful, how right, it felt to be joined with her in an embrace. And between them, even now, a new life was preparing for a grand entry. Jay could not let this family slip through his fingers.

His face was aimed over her shoulder at the dining area, and for a split second he thought he saw movement in the doorway.

A witness? Always, a father had witnesses.

The soft padding of feet up the stairs not only confirmed Todd's momentary presence; it underlined Jay's commitment to make this thing work.

TODD

His shin guards were still stuffed into his socks, sticky with sweat. Even though his knees were scuffed from slide tackling his team's leading scorer during the afternoon scrimmage, the attaboys from his coach had more than made up for the blood.

Todd liked being outdoors, even in the cold. Soccer was his favorite sport, and he'd played two seasons for the Sherwood Eagles.

But more than anything he loved imagination.

He peeled loose his shin guards and dropped them to the floor. He plopped down cross-legged on the carpet at the foot of his bed. He'd painted the papier mâché volcano yesterday, and now he was going to add tiny shreds of vegetation to the rugged slopes, using real leaves and grass from the backyard.

He reminded himself to keep his ears open for Mom's approach. He was supposed to be taking a shower before dinner. Not that he was really that dirty. Why did mothers stress so much about washing up?

Dad had been waiting for Mom in the living room, and maybe she'd sent Todd off just to get him out of her hair.

Parents needed time alone. Todd knew that.

He also knew that last night's argument was worse than normal, and so he couldn't help but eavesdrop as his mother went to sit on the couch. Todd couldn't hear all that was said. He saw enough, though.

Enough to know that Dad was acting . . . different, somehow.

Acting. That was the problem. Todd had seen his dad put on a show before—for customers, relatives, and people at church.

Todd glued down tufts of green and wondered how long his dad's change would last. Dad had made and broken promises before. Todd wanted to know this was for real before he was going to get too excited about it.

MAX

The message light was blinking on Max's machine when he got out of the shower that evening. He'd pulled out a fry pan and was heading to the garage to grab a bluegill from the freezer, when the red indicator snagged his attention.

"Better not be one of them telemarketers."

He punched the Play button.

"Heyya, Max. Garrett, here. Caught wind that you were wantin' parts for a '58 Triumph. Sure hope you're not tossin' good money at old cars. Then again, could be that age's playin' tricks on you." A throaty chortle. "Well, you gimme a call when you get round to this message. I don't talk money on people's machines. Shoot, then y'all might just hold me to it." Another chortle. "You oughta know where to find me. Same place you left me."

Max deleted the message after a second listen. His last encounter with Garrett had been in a pool hall downtown. A friendly game of billiards had turned into a heated argument—*Your cue ball touched the eight ball first, and don't you go tellin' me otherwise*—and both men had stood their ground.

Garrett knew about Max's bullet wounds, but not the pouch. As for Max, he knew he would never swing first, but so help him, if Garrett struck out, Max would have to put the man down on the ground.

In the end, they had both grumbled off through different exits.

That'd been two years ago, just about the time Max started working for Jay Austin Motors. Now here was Garrett, offering help with the TR3.

"Why should I even be surprised?" Max said aloud.

When God was at work, help could come from just about anywhere.

JAY

The next morning, Jay guided his SUV with the dealer plates into a parking space along the car lot's north end. He knew things needed to change around here, but the practical outworking of that remained to be seen. Today, his renewed commitments would be put to the test.

He climbed out of the vehicle and registered for the first time that he was wearing an orange-red shirt tucked into dark green pants.

Christmassy? Well, maybe.

It was one more reason, though, that he should not be getting dressed in the dark. Or, for that matter, be dressing himself at all. Best to defer to Judy's good judgment.

Inside the office building, he ran through the opening routine. He had a half hour till the beginning of business, and he knew his sales staff wouldn't roll in until the last minute. Sam and Max would be here shortly, yet their initial duties kept them busy out on the lot or in the garage. Oftentimes, he saw neither of them till a coffee break around 10:00 a.m.

Jay sat down in the copy room and opened his Bible atop the yellow-highlighted desk calendar.

Where to start?

This was like trying to make conversation with a friend he hadn't seen in ages. Should he go right to the serious stuff? Or get reacquainted through some basic Q&A time?

Psalms. That was right in the middle. As a kid he'd never been much of a reader, so his parents had advised that he stick to a daily devotion of one psalm as well as one of Proverbs' thirty-one chapters.

He'd never stuck to the plan for more than four or five days in a row.

He read aloud now, to seal the words in his memory: "'Blessed is the man who does not walk in the counsel of the wicked or stand in the way of sinners or sit in the seat of mockers. But his delight is in the law of the LORD, and on his law he meditates day and night. He is like a tree planted by streams of water, which yields its fruit in season and whose leaf does not wither. Whatever he does prospers. Not so the wicked! They are like chaff that the wind blows away. Therefore the wicked will not stand in the judgment, nor sinners in the assembly of the righteous. For the LORD watches over the way of the righteous, but the way of the wicked will perish.'"

He ruminated on these words.

What did it mean to delight in God's law? Was it mental enjoyment only? A state of contentment and rest? Or could it apply also to having fun on the job, to doing what was right while fulfilling your duties?

Almost opening time.

Jay walked out into the cold, hands in pockets, and scanned the rows of vehicles. The shadows were shortening, and the sun glistened off chrome and glass.

He said, "All right, Lord, this is Your lot. I will honor You with it."

Chapter 17

ONE WORD

BERNIE

Bernie showed up thirty-five minutes late. He blocked part of the service bay with his Chevrolet SUV and lumbered across the asphalt in his cream-colored vest and slacks. So what if he wasn't here on time? He had no appointments, and it wasn't like customers were pounding on the doors this early on a Tuesday.

"Max," he said to the man in the garage.

"'Morning, Bernie. You working on Central time today?"

"I needed the extra sleep, so sue me. Like Jay has any say in the matter." Walking by, he tossed his keys to the mechanic. "I'm a little low on transmission fluid. How 'bout hooking me up, man?"

Max looked down at the keys in his palm.

"You're Max-arvelous." Bernie hurried on, giving no time for an objection. He'd learned that tactic right from the beginning.

In the front office he found Vince on point, near the front door, reading the *Albany Herald*.

"Where were you this morning, Vince?"

"What're you talking about?"

"You said to be at the Corner Café at nine o'clock."

"No," Vince corrected. "I said to be at the Biscuit Barn at nine."

"The Biscuit Barn?"

"Yeah."

"So where're the biscuits?"

"I didn't feel like a biscuit." Vince straightened the paper. "So I went to Pearly's."

"What'd you get at Pearly's?"

Vince kept his eyes down. "A biscuit."

Bernie's lips curled. "You're a goober."

"I know." Vince grinned. "Least I got a biscuit. But I was there at nine and you weren't."

"I was at the Corner Café at nine, and"—he stabbed a finger toward Vince—"you'd better be there tomorrow at nine."

"How about being at *work* tomorrow at nine?" Jay said.

The boss man had slipped in unnoticed. His arm rested on the mantel beside the plaques and certificates. Did he think he appeared more intimidating with the accolades around him? They were empty awards, just slips of paper that anyone with a business license could dredge up.

Bernie refused to kowtow. He threw his hands up in mock surrender and donned a look of fear. "Oh, no. Jay's cracking the whip again. I think we better stop being lazy."

"You're admitting that you're lazy?"

"Well, no. I know it may look like it sometimes, but I . . . I like to think of myself as a hardworking man, trapped in a lazy man's body."

Jay seemed unconvinced.

Sam popped in from the kitchen area and took a seat, apparently interested in this conflict. He wore his usual cap, turned backward, and a leather necklace with a black onyx pendant.

Vince followed Bernie's lead. "I've always thought of myself as a tan bodybuilder," he said, "trapped in a chubby white man's body."

Bernie pinned him with a blank-eyed stare.

"Sam?" Jay said. "Anything we should know about you?"

"I'm just a black man in a black man's body, working with a buncha *strange* white boys."

Bernie smirked. At least Sam was keeping his good humor about this, whereas Jay Austin had his shorts all in a wad. Power politics would only backfire on him. He could try to enforce strict schedules, but this was a car lot—a *used*-car lot—and everyone knew that salespeople played by their own set of rules.

Or no rules at all. It took a special breed to survive in this business.

"Would you mind getting Max?" Jay said to Sam. "I'd like for us to have a little talk."

"Sure."

"With all of us?" Bernie checked.

"Yeah."

"What is this about? Are we in trouble or something?"

"I'll tell you when Max gets here."

"Listen." Vince scooted his chair toward Jay. "I'm planning to be here at nine tomorrow. I could get my biscuit earlier."

Bernie rolled his eyes. Already, the guy was schmoozing.

"Or," Vince added, "I don't have to get a biscuit at all."

Jay said, "It's not about the biscuits, Vince."

"Look, if this is about Bernie scraping the side of the Tahoe, that was an accident. I was there. He was only trying to park it between—"

"*Vince*," Bernie butted in. "Shut up."

"Were you gonna tell me about that?" Jay asked.

"Of course I was."

"After our meeting, I'll have you fill out a dents-and-dings report. That way we'll keep our inventory files accurate."

Bernie wanted to throttle his sales partner for opening his big mouth. They worked with vehicles, they tried to make sales, and sometimes they had to move things around without the aid of Sam or Max. So, there were the occasional minor incidents. Those were to be expected. Heck, Jay had probably made his share of miscues along the way. Who hadn't?

Sam and Max entered the room and took seats near the fireplace.

"Good morning, Max," Jay said. "Thanks for coming in. This shouldn't take but a minute."

"That's what he always says," Bernie murmured.

"I'd like to start by apologizing to each of you," Jay said.

"Apologizing? For what?"

"This is my business, Bernie. For the last two years, I have not been running it honestly or respectfully. I wanna say I'm sorry to each of you—for being a bad example."

Max was stoic, wiping his hands with a rag. Sam and Vince were all ears, lapping up these saccharine tones.

"No." Bernie shook his head. "You've gotta be kidding me."

"I'd also like to say to you that from now on we will be selling cars at honest prices."

Vince was confused. "What's that mean?"

"It means you get a fair commission off a fair sale."

"Okay," Vince said. "But who determines what 'fair' means?"

"Well, if you bought the car that you're trying to sell from another salesman, what would you feel okay with him making off it?"

"Oh." Vince looked away. "That stinks."

"Yeah, it stinks. What're you doing, Jay?" Bernie demanded.

"I'm changing the way we operate."

"By stripping our commissions away?"

"Not necessarily." Jay had shifted positions, propped against the edge of a desk. He looked calm—maddeningly, infuriatingly calm. If he had pranced in on a high horse, he could not have looked any more pious and *ridiculously* calm.

Bernie was ready to explode. "Oh, so we're supposed to accept your *humble* little apology, while you're cutting our salaries in half?"

"If you work hard at selling cars, you could make the same money you're making now—and do it with a clear conscience."

Sam and Max nodded their heads. A pair of yes-men.

What had this turned into? Bernie wondered. The Tuesday

morning ethics committee? Even politicians knew how to cut corners, how to word things just so. An idealistic approach would sink this lot faster than Jay Austin could say "No money down." Regardless of how squeaky-clean a corporation appeared, they all had their secrets. That was just life. So deal with it.

In fact, Bernie didn't know one human being who could claim, with a straight face, to be above reproach. That was the stuff of fairy tales.

And even if they tried to be honest here, buyers would still be liars.

"Jay, who cares about your conscience?" he fumed. "I have to make a living for my family, and you're taking food off my table."

"I'm not out to hurt your family, but—"

"So much for my vacation plans."

"But I do intend to run an honest business from now on."

"Jay, I sell cars for you. I organize all of your promotions. I make you look *good* in this community. I mean, you're practically famous around here."

"That's what worries me."

"You wanna be honest. Okay. *Honestly*, the last thing you should be doing is cutting my salary. I mean, I could make twice this right down the road at any of your competitors."

The room was stifling as they all awaited Jay's response.

"I don't disagree with that," he said, unflinching.

"Well, then why're you shooting us in the foot?" Bernie leaned forward in his chair. "Don't change anything. We're doing fine."

"I want a clean conscience before God."

"Aww, c'mon. This isn't a church."

Max peered over his glasses. "I don't think this is a bad move, Bernie."

"Of course you don't. You and Sam aren't salesmen, so your income stays the same."

"Yours could, too," Jay pointed out.

"Only if I work my tail off."

The second the words were out of his mouth, Bernie realized how weak they sounded, how lazy and incriminating.

Max sat back. Jay didn't speak or change his expression.

Only Vince seemed clueless to the deeper issues at stake. "So we're changing the prices on the cars?"

"We'll be doing that today," Jay said.

"No." Bernie felt anger chiseling lines into his face. "I don't like this, not one bit. Either you're gonna allow us to keep the same commission on every car we sell, or you're gonna raise our salaries to make up the difference."

Jay met Bernie's stare. The other guys waited.

"No."

That one word hung in the air. It was a death knell, the clanging *ding-a-ling* proof that Jay Austin had lost his sanity. The ship was going down. And its foolhardy captain would go down with it.

Bernie stood. "Well, you just got yourself one less salesman." He flung his name tag at Jay, then started grabbing his books and paperwork out of the top right-hand drawer of the desk.

He was outta here.

Chapter 18
HOOKED UP

SAM

This place was never boring; that was a fact.

"You're quitting?" Vince said.

"Yeah, I'm quitting. I'm not playing this game anymore. If you're smart, you'll quit, too."

Sam shook his head and watched Bernie Myers pack up. Though he had no real bond with the big guy, that didn't mean he wished him any harm. If nothing else, the sales boys provided the comic relief around this place.

Vince, on the other hand, was in an obvious quandary. He shifted his attention from his buddy's activity to his employer's solemn face.

Jay was a statue. He often got that way when trying to keep from saying or doing something ugly. Most days Jay was a cool cat, but Sam had seen him lose it once or twice. Each time, there had been a calm before the storm.

"You don't have to leave, Vince," Jay said.

"Don't be a fool," Bernie huffed. He leaned across the desk and eyed his sales partner. "You will never make a decent living staying here. He's going to make it impossible."

"Vince." Jay's voice was even and firm. "You can still be successful here. You've got twice the opportunity when Bernie walks out that door."

Sam had to give it to Jay: the man was standing his ground.

And doing so honorably.

Vince's gaze flickered back and forth, a man torn between respecting authority and pleasing his buddy.

Max got up. He eased past Sam, back toward the garage.

Sam worried about the old guy's ticker. When Max didn't know he was being observed, Sam sometimes noticed him grimacing, or staggering to his feet from under a car, or holding his side. All this drama was probably getting to him.

Not to Sam, though. What could you do but laugh? Sure, some days it got under his skin, but that's when he just put his head down and ground it out till quitting time.

His ears perked back up as the conflict continued.

"Don't even listen to him, Vince. What, you really think you're gonna stay here? Why waste your time?" Bernie said. "We could make twice what we're making here, right down the street at Bowers."

"Vince, you can stay," Jay repeated.

"C'mon, Vince."

The salesman seemed to be pondering the ramifications.

"*Vince*," Bernie barked out.

"I'm sorry." Vince Berkley stood and—probably to impress his friend—tried to remove his name tag with a flourish equal to Bernie's. Instead, he fumbled with it, stabbed his thumb, yelped, then freed the item and flung it onto the desk. "I can't do this, Jay."

The sales team, all two of them, headed for the exit. Bernie was laden with belongings, while Vince was focused on his wounded thumb.

Sam shook his head and saw Jay fold his arms across his chest.

Bernie flung bitter tones back over his shoulder. "You wasted two years of my life, Jay." He slammed the door, causing windows and blinds to rattle.

The sales office quieted. The tension dissipated. For the first time in minutes Jay took an audible breath, though he had to be wondering what would happen now that half his staff had abandoned him.

"Sam?" Jay wanted to know where his porter stood in all this.

Sam said, "I told you those were *strange* white boys."

A grin spread across his boss's face, and Sam had the sense that things were going to work themselves out just fine, like they usually did if you stopped fretting over all the details you could not control.

BERNIE

Bernie scurried outside with his partner—*former* partner—tagging along. "I'll tell you, Vince, Bowers is hiring, and I'm about to ride down there right now." He pointed a finger. "And you'd better go with me."

"You think we just did the right thing?"

"Yeah, I think we did the right thing. Unless *you* wanna stay here and work harder for less money." Bernie jerked a thumb toward the building. "This ship is sinking, man. Faster than the *Lusitania* or *Titanic*."

"Combined."

"Huh? No, that would take longer."

"What I meant was—"

"Doesn't matter what you *meant*, Vince. What you *said* doesn't make sense. You know, sometimes I don't even know how you manage to sell a car."

"I don't. Not enough of them, anyway."

"Not here, you don't," Bernie agreed. "Not anymore."

"I sure hope we did the right thing."

"Would you stop saying that? It's a new day, my friend, and I'm gonna make Jay wish he'd never gotten rid of me."

"Uh, well, he didn't really get rid of you. You just walked out and—"

"Stop. Please. Just shut up."

"Sorry."

They rounded the back of the building, where Max was finishing up with Bernie's Chevrolet SUV. He closed the hood as Bernie neared.

"Hey. Did you hook me up?"

"Yeah, I hooked you up." Max launched the keys back over his shoulder and walked away, swatting a rag against his leg.

Bernie's mouth wrinkled. Hmm. He got in and cranked the engine. Everything seemed to be in working condition. Time to go find himself a job where he could use the Touch without a do-gooder cramping his style.

MAX

Max sauntered back into the office building, gnawing on a piece of clove gum. He'd started chewing it years ago, to replace his pack-a-day smoking habit.

"Where'd you go?" Jay asked. "I thought you had left me, too."

"Nah, you know better than that."

"Yeah, Max. I do."

"Would you two quit it?" Sam gibed. "I'm getting all weepy-eyed."

Jay smiled. "Well, it's good to know who my friends are. It'll be different, but we can make this thing work."

Clearing his throat, Max stepped to the blinds and peered over the lot.

"What is it, Max? Customers?"

"Even better." Max was wiping a hand on his rag. "You guys better come to the window if you wanna see the big show."

"What? What'd you do?"

"I left Bernie a little parting gift." Max felt a mischievous grin split his lips as Jay and Sam rushed over. They had taken the bait. Time to reel them in.

On cue, Bernie's SUV drove into view, and his brake lights flashed.

Honnnk!

"What'd you do?" Jay said.

"I hooked his brake pedal to his horn."

"No you didn't."

Max lifted his chin and reveled in the prank's simplicity. From the lot, the horn blared again as Bernie neared the street.

Honnnk! Pause. *Honk-honnnk!*

Sam shook his head. "You guys're something else."

Through the glass, the three men watched Bernie jump from the vehicle's driver's seat and aim a fist at the office. His scream carried across the asphalt. "That's not funny, Max."

Max grinned, kept chewing his gum.

Bernie hopped back into the vehicle—*honnnk!*—and headed onto the side street, the horn sounding with each touch of his brake. They laughed as the sounds of his departure punctuated those of the midmorning traffic, each horn blast softer than the previous until the disgruntled former salesman was out of earshot.

"Sam." Jay turned from the window. "I need your help."

"Uh-oh."

"I'm gonna make you a car salesman."

"I'm not a car salesman."

"I'll give you a raise," Jay said.

That caused Max to lift an eyebrow.

"But then again"—Sam nodded sagely—"I might be a pretty *good* salesman."

"Don't think I'll be washing all the cars, Jay. That ain't gonna happen," Max clarified. "I got my hands full as it is."

"We'll all chip in."

"Okay. Long as we work together."

"Count me in," Sam said.

Jay looked down at his watch and couldn't help but smile.

"What are you grinning at?" Max asked.

"Max, it's 11:45 a.m. and it has already been an unforgettable day."

"Whaddya mean?"

"This morning, for the first time in my life, I started off by reading my Bible. Then I told God He could have this car lot. After that, I openly apologized to my sales staff for being a hypocrite, completely altered our company standards and selling philosophy, lost 66 percent of my sales staff, and gave Sam, my porter, a raise."

"Mm-hmm. So that's what's going on." Max smiled. "The first part of your day explains the second part."

Jay looked from Sam back to Max as if a lightbulb had turned on behind his eyes.

"I know something else," Max continued. "The Jay Austin that left here yesterday afternoon is not the same one who walked in the door this morning."

Sam studied Jay's eyes and began to nod in agreement.

Things were definitely different at Jay Austin Motors. Though many unresolved issues remained, it felt as though a fog had been lifted from the lot.

"So," Jay said, "I guess we've got work to do."

With that in mind, Max requested the dealer plate and explained that he had a lead on a flywheel for the TR3 convertible. "Need to run downtown," he told Jay. "Don't know if it's the right one, but I can't know till I take a look."

"Where downtown?"

"Little hole-in-the-wall place."

"Where?"

"It's a pool hall, Jay. Why does it matter?"

"Actually, I was just hoping you could pick us up something from Jimmie's Hot Dogs on the way back."

"Oh." Max shrugged. "Sure, I s'pose I could do that. As long as you're buying."

"Me? No, I'm thinking Sam's buying. I heard he just got a raise."

Chapter 19

POOL HALL BLUES

JUDY

"Lord," she groaned, "I just want this baby to come soon."

Judy had started the morning with another run to Starbucks—decaf chai, lots of whip. She had a limited clothing budget, drawn from Jay's salary, and by forgoing her usual after-Thanksgiving clothes sales, she could splurge on a treat twice a week.

Not like she needed more maternity outfits anyway.

To her relief, she'd missed the gossip crew in the coffee line. Spindly Blonde and Heavy Rouge must've been out collecting new data.

While sipping her drink, Judy had signed Christmas cards, addressed and stamped the envelopes, then run errands to the post office, bank, and Winn-Dixie. She was now back at home, snuggled on the couch. Her hips ached, and her feet were sore. She pulled a black wraparound over her rose-colored sweater.

Should she call Jay? She'd been thinking about him all morning. She felt—and this sounded funny even to her—like a schoolgirl, wondering if she should or shouldn't call, if she should tease or pursue.

There was just something about the way her husband had opened up to her last night, exposing his fears and his need, reaffirming his desire to nurture and protect, to be a godly head of his home . . .

It'd reached a spot deep inside of her. A spark. An ember.

This morning she was glowing.

Judy reached for the phone on the lamp stand, then blinked as the ringer chirped. When she checked caller ID, her pulse sped up. "Hi, honey."

"Judy, glad I caught you."

"You sound out of breath."

"I'm not even sure what I'm doing, but it seems right. I'm scared and excited, and . . . I guess I just wanted to let you know."

"Know what, Jay?"

"I told the Lord this was His lot. I gave it to Him."

"Okay."

"And now I'm trying to run it His way. No more lies, cheating, none of that."

"It's the right thing." She pulled her wraparound tighter. "But what're Bernie and Vince going to say?"

"They're gone."

"What?"

Jay said, "I'm not kidding. Both of them quit and walked out."

"So what're you going to do?"

"Sell cars by myself. Sam will be able to help some."

"Aren't you nervous about all this?" she said.

"Yes. But if I go under, it's because God allowed it. This is His lot now."

"Then run it in the way He would want, and don't worry about it."

"I'm trying not to." He cleared his throat. "What about you, Judy? We're gonna have another baby, and I know this seems . . . kinda crazy. I mean, it's only a few weeks till Christmas. The timing's horrible, isn't it?"

"I'm with you, Jay Austin. I love you. We'll do whatever we have to do." She wondered for a moment if they'd lost the phone connection. "Jay?"

"Thank you, Judy. I, uh . . . I needed to hear that, from you most of all."

"I mean it."

"Well." He chuckled. "Here's the first test then. With Bernie gone, I'm gonna be here till around seven, trying to catch up."

"Okay. Todd and I will work on his project. I'll see you tonight."

"Judy?"

"Yeah?"

"Would you mind if I brought your wedding photo to work? You know, to keep on my desk? It's in a frame, and I promise I'll be careful with it."

She shut her eyes, felt her throat constrict. She mumbled that yes, that would be okay with her. She would be honored.

"I love you," he said.

"Love you, too."

She disconnected the line and cradled the receiver against her neck. She then touched it to her head, trying to decide if now was a good time to place a call to the in-laws in Atlanta. She dialed the number, got an answer.

"Hello, Papa? It's Judy. Do you have a minute?"

MAX

"I was just fixin' to call you," Garrett said. "Didn't think you'd show."

"Here I am."

"Here you are. And we both know you ain't got any prettier, Max."

"Be worried if you thought otherwise."

Garrett guffawed. He was broad shouldered, with a beer belly that parted the folds of his leather vest. "C'mon in," he said, slapping Max hard on the back. "Be just like ol' times, what you say?"

Max followed the man through the swinging door with the single diamond-shaped window. The pool hall was a time machine, preserving everything just the way it had been for ages—same wood-paneled walls, flickering beer signs for brands that had gone out of business in the last century, and scuffed billiard tables stained dark green, almost black, from years of cigarette smoke. The smell of beer and smoke reminded Max of dozens of wasted nights, empty conversations, and a life that was now dead and gone.

"Garrett, I gotta be back to work soon."

"Work? Don't know what that is. I'm retired."

"Glad to hear it."

"You don't look none too glad."

"I am," Max assured him. "There's no hard feelings about what happened."

Garrett slapped his back again. "Good to know, good to know. Let's give 'er another shot, what you say?"

"Eight-ball, you mean?"

"You betcha."

"Kinda rusty. It's been two years."

"Took that last beatin' pretty hard, huh?"

Max felt pride swell in his chest and thought about duking it out right here, then reminded himself of his reason for coming. Just being in this place shifted him into old patterns of responding, but he wasn't that man anymore.

From the jukebox came the sounds of Creedence Clearwater Revival. "Garrett," Max said, "I'm really just here to look at that flywheel. If it ain't what I'm needing, I'll leave you be."

"And if it is?"

"I'll pay."

"You'll pay, all right." The words sounded threatening, yet Garrett showed nothing but good humor in his stance and tone. "Deal's this . . . One game o' eight-ball, and you get a peek at the part. If you win, it's yours for three-seventy-five. Tha's final."

"I wanna see it first."

Garrett shrugged. "Done told you the deal."

"Is it here? Tell me that."

"Near 'nuff I could spit on it."

"Rack 'em up then."

"Tha's what I like to hear." Another thundering backslap.

Max selected a cue from the wall rack, rolled it on the table to see that it was balanced and true. Garrett assembled his cue from a bag on a nearby table. Max won the lag, but he failed to drop in a single ball on the break, and his opponent took over.

It ended before it'd even started.

Garrett ran the table with masterful ease, calling the pockets and banking the eight ball into a corner. He grinned and joked throughout, never mean-spirited, just a retiree having a good time. He didn't rub salt in Max's wounds. He didn't gloat. He simply looked across the green felt when he was done and said he was sorry, he truly was.

"You've been playing," Max said.

"Could say that."

"Never had a chance, did I?"

"Could say that, too."

"So, what about the flywheel? No longer on the market?"

"Said no such thing." Garrett planted his cue on the floor and gripped the top end with both ends, leaning forward. "Bartender's got it behind the counter, in a box. Go have yourself a look."

Max was suspicious, but two minutes later he returned to the table.

"Whatcha say, Max?"

"That's what I'm looking for. Does three-seventy-five still hold?"

"Now, I done told you, that was only if you won. Which you didn't."

"I lost. I surrender. What now?"

Garrett shrugged. "That's all I wanted to hear. These days, my pride's worth more'n money. That beatin' you gave me two years back, it stung. I'm ownin' up to that, and I apologize. Figure I also owe you a thanks. That day made me madder'n heck. I played and played, till now I can whup just about anyone."

Max wasn't sure where this was leading.

"Nowadays, Max, I'm playin' for fun. Just a game, right? If you're ever lookin' for somethin' to do, stop in, and we'll rack 'em up again."

"I might do that," Max said. And he meant it. "Thing is, I really do need that flywheel, for a friend of mine. Please, if there's any way I could have it . . ."

"There is," Garrett said.

TODD

Todd checked the clock behind Mrs. Akridge's head and realized only six minutes had gone by since his last look. Clocks should be hidden out of sight, he thought. When he could see them, they didn't leave him alone.

On normal school days, he passed time by doodling. If that grew old, he came up with English challenges, writing lists of rhyming words or pairs of words that sounded alike but were spelled differently.

Read and *reed*. Or, *need* and *knead*.

This wasn't a normal day, though. It was the first of December, and that word alone was like neon flashing in his imagination.

Red, green, red, green . . . every other letter.

Christmas was coming. He'd get to go to Nana and Papa's in Atlanta, where he'd learn how to oil paint. How many kids knew how to do that? Most grown-ups didn't even know. He planned to do a painting for his mom, which he would wrap up as a late gift from Santa. Maybe she'd hang it on the wall in the living room if it was good enough.

Of course, even really good artists had to practice and practice. Practice makes perfect. Isn't that what Dad always said?

Maybe that's why he'd thrown Todd's picture in the trash. Maybe he was just pushing Todd to try harder, to do better.

Todd was going to work really hard to make his dad happy.

"Todd Austin?" His teacher's voice. "Are you listening?"

"Uh . . . yes, ma'am."

"And what did I just say?"

"I . . . don't know."

"Todd, I know you're an imaginative boy, but I need your attention up here. Do you think you can manage that?"

"Yes, Mrs. Akridge."

"Good. Now, boys and girls, I'm assigning a new project that'll be due when you return from your Christmas break. It'll include a written and oral presentation, and I'm telling you now so that you'll have plenty of time to work on it."

Although Todd tried to focus, her words began running together again. The clock hand was moving too slowly.

Too . . . and *to* . . . and *two* . . .

Too many days before he got *to* see his *two* grandparents.

Chapter 20

HANDS

JAY

What a mess. Bernie's files were incomplete, disorganized, and a general reflection of the way he had done business. Jay realized that some form of basic accountability would have to be implemented in the future.

Jay clasped his hands behind his neck. His shoulders felt tight.

"Getting nowhere fast, by the look of it," Max said as he wandered into the office. "I'd help, but I'm no good when it comes to all them numbers."

"Thanks anyway."

"Sam sold any cars yet?"

"Whoa. Give the man a chance, Max. He's been a salesman all of maybe three hours. Once he settles in, he'll do just fine."

Jay returned his attention to the documents in front of him, his fingers tapping at the adding machine. He saw Max at the edge of his vision, still in the doorway. Jay was wondering if the man had something else to add, when his nose detected the parade of aromas from around the corner.

"The hot dogs!" he exclaimed. "You brought them."

"Right here in the kitchen."

"Why didn't you say something?"

"We're all adults around here," Max noted. "Now that we've got rid of them other two jokers. Receipts and change are on the counter."

"Appreciate it."

Sam appeared in the front office. "Mmm. Now, that smells good."

"We love our Jimmie's," Jay mumbled through a sloppy, delicious bite.

The three men indulged their taste buds, taking part in the goodness that had been a fixture in Albany's history since 1925. Not many places could make such a claim. Eight decades of memories. Nostalgia passed from one generation to the next to the next.

Jay thought about his own children. He and Judy had chosen to be surprised by the gender of their second, which only intensified the longing for the birth. Would Todd have a brother or a sister? Would there be more baseball pennants and race cars? Or frilly pink dresses and Easter bonnets?

Life and birth . . . what miracles. Each individual a lump of clay fashioned into something unique by the Potter's hands.

"Jay, when you're done there . . ."

"Yeah?" He ran a napkin over his mouth, caught a diced onion before it cartwheeled from his chin.

"You might wanna come look at what I got outside."

"Don't tell me, Max. The flywheel?"

Max tilted his head.

"That's it, isn't it?" Jay said.

"You said not to tell you. Guess you'll have to see for yourself."

Jay herded his mechanic through the side door into the garage, with Max obviously enjoying every second of the torture he was imposing. Max stopped at a cardboard box beneath the carport. He folded back the flaps, revealing a silver-colored flywheel with teeth around its outer edge. Rather than rusty and stained, as Jay had expected, this one looked clean and new.

"That's for a TR3?"

"Yep," Max said. "That's the real thing."

"Same model?"

"Same model."

"Where'd you get it?"

Max wore his inscrutable smile. "Aww, a friend of mine had it at his shop. No charge. Long story short, he didn't care about the money." Max opened his hand, palm up. "All I had to do was ask."

This was incredible.

Jay punched an enthusiastic fist into his own hand. He wondered what the convertible would sound like the first time it started up. Would it be a throaty growl, or a refined British purr? Talk about a wild day.

The day had one more surprise for him.

JAY

He was in the copy room, still filtering through the hodgepodge of transactions left by the late great Bernie Myers. His mind was elastic and raw, stretched farther than was comfortable.

The front door chimed.

Jay looked at his watch: 5:50 p.m. He got up, wondering if this visitor knew that the lot had closed already. He stopped at the sight of his father.

The senior Mr. Austin stood just inside the door, tentative, with a cane in hand. He was graying, yet stately. Spots of sorrow smudged the kindness in his eyes. During their last meeting, Jay had uttered some harsh words, and they stared at each other now as though reevaluating that moment in time.

"Dad?"

"Hello, Jay."

"What're you doing here?"

"I wanted to come and talk to you, if you have a minute."

Great. The man had come to collect his money, the same way the banker, Mr. MacDonald, was threatening to shut down the car lot if he didn't get *his* payment.

While here in Albany, Jay had tried not to dwell on his past, his mistakes, or the people he had hurt. He was a forward thinker. No time for wallowing.

In this moment, however, he felt exposed. He should've never tapped his father for that twenty thousand in start-up cash. His brother, Joey, had needed money, too, while finishing dental school, and instead Jay had weaseled in and played the sympathy card.

Jay. Short for Jacob. Like his biblical namesake, he had edged in on his older brother's birthright for his own selfish gain.

He said, "You drove down from Atlanta just to talk to me?"

His father nodded. "I did."

"You wanna sit down?" Jay gestured to the chair by the sales desk and found his own seat on the other side.

"Yes, thank you."

"Is, uh . . . Is Mom okay?"

"She's fine, Son."

Not only had Jay disappointed his father and brother; he'd let his mother down by dropping out of Georgia State after his junior year. A schoolteacher, she still taught fourth and fifth grades, so his leaving school had hit her especially hard. At the time she could not understand the allure of a dot-com venture. She just didn't realize the obvious fortune Jay was about to make.

What a fiasco that'd been.

After losing a bundle of investors' capital, Jay had moved from job to job and dragged Judy and Todd in his wake.

"It's good to be here," Mr. Austin said.

Jay looked down, studying the wood grain on his desk.

"I wanted to come down to see you today. Hope it's not a bad time." Mr. Austin adjusted in his chair, hands clasped over the top of his cane. "I got a call from Judy this morning, and she told me about some decisions you've made. She said you've made quite a change in direction, and you've even decided to make Jesus the Lord of your life."

"Yes, sir."

"Jay?" His father peered over the desk. "Did you really mean that?"

"Yes, sir."

"I have to admit I was thrilled when I got that call." Mr. Austin smiled and blew out a breath. "Your mom and I, we've prayed about this for a long time."

"Dad, I . . . I know I've been difficult. And I know I've been stubborn."

"There's no denying that."

"The things I said last time . . . I was wrong. You have been a good father to me. I'm just . . . I'm . . ." Remorse welled in Jay's throat. "I'm sorry I was that difficult."

"Jay, I didn't come for an apology. I came to encourage you, and to tell you how proud I am of you."

Proud? Of what?

Jay returned his gaze to the desktop. He blinked. There was still no mention of the debt owed or his past failures. He felt no underhanded condemnation in the man's statement, only the loving tones of a father.

Across from Jay, Mr. Austin stood. He moved carefully, yet with purpose, coming around to Jay's side of the desk. He propped his cane against the wooden edge, then rested one hand on his son's shoulder, the other on his head.

"Lord," he prayed, "I thank You for my son, Jay. And I thank You that he's turned his heart to You."

Jay felt warmth pouring down through those cupped palms. His eyes were still open as he recalled Old Testament stories of fathers pronouncing blessings over their sons—Abraham, Isaac, and . . .

Yes, even Jacob.

Jay swallowed hard. He wanted all that God had for him and his family. He was done fighting on his own, tired of trusting in his own wisdom.

"Thank You for receiving him," Mr. Austin continued, "and for cleansing him and directing his path. I praise You, Lord, for what You've done in him. Now, Lord, in Your name, I bless him with courage, with faith, and with integrity. Lord, I call him a man of strength, of love, and grace."

A tingling sensation spread over Jay's scalp, a soothing balm, the feel of sun-warmed olive oil running down through his hair and across his skin. He let it flow. He basked in the sense of his earthly father's blessing and the heavenly Father's acceptance.

He didn't deserve this. He had been so prideful, so stiff-necked. Yet here it was, the love of a father for his son.

Not earned. Freely given.

Jay's mind raced through images of his failures, his pride and dishonesty, and how empty his life had become. Then there was last night's prayer. More than a wish to the wind, it was a surrender. He had bowed his heart before Christ, who would make all things new.

Jay touched a fist to his own lips as tears pooled along his eyelids and began to fall. He felt something breaking within, breaking free, even as his dad continued praying.

"I ask, as Jay's earthly father, that You would rain down favor on him, that he would know he is loved and treasured, that You would bless whatever he touches. This is my son, Lord, and I give him back to You. Lord, I love him. Keep him and bless him. In Jesus' name, amen."

Jay was crying openly, his cheeks wet with tears. There was no shame in this. Shame was washing away in each droplet.

Mr. Austin took hold of his cane. "I love you, Son."

Jay covered his face and wept as his father slipped away.

Chapter 21

WORKING FOR PEANUTS

TODD

Dad was late coming home from work again. Last night he had said all the right things to Mom, sounding like he was going to change, but already he was doing the same stuff he'd always done.

Todd didn't care. He felt sorry for Mom, though, since she'd probably got her hopes up. Todd knew better.

He flicked on the reading lamp that was clipped to his headboard, then opened his textbook. History. Ugh. This stuff was boring. He toed his shoes from his feet and let them thud to the floor.

"Todd, honey? You okay?"

"I'm fine," he called back through his open bedroom door.

From the driveway, the sound of tires on gravel signaled his father's arrival. He eased off the bed and moved to the landing at the top of the stairs. From there, he watched his dad come through the front door with a paper tucked under his arm. He was not only late; he was bringing work home with him.

Mom met him there in the foyer. Dad didn't make any excuses. Didn't start apologizing or any of that.

He said, "Judy, I'm glad to be home."

"I'm glad you're home, too."

They embraced, gave each other a kiss. Todd looked away, even though he was glad to know they could still be lovey-dovey sometimes.

"What a day," Dad said. "And guess who stopped by the lot?"

"Hmm . . ." Mom put a finger to her lips.

"I think you know, you rascal. Thank you, Judy. It was really good to see him. Thank you."

"I want to hear all about it. Can we go into the living room? My feet are . . . It'll just help if I can sit down."

Todd's eyebrows pushed together as he watched his parents slip from sight. He had to admit that something seemed different. Not like one day could prove anything, but it was a start.

He trudged back to the dreaded history book on his pillow.

Later, Dad's heavy footsteps came up the stairs and down the hall. He knocked on the door frame, then found a seat at the end of Todd's bed.

"What're you reading?"

Todd turned on his side. "A book on Vesuvius."

"Vesuvius? What's that?"

"It's a volcano that destroyed a whole village in Italy."

"I didn't know you were interested in that. Why're you reading about that?"

"It's for my science project." Todd pointed to his finished volcano in the corner of his room.

Dad turned. He got up and walked over to the structure, crouching down to study the details of trees, ridges, and a village Todd had put together at the mountain's base. "It's amazing, Todd. When did you do this?"

"I've been working on it for a few days. Mom helped me."

"It's incredible."

Todd cracked his knuckles.

Dad kneeled at the side of the bed, his arms folded over the comforter. "Todd, I don't think that I have been a very good dad to you. And, uh . . . Well, I want to be. So, I have asked God to help me do better. And if it's okay with you, I would like to hang out with you a little bit more."

Todd gave a slight smile, still knuckle-popping. "Okay."

"Okay. And I wasn't kidding. I really am impressed with your volcano."

"Thanks."

Dad stood, then reached a hand behind his back. "I know you need to finish your homework, but there's one more thing. I found this in the office at work, and I think it's pretty amazing." He brought into view the colored pencil drawing of the race car. Black numbers stood out against the orange door panel. "I have to admit, Todd, at first I didn't realize what I had in my hands. I threw it away, and that was a big mistake."

"You laminated it."

"I did."

"You're not supposed to laminate artwork."

"I wanted to protect it, Todd. To make sure it stays around. Seems we have a budding artist in the house, and someday this might be worth a fortune. You never know—it could sell for millions at an auction, even help pay for my false teeth when I'm old."

A wide grin spread across Todd's face.

"I just wanted to tell you thanks," Dad said. "Sorry it took so long."

"It's okay."

His father patted him on the shoulder. "Good night, buddy."

JUDY

Judy dumped an armload of clean laundry on the side of the bed. She waved away the residual dryer-heat and scent of fabric softener. She'd bought the softener herself. Tested the smell with her own nose. Yet now, with the pregnancy, it gave her a headache.

"I'm really outta touch with my son," Jay said, coming in from the hall.

"Why do you say that?"

"Do you even have to ask?"

"Well, Jay, you know that can change."

"It *will* change." He joined in with her, folding towels.

Hmm. Another first. Judy was surprised, especially since he'd had to stay late at work to cover Bernie's absence.

"Will you be able to handle the lot without more help?" she said.

"I can't afford more help. I've already given Sam a small raise to help me sell. So, unless there's some hardworking guy willing to work for peanuts, we're on our own."

"Why don't you ask God for someone like that?"

"Well, I *can*." Jay stared across the bed. "But who would do that?"

JAY

The next morning, Jay arrived at the lot the same time as Max and Sam. They gave one another knowing nods, then headed to their respective positions, three men preparing to defend their turf against insurmountable odds.

"Here I am, Lord," Jay said through chattering teeth.

Despite the sunshine, winter was baring its fangs and stripping trees of their foliage. Frost shimmered in patches where the shade was thickest.

I hope you know this address, he added silently from the chair behind the sales desk. *Because the bank certainly does.*

The puttering of a compact car cut through his thoughts. He watched the vehicle zip into a spot alongside the building, saw a young guy in Converse tennis shoes pop into view. The kid shouldered a book bag and bounced up the wooden front steps. A college kid in need of new wheels? Or perhaps one of those overeager, door-to-door, candy bar salesmen.

The kid pushed inside.

"Good morning," Jay said.

"Hi, uh . . . I'm looking for Jay Austin."

"You found him."

"Oh, hi." They shook hands. "I'm Kevin Cantrell."

Kevin's appearance was tidy, if not a bit understated. His smile seemed genuine, and intelligent eyes glowed with enthusiasm behind his glasses. The strap of his bag was as wide as a bandit's bandolier in an old Western, but he looked harmless. Like he should be out mowing lawns.

Still, there was also something off about the guy.

Well, not *off* . . . Maybe goofy.

"Hello, Kevin Cantrell. What can I do for you?"

"Well"—Kevin flashed a wide, crooked smile—"you can give me a job if you have an opening."

"You're looking for a job?"

"If you're hiring."

Jay gestured. "Why don't you have a seat?" He moved around to his chair, while the kid slipped the bag from his shoulder and settled across from him.

"This is it, huh? This is where it all happens?" Kevin scanned the office. "I'm between semesters, and I've got about six weeks, and I've always wanted to see how I'd do at sales."

"So, you're looking for a job for six weeks."

"Right."

"Well, Kevin." Jay leaned back. "I could use some help around here, but I'd need it for a little more than six weeks."

"Oh, I understand. But I'm a really fast learner, and I want to have my own lot one day, so I'd work really hard for you."

"But, six weeks?"

"You can pay me minimum wage. I wanna sell a car so bad I can *taste* it."

"Minimum wage?"

"That's right."

Jay weighed the possibility. He could almost hear Judy reminding him of their conversation the previous evening, pointing out the impeccable timing of it. Sure, it could be a coincidence. It could also be a direct answer to his prayers.

But did God even endorse Converse?

"Jay—can I call you Jay?—it's obvious you want me here," Kevin said.

"Like I said, we do need the help."

"Then what're you waiting for? Here's my résumé and references. I'm available anytime you can schedule me."

Jay stared at the papers, then at Kevin. "Six weeks?"

The goofy smile stretched earlobe to earlobe. "Minimum wage."

"Hmm."

"Whaddya say? If I can talk you into this, then I'm bound to be able to sell cars, don't you think? I mean, how hard can it be?"

Chapter 22

RULE #1

JAY

At Jay's direction, Kevin backed a Chevy into a parking spot. They were rearranging the inventory, giving the front line a new look, in hopes of catching the eyes of passersby. The weather was holding up, with clear December skies and crisp afternoons, and that meant better-than-average foot traffic.

Still, Jay knew he was far from reaching the sort of numbers he would need to stave off the creditors.

Time was ticking.

In the week that Kevin had been with them, he'd shown a willingness to learn and some nifty mathematical skills. He'd sold two cars. He got along well with Max and Sam and arrived each day on time, dressed, fed, and ready to go.

"Whoa." Jay held up a hand. "That's good. That's it."

Kevin set the brake and hopped out.

"All right, we're gonna do the same thing with the Taurus. We're gonna put it right here." Jay gestured to the empty space he was standing in.

"Okay."

Jay watched Kevin jog off in his tan Dockers for the next car. He shook his head at the kid's boundless energy. Again, he thanked God for this unexpected blessing.

It was too bad that Kevin Cantrell would be gone in five weeks.

Of course, Jay Austin might be out of a job by then, too.

Jay's ears perked up at the sound of an engine cranking over. The sound emanated from the carport. He waved to Kevin. "Hey, I'll be right back."

He turned and walked around the corner of the service garage. There, in the driver's seat of the Triumph TR3, Max was leaned back. He had the top down, the gleaming white door open, and he was listening as the engine coughed, sputtered, then settled into a healthy growl. It wasn't the low rumble of an American-built sports car, not quite that meaty. But it filled the space beneath the overhang and vibrated the concrete under Jay's feet.

Jay stepped closer, letting the sound wash over him. "Oh yeah, baby."

Those words just about covered it.

Max cocked his head from behind the windshield and smiled. Jay pointed a finger, as if to say, "You're the man."

Max held up a finger, indicating there was something else.

He removed his wire-rimmed spectacles, replaced them with a pair of aviator sunglasses, then pulled on a touring cap. Jay arched an eyebrow, folded his arms, and leaned against the garage. This was too much.

Max closed the driver's door and resituated himself in the seat. He pointed back at Jay. Jay laughed and pulled his fist to his mouth.

Amazing how one part out of order had thrown everything off.

The car that had been good for nothing weeks ago was now a classic convertible, ready to rock and roll.

KEVIN

Kevin liked Jay Austin. He got a good vibe off the guy—and usually Kevin's vibes were right. Of course, you never could tell these days. All you had to do was open a newspaper to find that out for yourself.

Trust no one. That was Kevin Cantrell's Rule #1.

He leaned back against the Chevy he had parked earlier, adjusting his book bag, and observed Jay's approach across the pavement.

"Hate to say this, Jay, but that's a terrible sweater."

"Hey."

"Looks like something from the eighties."

"It *is* from the eighties. My deceased grandmother made it for me, so go ahead and laugh all you want."

"I didn't know dead people could knit."

"You are sick and wrong."

"Or maybe she gave it to you because *she* didn't wanna be caught dead in it." Kevin laughed at his own joke. He knew Jay could take it. Wasn't thick skin a prerequisite for any salesperson?

Jay said, "Don't you have work to do? What do I pay you for anyway?"

"You pay me? Oh yeah. Minimum wage."

Jay propped himself against the low metal fence a few feet from Kevin. Kevin tucked one hand in his pocket, the other into the buttoned folds of his shirt. He was getting chilled now that he'd stopped running around.

"So," he said to his boss. "How long've you been here?"

"I've been here about two years."

"You like it here?"

"I do," Jay replied. "Albany's a good-sized city that still has the feel of a small town. I like the pace. Just wish I could sell more cars."

"Hope you're not slamming my sales skills. It's only been a week."

"Nah. It's nothing to do with you."

"Speaking of selling cars, I wanted to ask . . . You don't seem to be getting as much as you could out of some of these. If I sold one for a little more, could I keep the rest as commission?"

"Kevin, we're not going to go that route." Jay turned his head to meet Kevin's gaze. "We're gonna charge what we would feel good about being charged. I'm gonna stick to the fair market value."

"You can get away with pushing a *little* bit." Kevin straightened from the car and took a step forward, his voice low. "I mean, don't you need the money?"

"I do. But I've gotta live with how I run this place."

"What about the competitors? I mean, how can I make a living at this?"

"That's a good question, one I'm still trying to figure out. I do know, I just don't want any more regrets. I'm sticking to the highest standard I can. You treat people right, it'll come back to you."

"You really believe that? Seems like a nice idea, but a little naive."

"You're a good kid," Jay said. "Try not to become too pessimistic, all right? Cautious and callous. Those are two very different things, Kevin."

"I'm not so sure about that. And I don't know that I care."

"Well, you should—"

"Kidding, Jay. Don't you get it? 'Not so sure . . . don't care' . . . Never mind."

Jay offered a weak smile. He looked toward the carport area, then down at his wristwatch.

Kevin followed his eyes. "You're dying to drive that car, aren't you?"

"I am."

"Why don't you take off? I can lock up."

Jay seemed to consider that. "You sure you remember how to do the paperwork if someone buys a car?"

"Sold the Bronco yesterday, and I didn't have a problem."

"Okay. But if you have any questions, you ask Sam. All right?"

Kevin waved a dismissive hand. "I'll be fine."

Jay stood and headed toward the garage. "Just lock both doors and don't forget the alarm," he ordered over his shoulder.

Kevin meandered along the line of cars, cataloging a few of the sticker prices in his head. He jogged up the steps into the modular office building, his book bag hanging from his neck. He peeked into the kitchen area.

No sign of Sam. No Max.

He checked the washroom, the sales office, then slunk into the copy room where rows of filing cabinets stored customer info and vehicle specs. He opened the top drawer of the first cabinet and began picking through the files.

PART THREE

"The flywheel, see, it helps start the car,
then stores up all this rotational energy
during engine impulses."

—MAX KENDALL, MECHANIC

Chapter 23

OUT OF TIME

JAY

The dream world was over. Five weeks had passed quickly—much too quickly—and reality was about to kick back in.

Jay glanced at his watch. *Ticktock-ticktock* . . .

He had to believe Kevin Cantrell had been a godsend, and yet it'd made no real difference in the larger scheme of things. Kevin had earned a few bucks, Jay had sold a few more cars, and that was that.

Kevin was still leaving, as planned.

And the banker would be coming by later, like some financial coroner, to pronounce the demise of Jay Austin Motors.

On the small office TV set, a local commercial was running. Jay turned up the volume and heard the sound of screeching tires, followed by the manufactured excitement of the narrator.

"Butch Bowers AutoWorld!" A large man wearing a tie and glasses filled the screen. It was Bowers himself. "Check out this '02 Yukon, for just $25,995." Bernie Myers flashed into the picture next, staring up from the competitor's sales lot into a bird's-eye-view camera. "It's *phenomenal!*" he yelled.

It was phenomenal that Bernie could even sleep at night.

Not that Jay was any better, left to his own devices. How had he managed it for the previous two years? No wonder he had started losing hair and having stomach problems. Thankfully, the digestive issues had disappeared.

As for the receding hairline? He would have to live with that.

Bowers cut back in. "See this '99 Mustang GT, sliced down to $10,950. How 'bout this '02 F-150 diesel, for just $28,995? And if you act now, we'll throw in a free chassis treatment undercoating, guaranteed not to rot, rust, bust, chip, pop, stain, crack, or peel. Unless," he added quickly, "it comes in contact with water."

"*What?*" Jay laughed.

Bowers pointed at him through the screen. "That's a Butch Bowers factory guarantee. Butch Bowers AutoWorld!" A Chinese gong reverberated. "You won't find a better deal anywhere. I'm Butch Bowers, and you can *bet* on it."

Jay shook his head.

I'm trying to do it Your way, Lord, but this guy's walking all over me.

He knew through the grapevine that Butch Bowers lived in an upscale gated community and golfed with the local celebrities. Word was, he'd even taken Dick Cheney quail hunting a few years back, on his property outside of town.

The door chimed as Kevin entered. He plopped down across from Jay. "Whatcha watching there?"

"The competition."

"This business is tough, isn't it?"

"Unless you wanna sell your soul," Jay muttered.

"Well." Kevin shrugged. "I've said 'So long' to Max and Sam."

"Kevin, I hate to lose you."

"I'm just sorry I couldn't sell more cars for you."

Jay opened a desk drawer. "I didn't sell many either. But you kept your word, worked hard for me. I appreciate it." He slid Kevin's final payment in an envelope across the desk.

"Thanks for the opportunity. You know, I have to admit that working here's been a little bit, uh . . . different than what I expected."

"What'd you expect?"

"I don't know. I guess I halfway expected you to be a little more . . . *strategic* in the way you sell cars."

"Strategic?"

"Okay." Kevin grinned. "Devious."

Jay emitted a chuckle. "I understand."

"Well, you're not a bad guy. I'm glad I met you."

"I'm grateful for your approval." Jay shook his hand. "Drop us a line sometime."

"I will."

Jay waved. "Take care of yourself."

The phone rang as the door closed behind Kevin.

Oh, boy.

Another ring.

Here goes nothing.

On the third ring, Jay picked up. "Jay Austin Motors. Yes, hello, Mr. MacDonald. How're you? Yes, I realize that. That'd be fine. You can come whenever's convenient. Very good."

He hung up. He drew in a deep breath. He began second-guessing the decisions he'd been making, everything from the trade-ins he'd accepted to the tithe envelope he'd put into the offering plate last Sunday—with an actual check inside. He'd known it was the right thing to do, yet it had left him short on his mortgage payment. And the holidays had been rough.

If he was doing things God's way, why was it all falling apart?

JUDY

So much for the decaf chai.

When Judy had agreed to stand with her husband in his commitment to do things right, she had no idea their livelihood would be threatened so quickly. She'd heard the statistics about how most Americans lived paycheck to paycheck, how most households teetered only a penniless month or two from disaster.

But the Austins were different, weren't they? She had a 401(k) from her previous job, and Jay had savings bonds that he'd received from his grandparents that'd been maturing for years.

None of that paid for the groceries, though. Or the electric bill.

Thank goodness Todd's visit with Nana and Papa had made up for the Austins' lean Christmas. They'd barely come up with stocking stuffers.

How could she even think about something as frivolous as a visit to Starbucks?

Judy wiped the tears from her eyes as she prayed on the phone with an elder's wife from the church. She didn't go into the details, just enough to make sure they could be united in their petition before God.

"Thank you, Christina. I really needed that," Judy said.

"Anytime."

"It's just nice to talk to an adult sometimes. I know that sounds funny, but there are hours that go by when this baby's the only one I have to talk to. If they could see me on video—pacing through the house, blabbing to my tummy."

Christina's laughter bubbled with reassurance. "Oh, Judy, we have to get you out of there. Tell me this: are you a Starbucks girl?"

"A what?"

"Let's say we meet there in twenty minutes. That gives you some time away, before Todd gets home from school. Isn't that right?"

"Yeah, but—"

"Do you have other plans?"

"No, but—"

"I won't accept any excuses, do you hear? And the treat's on me."

Judy hung up and shook her head, smiling. She felt sometimes as if God were winking at her from heaven. Amazing how He seemed to be aware of even the littlest, most trivial things.

"Thank You," she whispered.

JAY

Mr. MacDonald arrived before noon. Though he accepted the seat Jay offered him, he wasted no time getting to the point.

Jay listened. Nodded. The banker's face was firm but not without empathy.

"The bottom line," he said in closing, "is that twelve thousand is a good start, Mr. Austin, but that's only about a third of what you owe. You're behind with your floor plan, your mortgage. Your checking account's overdrawn, and your insurance is fixin' to lapse."

"My insurance? I didn't know about that."

Jay couldn't meet the man's eyes. Instead, he gazed down at the desk calendar, where he had penciled in plans for spring break in Atlanta. Todd was so excited about seeing Nana and Papa again after his Christmas session with them, but Jay couldn't even afford the gas now. Not to mention his hopes for a day at Six Flags. Last year, he would've charged all to the business credit card—then written it off on his taxes—yet that would violate his newly reinstated principles.

"I don't know what to tell you," Jay admitted.

"Do you see any way of coming up with the money?"

"Well, we didn't . . . we didn't sell cars like we normally do this time of year. Um, that's why I'm behind. I don't suppose I can talk you into a few more weeks to catch up?"

"Mr. Austin, the bank's been gracious already in giving you some extra time. But unless you have the money by Friday, I'll have to come get your cars."

"I understand."

Time of Jay Austin Motors' death: *Friday, late January.*

"I'm sorry it's come to this," said Mr. MacDonald. "I wish you luck. I appreciate you meeting with me today."

Jay needed more than luck. He needed a miracle. Through the blinds, he watched the banker stroll outside to his black BMW, and he couldn't help but wonder if Butch Bowers ever went golfing with the man.

From the side door Max Kendall walked in, hitched up his pants, and took a seat near the fireplace. He folded and smoothed his grease rag over his left thigh. "So, what's the plan?"

"Max, I never thought I'd be saying this . . . We might not have a lot next week. We'd have to sell almost every car out there to pay our debts and bills. I'm not sure what I'm gonna do."

"Well, I'm going fishing."

Jay smiled. "I gave this lot to the Lord. I know there are consequences for the way I ran it, but I guess I was secretly hoping He would get us back on solid ground. I guess He can do whatever He wants to with it."

Max sat forward. His voice was quiet and confident. "Don't you quit yet. Let's see what the Lord does."

"I wish I had more faith. He's running out of time."

Chapter 24

TAILGATES AND TITLES

JUDY

Jay was seated in a stuffed armchair, his face lit by pale daylight that oozed through the sliding glass door. He was reading a Bible. He was dressed in a sweatshirt, instead of one of his dress shirts or sweaters. To Judy, seated on the couch across from him, he looked awfully handsome.

This was her husband. Her life-mate.

She could still remember their first meeting at the Atlanta Auto Show. Mr. Jay Austin, full of swagger and youth, ready to take on the world . . . He had tapped her on the shoulder. She had turned.

First words out of his mouth: "Are you a Panther?"

"If you mean, do I go to Georgia State . . . then, yes. But even if I didn't," she added, "you still better watch out."

He was putty in her hands after that.

Of course, life had a way of breaking people down. Judy's father had worked in construction, operating a cement truck, and he used to compare people to rocks inside that huge grinding mixer. If you rolled with the junk that came your way, it smoothed and polished you. If you resisted, you got thrown against the unforgiving walls, where you cracked and became jagged. And what good was a bunch of rough, stubbly concrete?

Judy missed her dad. He'd passed away not long after her wedding. Her mother had remarried six years ago and migrated south to Florida.

Judy could still picture her dad, a big, burly man with a heart of gold beneath his stained and stretched-out T-shirts. He would've approved of the Bible-reading man now across from her.

"Anything interesting?" Judy prodded.

"Yeah," said Jay. "Listen to this, from Proverbs chapter 3, verses 5 and 6: 'Trust in the LORD with all your heart and lean not on your own understanding; in all your ways acknowledge him, and he will make your paths straight.'"

"See? So why're we worrying? It says, 'Trust in the LORD with your heart.'"

"That's not the part that hits me so hard. It's the 'lean not on your own understanding' part. I definitely don't *understand* why we're in the hole with our checking account."

"Because we didn't—"

"I mean, I understand the immediate reason. The financial explanation. I just don't get why it seems like we're making right decisions now, and it's only making things worse."

"I don't have any easy answers for you."

"'He will make your paths straight.'" Jay tapped the page with his finger. "I've walked crooked so long, I don't even know how to follow a straight line."

Judy rested her hands on her belly. "You're not thinking about getting another emergency loan, are you?"

"No. It's crossed my mind, but I know that's not the answer."

"It's His lot, Jay."

"It's His lot." He looked up. "I'm tired of worrying about money anyway."

"That's because it's always been *our* money."

"What? Instead of God's money that He allows us to use?"

She pursed her lips. "Now, there's a thought."

"I know that's the right mind-set. It just feels so *back*wards to think that way."

"Or maybe it's the *normal* way, and we've just been doing it backwards this whole time."

"I've been going backwards so long, it's a rush to go forwards."

"Are we still planning on tithing?" Judy asked.

"Whoa. Now, that's one way to put the brakes on a conversation."

"I'm serious."

"If you mean tithing on our diminishing income . . ." Jay lifted his Bible from his lap, as though to say he could only do as he was told. "Yep."

"Good. I think we should tithe until there's nothing to tithe off of."

"That day may be coming, sweetheart."

Judy paused. His statement, though playful, scared her. It was so easy to get wrapped up in her worries over this baby.

Her thoughts dashed back to Christina's unexpected treat this morning, the way God had come through in even the smallest of areas, the thing she never would have thought He had time for. And the chai had been out of this world.

"This is from Psalm 37," she said, reading from her own Bible. "'Delight yourself in the LORD and he will give you the desires of your heart. Commit your way to the LORD; trust in him and he will do this: He will make your righteousness shine like the dawn, the justice of your cause like the noonday sun. Be still before the LORD and wait patiently for him.'"

Jay gazed out the window, where shadows played over the deck.

"The desire of my heart," he said, "would be to finish well. If I have to change jobs, I'd want to do it in a more honorable way—instead of getting kicked out because I couldn't pay my debts."

"All you have to do is be still."

"For a man, that's about the hardest thing in the world."

JAY

Jay and Todd sat on the cold tailgate of a lot pickup, separated by fountain drinks and a bag of Sun Chips. With Sherwood Christian Academy's scheduled half day, Jay had suggested that Judy drop off Todd so he could hang out for the afternoon on the car lot.

"So how's it feel to be a celebrity?" Jay inquired.

Todd's legs dangled over the tailgate. Dressed in jeans, tennis shoes, and a hoodie, he squinted into the winter sun. "I'm not a celebrity."

"You won first prize at the science fair with your volcano. I'd say that makes you a pretty big celebrity."

Todd took another bite of his sandwich.

Jay was trying to get a dialogue going here, some father-son banter, but his nine-year-old was solemn. At the same age, Jay had already been a big flirt and a soon-to-be jock. His friends were giggly girls and other young studs. He remembered kids like Todd—but not very well. They were mostly off the radar of a kid too cool for school and for solitary hobbies.

Boy, Jay said to himself, *does my arrogance go back that far?*

Todd appeared ready to speak. Jay's wind-numbed fingers shoved in a helping of chips as he waited for his son to voice what was on his mind. Traffic zipped in both directions along North Slappey Boulevard.

"Dad?"

"Mm-hmm."

"Are you really going to stop selling cars?"

"If that's what God wants."

"What's Mom think?"

"She wants whatever God wants."

"What're you gonna do?"

"I don't know, Son."

"I wanna be an artist someday."

Jay thought of all the reasons to discourage such a fickle

pursuit—hadn't Vincent van Gogh died poor and unknown?—but set them aside for another time.

He said instead, "Maybe you could teach me to make volcanoes, Todd. Then every kid who needed a volcano could buy it from me, and I could make a lotta money that way."

"Well, first you gotta pay me a lotta money so I can teach you."

"Listen to *you*." He messed his son's hair.

Max walked over from the garage. "Hey, man, what's all this sloughing off?"

"I can do whatever I want to. We may be closed by this time tomorrow anyway." Jay bit into his sandwich.

"You don't look too stressed-out about it."

"I'm learning how to be still, and to trust. That's what Judy told me I needed to do, but it's harder than you'd think."

"Yeah, I agree."

"In fact, I thought of you, Max."

"Oh, no."

Todd wore a closed-lip grin.

"I was thinking about that flywheel," Jay explained, "and how the car had to just sit there until you could tear it apart and put it back together. All that time, it was probably wondering what was taking you so long."

"Hey. Things went quick once I got my hands on the part."

"Just an analogy, that's all."

With jaws working on that clove gum he liked so much, Max looked down past the rim of his glasses. Jay gave him a smile. He was going to miss their daily joking run-ins. Max Kendall had been a faithful employee, a stand-up individual, and a true friend.

"Max, just so I know I've said it . . . I appreciate you very much."

"Well, just so I know I've said it . . . You ought to. There aren't many left like me." With that, Max pivoted on one foot and strutted off, his arms swaying in a playful rhythm.

"Wh . . . what?" Jay choked on his bite of food. "Hey, pride goes before a fall, you old geezer."

Max never turned. He wagged a finger in the air and kept strutting.

Jay chuckled, then froze. He realized his son had been listening to every word. "Hey," Jay said in his sternest fatherly tone, "don't you ever talk to an old man like that. It's rude."

TODD

Later in the afternoon, Todd and his dad took up positions on the copy room floor. Todd sat cross-legged, leaned against the photocopier, and worked on another drawing. His dad's legs were stretched out, his back pressed against a file cabinet.

"Huh," Dad said.

Todd looked up.

His dad lifted a typed, official-looking paper. "What's this doing here?" he mumbled. "It's a contract from one of our files, wedged right next to this cabinet, like it fell out or something. Bernie better not have come sneaking back in here. I can just see him, taking down the phone numbers of all his previous buyers."

Todd added a shadow to his artwork.

"If I knew we'd be open much longer, I'd get all the locks rekeyed."

"Look," Todd said. "My car has rockets coming out the back."

"Oh, yeah? Well, my car's got a missile on the top."

"Yeah? So mine goes faster."

Jay looked up, and they gave each other steely-eyed glares. "Lemme see that," he said, grabbing Todd's drawing. He studied the dimensions, the colors, the shading. "Hey, that's not bad. Where'd you learn to draw?"

Todd cracked his knuckles. "I don't know."

"That's pretty good. I'm gonna have to put that on the wall when you're done."

The front door chimed. "Hello?" A woman's voice.

Dad set down his papers and got to his feet. "You stay right here, okay?"

"Mm-hmm."

Todd watched his father smooth his sweater and head out into the sales office. He could see the desk from here, and he recognized the lady who had come in. That was Derek's mom. Derek had played on the soccer team last year.

"Hey, Mary," Dad greeted the woman. "How are you?"

She clutched her keys, looking worried. She was pretty, with dark hair pulled back to show off her earrings, and her gray eyes contrasted with a black top. Todd noticed those types of things, since they were elements of his artwork.

"Fine," Mary said at last.

From his spot on the floor, Todd saw her join his dad at the desk.

"All right, Mary . . ." His dad pulled out a ledger book and thumbed through it.

She fidgeted and sighed. "I'm not here to make a payment."

Dad stopped. Looked across the desk.

"I'm, um . . . I'm here to give the car back."

"You what?"

Mary pushed the keys onto the desk.

Todd held his breath for his dad's response. He'd seen his father acting differently at home, but he had to see how that worked here in everyday life. He wanted to believe the best about him, but he'd sat here in the past and heard things said at that very same desk that didn't seem right, even to Todd's ears.

"Can you tell me what's going on?" Dad's chair squeaked as he leaned back.

"I'm so far behind on payments," Mary said. "I . . . I can't get caught up."

"Mary, you only owe twelve hundred and sixty-five dollars. The car's yours after that. You're so close."

"I know." She pressed her lips together and looked away. Her voice cracked. "I just can't afford it, because my husband's been out of work for a couple of months and all. It just seems like every week there's a new bill, one on top of the other. We just can't get caught up. My son, he's . . . he's sick. And we're going back and forth to the doctor in Atlanta. And . . . I don't know what else to do."

Todd believed her. He'd heard about Derek and the doctors. That's why the kid wasn't playing soccer this season.

"I don't know what we're going to do," Mary continued. "The car's been great. I just . . . I don't know what to say. I'm so sorry."

Dad stood and moved to a cabinet behind his desk. He didn't speak.

For a moment, Mary looked defensive. Like she'd made him upset or something. "I mean, I just feel like I'm making the right decision here, Mr. Austin. I'm . . . I really . . ."

Todd heard her voice trail away. He saw her draw in air, then sigh. She deflated in her chair, sinking lower.

Todd's dad came back to the desk. He had a file in his hands, probably the paperwork on the lady's car. Her eyes were fearful, and Todd wondered how his father was going handle this. Did he have the power to add on late fees? To take the car away, just like that?

"Mary . . ." Dad started writing.

Her forehead wrinkled with grief as she aimed her eyes into her lap.

"Mary, I believe you. I know you're behind, but you have been one of my best customers. I just pray that God helps you with what you're going through." He pushed a pink-tinged piece of paper across the desk, along with her set of keys. He closed the ledger and put it away.

"This is the title?" she said, voice quivering with astonishment.

"The car is yours. You're paid in full," Dad said.

Mary swallowed and sat, stunned.

Todd could hardly believe it either. He waited for someone to say something. *Title* and *tidal* . . . The two words sounded almost the same, and both had a similar effect on the lady at the desk. Tears brimmed on her eyelids, about to come flowing down in a wave.

Obviously uncomfortable with the charge of emotion in the air, Dad looked at Mary, glanced away, then excused himself and closed the door on his way into the adjoining washroom. She was left to take it all in, to receive what had been freely given to her.

Paid in full . . .

Todd liked the sound of that. His chest was bursting with pride.

Mary turned to go and seemed to notice Todd for the first time. She tried to gather herself, then said, "Your daddy's a *really* good man."

Still cross-legged on the copy room floor, Todd Austin beamed.

Chapter 25
THE GUY TO BEAT

JAY

Low, roiling storm clouds chased Jay home from the car lot. He was ready for a cozy evening indoors. He picked up Thursday's mail from the stand in the hallway, scanned through it for any sign of a sweepstakes million-dollar check, or a surprise windfall from the bank, or—

Anything that could lift his burden of gloom.

Tomorrow was the day. The end of the car lot. He could live with the choices he had made, but it was harder to accept that his wife and children would suffer the consequences as well. Why hadn't he considered them at the time?

He used to tell himself he *was* thinking of them when he fudged the numbers to gain an extra thousand dollars. Wrong. He'd thought only of himself.

"Hey, honey," Judy said from behind the black marble countertop she was wiping down. She smiled at him. A cross hung from a chain around her neck.

Jay stepped into the dining area, still filtering through the junk mail in hand. "You know, if we took all our credit card offers and put them end to end, I'm convinced they'd go to the moon and back."

"Or you could take the cards and *buy* me the moon," Judy said.

"Sounds like you're flirting now."

"Maybe I am, Mr. Austin."

"You really want the moon?"

"Well." She looked up at the ceiling. "I don't know where I'd put it. Probably just have to leave it exactly where it's at."

"And we'd never pay it off."

"Yeah."

"Yeah," Jay echoed. "Is Todd still at Jeff's house?"

"Yep. They're going on that field trip tomorrow, so I let him spend the night. We've got the house to ourselves. I was thinking maybe a nice relaxing evening, just you and me, cuddling on the couch and watching some TV."

"Cuddling?" Jay gave her a sly grin. "Is that allowed in your condition?"

"I hope you're joking, Jay Austin."

"I . . . uh . . ."

The sound of the phone came to his rescue.

He picked up. "Hello? Yes. Uhhh, no, actually we don't need another credit card right—yes. Oh?" Jay widened his eyes as

Judy smiled in the middle of her work. "Oh, it's a *mind*-blowing rate. Unbelievable. I'm still not gonna take it. Thank you. Uh-huh. Thank you. *Thank* you." He slammed the receiver back onto the wall base and groaned. He snatched the phone back, turned off the ringer, and set it near the china cabinet. "We don't need any more calls tonight."

"Just the two of us," Judy said.

He faced his wife across the dining bar, admiring her sweet smile and beautiful glowing skin.

"So," she said. "Tomorrow's the day."

"It is."

"How're you doing?"

"I'm not sure. I've got some anxiety, but it's a peaceful sort of anxiety."

"A *peaceful* anxiety? Can you have peaceful anxiety?"

"Well," Jay said, "what do you call it when you feel like your life's turning upside down, but you still think God's in control?"

"It's like a . . ."—she tilted her head, thinking—"a serene . . . chaos."

"A serene cha—what's the difference between a peaceful anxiety and a serene chaos?"

"Serene chaos is better."

Jay shrugged. "Well, there you have it."

He moved into the living room, picked up the newspaper. He moved a pillow from behind him—really, what was it with women and all these fluffy pillows?—and turned on the TV.

A newscaster was introducing an upcoming news report: ". . . and a look at the latest craze in weight loss. With a growing number of new energy-giving weight-loss drugs available, is the health risk going up to trim down?" A handful of pills was shown at close quarters, followed by a shot of a man's belly rolling over the belt of his pants.

Jay shook his head and spread out the paper, seeking the sports and classifieds sections. He'd been perusing other career possibilities, in light of what was sure to come.

"Those stories and more," the narrator continued, "on the *NBS Nightly NewsWatch*. And now from our studios in New York, here's Tom Jennings."

The scene shifted from an obese man patting his belly to a news anchor propped on a stool and facing the camera in a no-nonsense manner.

"Good evening," Tom Jennings said. "Our top story tonight is about the car business, or specifically the sale of used cars. Each year in America, over half a million cars are sold, and the number of used-car lots in this country has risen dramatically over the last year. But how much do we really know about buying a used car?"

A lot less than most people think, Jay said to himself.

"Most Americans take for granted that any markdown in price at all is a deal, and although there are many deals to be found, experts say that most Americans are unaware of just how easy it is to be deceived."

You can say that again.

"For the last six weeks, *NBS Nightly News* has conducted an undercover investigation into the used-car business. We have to begin with a warning: You won't like what we found."

"Oh, Lord," Jay mumbled aloud. "Maybe I *should* get another career."

"Really?" Judy piped in. "Maybe you're right."

"Maybe it's a sign."

But Tom Jennings wasn't done, not even close.

BERNIE

The pool hall was smoky, especially now that guys were getting off work and slapping down their quarters for next-ups. Cones of lemon-colored light illuminated each billiard table. In the corner near the bar, a TV blared despite the fact no one paid it any mind.

Bernie Myers had never been to this place before, but he'd followed a few of his coworkers in for happy hour—a few games of eight-ball and a chance to buddy up with the top dogs at Butch Bowers.

"I'm told you're the guy to beat," Bernie said to the man at table one. "That true?"

"Ain't no slouch."

Bernie smirked at the burly, wrinkled man in the leather vest. Who'd the guy think he was, some Old West gunslinger? Regardless, if Bernie managed to beat the best guy in here, his fellow sales associates would pass the word around, and he would earn big-time respect at the new job.

Which could transfer into a better office, more money, and . . .

"Let's rack 'em," he said.

"How much?"

"Just a friendly game. I'm not a gambling man."

"Sure ya is. We all got a little o' that in us."

"What's your name, first?" Bernie said.

"What's it matter to ya?"

"Well." He grinned, imagining his last set of buyers. "I never take money from someone till they've given me their name. Just common courtesy, I guess."

"Garrett."

"Okay, Garrett. I'm Bernie. Let's play for twenty."

"Forty."

"You got it on you?"

Garrett patted his vest, his jeans pockets, stumbled against the table as he reached into his left boot. Two wrinkled twenties appeared in his hand. Probably smelled like old socks, but Bernie figured if they were green they were clean. And he was convinced the cash would be his shortly.

The first game was a seesaw affair, which Garrett won on a lucky shot.

"Again," Bernie said.

"Double or nothin'. Tha's the stakes."

Bernie pointed at him. "You're on."

That's when he turned and caught the closed captions on the bottom portion of the TV screen. Something about car sales. A special report.

". . . We decided to do an investigation of six used-car lots picked at random across the U.S. And we begin tonight by taking you to a lot in north Arkansas. Bud Morris Auto Sales has been around for almost thirty years, with a seemingly solid reputation. But after an undercover reporter spoke with a sales associate behind the scenes, what we found was a different story."

The hidden video was grainy, black-and-white. It showed a guy in his office, holding a coffee mug. He was in shorts, his feet up on the desk, sunglasses propped on the brim of his baseball cap.

Female reporter: "I mean, how do you do it? Is eight thousand the most you've ever cleared?"

Sales associate: "No. Bud got this lady to pay sixteen thousand for a Cadillac that we just got for five."

"Sixteen?"

"Oh, yeah. We made eleven thousand off of her. And she left here thinking she got a great deal."

"Does that happen very often?"

Associate: "Uhh . . . No, usually we just end up making about two or three grand more than we ought to."

"On every car?"

"Yeah, you can tell pretty quick who's done their homework." A shot of sales sheets and contracts came onto the screen. "If they don't know how much a car should cost, we'll get 'em."

Bernie smirked at that, then turned and saw the old guy, Garrett, propped on both arms against the billiard table. He looked patient enough. A little red eyed.

The next game was gonna be all Bernie's. He was sure of it.

JAY

". . . If they don't know how much a car should cost, we'll get 'em."

Still facing the TV, Jay felt indignation and shame rise in his throat. To think that he had been a part of this often-shady industry, a willing participant in other people's misfortune.

Tom Jennings came back into view: "And get them they did. After obtaining information on a dozen cars sold to unsuspecting customers, *NBS Nightly News* found that, on average, each car sold for thirty-five hundred dollars above the acceptable range."

That used to seem just fine. What was wrong with me?

Behind him, Jay heard Judy slicing fruit on the cutting board.

Jennings: "Next we go to the state of Utah, where we had an undercover reporter pose as a customer with seemingly no idea as to what her car of choice would cost. Experts say this 1988 Chevrolet Blazer should run between twelve and fifteen hundred dollars. But listen to what the salesman tries to sell it for."

The mustached salesman was in a sweater and a golfing cap. His eyes were hidden by sunglasses. The low-grade video showed him in the passenger seat of the Blazer, talking so fast that the customer couldn't even ask a question: "This is a very, very popular car. Great ride. You drive it. I promise, it's a great ride. Great stereo system. It'll hold its value. It's American-made."

The next shot showed the same man standing outside the driver's-side door, referring to the sticker posted in the window. "We've got about seven thousand in this one," he said. "But I, uh . . . I can get it to you for about six."

Jennings: "Six thousand dollars? Even in great condition, our experts say that's a rip-off. As a matter of fact, of the six lots we investigated, only one proved to deal honestly all the time."

Oh, this should be interesting, Jay thought.

"We now take you to south Georgia, to the city of Albany."

No way.

"It's a small car lot, with at most thirty-five cars."

What? Well, I'm not the only small lot in town . . .

"This time, what we found was a different story. We were able to get a detailed look through the eyes of our undercover reporter, who was actually hired and trained to sell cars at Jay Austin Motors."

Jay rocketed forward. He heard Judy drop something in the kitchen.

Chapter 26

DANCE PARTNERS

JUDY

The knife clattered from the cutting board into the stainless-steel sink. Judy gawked over the marble counter, past Jay's place on the couch, at the living room television.

An undercover reporter?

Judy couldn't even imagine who they were referring to.

On the screen, a grainy video of her husband appeared. Whoever had been holding the camera had it at hip level, angled upward. Jay was leaned back against the low metal fence at the lot.

"Kevin *Cantrell*?" Jay threw down the newspaper and stood.

The college kid? Judy questioned. *That* Kevin?

The voice that played through the speakers confirmed their suspicions: "Speaking of selling cars, I wanted to ask . . . You don't seem to be getting as much as you could out of some of these. If I sold one for a little more, could I keep the rest as commission?"

"Kevin," Jay responded, clearly unaware he was being recorded, "we're not going to go that route. We're gonna charge what we would feel good about being charged. I'm gonna stick to the fair market value."

"You can get away with pushing a *little* bit. I mean, don't you need the money?"

"I do. But I've gotta live with how I run this place . . . I do know, I just don't want any more regrets. I'm sticking to the highest standard I can. You treat people right, it'll come back to you."

Tom Jennings: "That's a good philosophy, and one that he apparently lives by. In six weeks, the profit averaged out at fifteen hundred dollars per car, an amount considered completely acceptable."

Judy joined Jay in front of the couch. Her initial sense of betrayal and shock was changing to one of rejoicing. She turned toward her husband, but his face was fixed straight ahead, unblinking, only the movement of his nostrils giving any indication he had not turned into stone.

Be still . . . Isn't that what she'd told him?

This was a little *too* still.

Judy walked to the dining table, grabbed her Bible, and hurried back.

"In fact," the reporter went on, "Jay Austin Motors even paid for repairs to cars that had problems soon after being sold—a gesture not often seen in the used-car business. And whereas he may not be rolling in the dough, his honesty comes as a refreshing reminder to treat others as you want to be treated. When we return, we'll—"

Judy clicked off the TV and began reading aloud what they had gone over just the night before: "'Delight yourself in the LORD and he will give you the desires of your heart. Commit your way to the LORD; trust in him and he will do this: He will make your righteousness shine like the dawn, the justice of your cause like the noonday sun. Be still before the LORD and wait patiently for him.'"

Jay blinked. Finally. His eyes were wet.

"I am so proud of you," Judy said. She touched his chin and turned his face toward her. "Did you hear me? I am *sooo* proud of you."

He looked down. "I just wanted to finish well."

She wrapped herself around his waist and leaned into him. "You may not be finished yet."

He pulled her close. He didn't say a word.

She thought of that old joke about knowing when a salesman was lying by the fact that he was moving his lips. Maybe it was best that Jay remained quiet. And her, too. She'd done her share of nagging in the past, trying to do the Lord's work for Him. Right now, they'd take a moment to bask in what God was doing.

BERNIE

In the course of one investigative report, Bernie had lost two games of eight-ball and a quick eighty bucks. Even worse, as closed captions scrolled down the pool-hall TV screen, he watched a national news program laud the integrity of the goateed, bad-sweater-wearing Jay Austin.

Jay. The man who had taught him the Touch.

No one seemed to be paying any attention to this broadcast. Didn't they realize the injustice of it all? Who had Jay paid off this time? *NBS Nightly NewsWatch*? This had to be a joke.

"No," Bernie said aloud. "What a buncha bull."

"'Scuse me?"

"You heard me. What a low-down, dirty, rotten cheat."

"Now, you ain't got no place callin' names," Garrett said.

Bernie wobbled around. "Relax, buddy. Wasn't talking about you."

"What? You think I'm deaf, too? I done *heard* whatcha said."

"Hey." Bernie held up both hands. "Not you," he reiterated. "I'm talking about . . . 'bout the TV there, the report. And Jay Austin."

"Jay Austin Motors?" Garrett said. "Know a guy that works there."

"Buncha liars. Every last one of them."

"Nah, not this one. He's good people."

"*Ha.*"

"You best hold your tongue, mister."

"Listen, G-man—"

"What'd you call me?"

"Believe me, I know all about the guys down at that lot." Bernie saw a black light swelling in the burly man's eyes, but this wasn't the Old West, and he refused to be intimidated. Bernie had his own share of weight to throw around, more than enough to pack a hard punch. "Those guys'd cheat you quicker than—"

In one motion, Garrett lifted his cue stick in both hands and shoved Bernie back against the padded bar. The polished wood rolled up his chest and into the folds of his neck, halting his flow of words.

"Now, what'd I tell ya?" Garrett growled.

"Oh, no you didn't," Bernie squeaked. "You . . . you picked the *wrong* dance partner."

MAX

Though Max didn't show it, he was frightened. It was a strange feeling for him, one he hadn't encountered since those weeks at the hospital after the shooting. Even then, he wasn't overly worried about dying. He knew the good Lord was waiting on the other side.

And his good wife, too.

No, what scared him more than death was the idea of being alone.

At work, he'd found a fishing buddy in Sam Jones. They'd shared many an evening on the riverbank, even taken a trip last summer to the North Flint River where the shoalies were things of legend.

He'd also found a friend in that scoundrel Jay Austin. Though nearly forty years separated them, they shared a camaraderie that reminded Max of his army days—poking fun, talking shop, and telling the truth even when the truth wasn't easy to take.

Every man needed that now and then.

And the last few weeks had been the best yet. Jay, Sam, and Max had bonded and locked shields while fighting to protect the future of this lot. They'd talked and shared more than in the previous years put together.

Now, within twenty-four hours, it would all be stripped away.

Oh, sure, they'd tell each other to call, to keep in touch, and all that nonsense. Nobody did that, though. Not anymore. Not with the Internet and cell phones and other contraptions that masqueraded as ways of communicating. Seemed people these days were always brushing by, hurrying to the next thing, never really stopping to know a person.

Then again, maybe Max Kendall was just getting old and cynical.

Or even worse . . . senile.

Well, enough of all that. He'd gone fishing earlier. Given his concerns to the Lord. What more could he do?

Max eased onto the sofa and turned on the TV. The one show he watched regularly was the late local news. He pulled his wife's shawl across his legs and let the worries of the day roll off his back.

Drifting, drifting . . .

Suddenly his eyes snapped open. Something had jolted his subconscious. He pushed his glasses back up on his nose and focused. There, beneath the rabbit-eared antennas, plastered on the twelve-inch screen, a familiar face appeared.

". . . and in an altercation earlier tonight, things turned ugly when one Bernie Myers lost his temper at a local pool hall. Known to many through his used-car-commercial appearances,

Myers claims he was assaulted by a patron, while others say that's simply not the case. Garrett Drake, a retiree and regular at the establishment, told police officers that he was protecting another man's honor and that Myers was the first to throw a punch. Both men were issued citations for disturbing the peace and await their chances to stand before a city judge. When we come back . . ."

Max shook his head. Why should he be surprised?

Adding to the moment, the first advertisement to blast through the TV was for Butch Bowers AutoWorld. There he was, Bernie Myers in his sunglasses.

"It's *phenomenal*."

"Got that right," Max answered back. "Sure is."

Chapter 27

BACKUP

JAY

Let the countdown begin. This was it, the last day.

Jay rolled along a side street and parked beside the sales office. "I turned this lot over to You, Lord. Next, I get to turn it over to the bank."

He stepped out of the vehicle. He had one hope: that he could bring in enough to cover Max's and Sam's final paychecks. He could not—would not—cheat those guys. They'd busted their backsides to keep this place running ever since the ignoble departure of Bernie Myers and Vince Berkley.

Of course, Jay had reason for his hope.

Last night, God had stood on his behalf. The timing was too perfect. And if a few local viewers were impressed, Jay might just sell some cars today.

He walked around the building, drawn by the sound of voices. He reeled back in astonishment. Sure, he'd expected a few early buyers, but this was . . . Well, it was ridiculous. Upward of thirty people were milling between the cars, peeking through windows, examining tires and paint jobs.

Jay stepped over the low fence and approached the throng.

A man in jeans and glasses met him, midstride. "Mr. Austin, I saw you on the news last night, and I was looking to buy a car. I was wondering if you could show me this Tracker over here."

"Ex*cuse* me. Ex*cuse* me." A woman holding a toddler in her arms leaned forward. "You were *not* the first one here. I've been here since seven thirty."

"Okay, uh . . ." Jay panned the crowd. "Are you all here to buy cars?"

A chorus of replies: "Yes." "I am." "What else do you think?"

A few hands were raised.

Jay grinned. This was looking like church, right here in the sales lot—lifted hands, sun shining down, and hope burning bright. "Uh . . . Lemme run in real quick and open up. And I, uh . . . I need to make one quick call. Would you mind staying here for just a minute?"

"I ain't buyin' a car nowhere else!" one man shouted.

"Okay. Well, you stick with me." Jay made eye contact with scattered individuals. No need to manipulate, but no need to avoid dealing with human nature either. If he left for a few minutes, some of these customers might scurry off on other errands. "Don't go anywhere," he urged. "Look around and find something you're interested—"

"Already know what I want."

"Good. Then I'll be right back to talk."

He dashed toward the sales office, tripped, slipped, regained his balance on the steps. After fumbling with the lock, he made sure to disengage the alarm and then pulled his cell phone from his pocket. Time to call for backup.

JUDY

"Hello?"

Wrapped in a bathrobe, Judy answered the phone on her way out of the shower. She'd woken early with a compulsion to clean house, to set things in order. She'd spent two hours scrubbing, polishing, dusting, and rearranging, until a shower had been a matter of necessity.

Much better. The scents of soap and shampoo wafted through the towel still coiled around her head.

"Judy."

"What's going on?" She tightened the belt of her robe. "You sound like you've been running, Jay."

"Just"—deep breath—"getting started."

"Did Mr. MacDonald send the repo guy already?"

"No, I—"

"Are you okay? Jay, did they send someone after you?"

"Nothing like that." The strength returned to his voice. "Listen, Judy, I need a favor. I need you to get on the phone with Max and Sam, and get up here as fast as possible."

"What's going on?"

"I've got thirty people outside, waiting to buy cars *right* now."

"Did you say thirty?"

"Thirty."

She must've heard incorrectly. "Thirty?"

"*Thirty.*"

She held the phone away from her mouth and screamed. The receiver almost dropped. She caught it and tried to collect herself.

"I need you to call them," Jay said, "and get them up here as soon as you can. And I need your help, too, okay?"

"What? I'm not a car salesman."

"Well, you are today. I gotta get going."

The call ended.

With one hand resting on her stomach, Judy held the phone to her ear for a full thirty seconds, willing her husband to come back on the line and tell her this was a prank. The towel began to slip from her head, and a curtain of wet hair fell in front of her eyes.

Time to pull yourself together, she thought. This was a good thing, a *very* good thing. There was no way she would let her fears stand in the way.

JAY

The next hour sped by, spurred along by Jay's excitement.

He was in the zone, in the sweet spot.

The appearance of his faithful employees added to the adrenaline rush. They could do this. They could beat this thing. He was reminded of the pickup basketball games he used to play in college, three-on-three. There was nothing better than a fast break, when all three players were dialed in, weaving, passing, taking the ball to the hoop.

Where was Judy, though?

Jay showed the Tracker to the man who had expressed interest. Next thing he knew, they were doing paperwork on the hood. Jay pointed Sam to a man at a Chevy pickup, and Sam headed that way. Soon after, the Tracker was rolling off the lot with a new owner at the wheel.

Jay moved to a couple with a child, standing beside a sedan. The woman explained that she did local catering and needed a second vehicle now that her hobby had blossomed into a full-time job.

"If you can believe this," she added, "I was even contacted by some local filmmakers to cater their latest production, the cast and crew and all."

"Really?" Jay said. "What sorta film?"

"It's a high school sports movie. I just hope it turns out well. You know, they're hoping it gets in the theaters."

"Sounds like they're facing a giant of a task. Now, tell me, what're your thoughts on this car?"

A few minutes later, Jay left her to talk it over with her husband. His eyes swept the lot and found Max pulling out the oil dipstick for a sour-faced customer with his hands folded high on his chest. No problem. Max could take care of himself. Farther along, Sam, in camouflage pants and his usual hat, was working a deal on the truck. Minutes later, Sam was shaking hands with the customer and pointing toward the sales office.

Another sale. This had never been so easy.

Jay checked his watch. When was his wife going to . . . ?

"Judy," he said as she scurried into view.

"Sorry, Jay. I know it's important to look good for the customers, so I—"

"Nobody cares about that," he said. "Not today."

She looked crestfallen.

Jay knew he'd said the wrong thing. He started to apologize, but the sour-faced man inserted himself between them, his nose nearly touching Jay's, his nicotine-stained teeth showing between chapped lips.

"That man"—he stabbed a finger in Max's direction—"he keeps tryin' to sell me a stinkin' car."

"Uh. Okay."

"Nosiree, it's not okay. I don't wanna buy a stinkin' car, and I don't 'preciate you high-pressure sales folk tryin' to tell me different."

"This is a sales lot, sir."

"That don't mean you need to ambush every Joe, Dick, and Harry that comes wanderin' 'cross your property."

Jay recalled dealing with this man a few months ago—the same complaints, same silliness. He was a visual reminder of what Max could've been if Max had chosen a road of bitterness.

"So, why *are* you here?" Jay probed.

"Well, if you gotta know, I'm just lookin'."

"Last time I was 'just lookin',' I ended up married." Jay stepped around the man and wrapped his arm around Judy's waist. "To this lovely lady, right here."

"Humph."

"There's nothing prettier on this lot, but if you find something you *do* want, you let us know. Otherwise," Jay assured him, "we won't be bothering you."

The old character shuffled away.

"Thank you," said Judy.

"I meant it. You look great, sweetheart."

"So what can I do to help?"

He encouraged her to be her usual, friendly self. He assured her that all the cars in stock were in good mechanical condition. If she had any questions, she could come ask. He introduced her to a couple at a white GMC, patted her on the back, and left her standing stiff-armed but determined to succeed.

Jay returned to the catering lady with the young child. Her husband wanted to know what sort of down payment Jay would accept. Once that was resolved, they shook hands, and Jay went to fetch keys and paperwork.

More deals followed.

The woman who'd "been here since seven thirty" found a suitable vehicle.

Later, Jay turned to a middle-aged lady in a red sweater. He handed her papers to sign, then realized they were for the teenager behind her. The boy signed the agreement, while the lady pointed out her car of choice.

Jay stood with hands on his hips and surveyed the emptying lot. Judy, Max, and Sam were all still engaged with people.

The day wasn't over yet.

SAM

"I like this Oldsmobile," the man said to Sam. He had introduced himself as the orchestra leader for the local school's music program. Maybe he hoped for an educator's discount or something. "How much for it?"

Sam thought it over. "About seven thousand dollars."

"Would you take sixty-five hundred?"

Sam remained deadpan. "All right."

"You will?"

"I guess so."

"All right." The man reached out and shook his hand.

"If that's what you wanna pay," Sam added.

His basic knowledge of the vehicles and their values had increased over the last month, and the sales tactics were getting easier. In fact, he kinda had fun doing this. He started toward the office.

"Uhh . . . Well, hang on," the man said. "How 'bout six thousand?"

"No. You done said sixty-five. I know you got it, or you wouldn't have offered it."

"What if I have a trade-in?"

"Sorry. Today's our last day, so we aren't taking trade-ins."

"Well. Okay."

"Good." Sam turned. "I'll get the papers."

Shaking his head, the man pushed his hands into his pockets. "Aw, man."

JAY

Jay faced a no-nonsense buyer over the hood of the red Isuzu Trooper. Stymied by the man's barrage of questions, Judy had called for reinforcements. The moment he bagan talking, the man reminded Jay of his brother, Joey, in how he haggled.

"Miles?" the man demanded of Jay.

"One-twenty."

"Highway?"

"Some."

"Wrecked?"

"No."

"Smoker?"

"No."

"Cruise?"

"Yes."

"Price?"

"Eight."

"Seven."

"Seven-five."

"Done." The man smiled and met Jay at the front end, where they sealed the agreement with clasped hands. "I like the way you deal."

JUDY

Judy felt so out of place doing this. Jay was in his element, while Max looked comfortable talking to customers, as did Sam in his camouflage attire.

And she had been worried about her mascara?

The day was passing quickly. She told herself not to worry about Todd, since he had an extra key. He would make himself a snack and be just fine.

The hard ground was pushing up through her legs into her spine. She held her back and approached a man who had been studying a particular car. She almost asked, "Can I help you?" then reminded herself she was supposed to leave no room for yes or no answers, only answers that opened up discussion.

"How can I help you?" she amended.

"This here . . ." He tapped the windshield. "This looks pretty good for this price, huh?"

"Yeah, I guess so."

"And it's pretty clean."

"Seems to be, yes."

"Most of the miles are probably highway miles, right?"

"I really have no idea." She grimaced as a spasm knotted her lower back muscles. "Would you mind if I went into the office and sat down?"

"All right, you talked me into it." The man clapped his hands together. "I think I'll take it. So, I guess I oughta follow you indoors then?"

Judy smiled through her pain. Jay would be proud.

MAX

Max stood in the center of the lot. Jay and Sam joined him. Aside from two remaining vehicles—a Toyota pickup and an old Lincoln—the view was unobstructed across the tire-marked pavement. He figured this was about as good as it could get. If they had to go down, at least they'd go down swinging.

Without saying a thing, they exchanged glances and began laughing, right up till their sides hurt and their cheeks were tight as acorns.

Sometimes, there was just no need for words.

At last, Max asked Jay what time the bank was coming over.

"Four," Jay replied.

"It's three fifty. I'd have that check ready if I were you."

The sour-faced man from earlier on shuffled toward them. "Hey, there. Hey, you three. What's it take for an old man to buy a stinkin' car round here?"

Max and Jay rolled their eyes at each other.

Sam said, "You got just two to choose from."

"Don't want two. What good'd that do me? I want that Lincoln right there. And I don't want no hassle, you hear? Got cash, so you can take it or leave it."

"Well, sir." Sam wore a wry grin. "I guess we'll take it."

It was now 3:53 p.m. They needed one more buyer, just one more.

Chapter 28

PAYBACKS

JAY

"Let's hear it, Judy. What's the verdict?"

Head down, she held up her left hand and used a pencil eraser to continue tapping figures into an adding machine.

Jay, Sam, and Max waited around the sales desk. The bank should've been here half an hour ago. Jay watched the wall clock tick off another minute, his anxiety in direct opposition to the hope that had crested over them as the Toyota pickup sold to a landscaper in need of a second crew vehicle.

The lot was empty. Not one car remained.

But once numbers were crunched and expenses paid, what did it mean?

Judy transferred an amount from the machine's display into the ledger, then lifted a mysterious smile to the waiting trio.

Jay huffed. "Sweetheart, c'*mon*."

"Thirty-eight thousand, four-hundred and fifteen dollars," she said.

Jay smiled and folded his arms across his chest. He shot the guys a congratulatory look. Sam nodded and returned the smile, his elbow resting on the mantel. Max leaned forward in his seat, still not ready to celebrate.

"And that's *after* covering the cost of the cars," Judy added.

Chewing his clove gum a little faster, Max grinned.

MR. MACDONALD

In his black BMW soft-top, Mr. MacDonald made his way north toward Jay Austin Motors—soon to be the property of Franklin Bank and Trust. He hated to do this. He knew the toils of running one's own business. He knew even better the way a failed venture could shatter a man's pride and destroy a household. His own father had become a shell of his former self after a debilitating stock market gamble.

That wouldn't be the fate of George MacDonald.

In his teens, he had set aside his golfing aspirations and chosen instead the road to stability and security. Did he regret it? Did he ever pine away for the unfulfilled dreams of his youth?

No, he certainly did not.

Most dreams, in his staid opinion, only led to nightmares. Best to keep your eyes wide open and play it safe.

Mr. MacDonald downshifted and panned the sidewalk ahead, searching for the long row of automobiles that would soon be part of the bank's assets. They'd go to auction, turn a small profit with any luck, and the real estate would be put up for sale. Easy come, easy go.

Life, he knew, had a way of separating the men from the boys.

He squinted through the windshield. Hmm. Yes, this was the address. The sign read "Jay Austin Motors." Colorful pennants flapped in the evening breeze with cheerful abandon.

So where were the cars?

He slid into a space next to the office, climbed out, and put a hand on his waist. His gold watch glinted in the waning sun. This was the right place, no doubt about it. It was nearly four forty, and the lot should still be open.

What had Jay Austin done?

During his banking career, Mr. MacDonald had witnessed deceptions and subterfuges of all sorts. He'd sent out his repo guys, only to hear back about car owners who'd hidden their vehicles in relatives' garages or on neighboring blocks.

But this? With thirty-plus cars to be repossessed, this had to be the largest-scale deception he himself had ever come across.

He walked across the bare lot. He had a cell phone on his belt and considered calling the police. Yes, that would be the sad but certain conclusion to Jay Austin's delinquency on his accounts.

He was reaching for his phone when the click of a door and the sound of footsteps stopped him. He turned to see Jay approaching at a fast pace from the sales office. For a moment, he feared an assault.

Then he spotted the envelope in the man's hand.

"Mr. MacDonald," Jay said.

"Yes?"

"How're you doing?"

"Hi." Mr. MacDonald kept his voice stern. "How're you?"

Jay shook his hand. "I'm doing fine." He handed over the envelope. "Uh, that's for you. I think that, uh . . . that should about cover what we owe."

"Where are the cars?" he insisted.

"Well, uh . . ." Jay put his hands on his hips, looked around, then turned back. "We sold them."

"What do you mean, you sold them?"

"Uh . . . We had a real, *real* good day today."

Mr. MacDonald reached into the envelope, half expecting a death threat—he'd seen them before—or a small check with a note begging for more leniency. Sorry. Barring an act of divine intervention, there would be no more grace.

The amount on the check hit him with near-physical force. *What?* His eyes widened. *This is impossible.*

Mr. MacDonald prided himself on his stoicism, but there was no denying the moment's impact. He stared at the row of numbers, then swiveled his gaze back to the man at his side. He knew the check could be bad, could bounce higher than a man in antigravity boots, but something in Jay Austin's serene expression told him that would not be the case.

JAY

"Todd's passed out on his bed," Judy said.

"I know how he feels."

What a week. An unforgettable, mind-blowing, hold-on-to-your-hats kinda week. A thank-God-for-grace week.

Jay was worn-out. Even while rejoicing, he was reminded of his mortality as his body shut down beneath the overload of emotions he had endured. He was stretched out now on the master bedroom floor, feet propped on a padded footstool, switching between news broadcasts on the TV.

On one channel, a male reporter asked, "Do you trust used-car salesmen? They don't always have great reputations, but one here in Albany is earning respect. A national news organization recently investigated Jay Austin Motors and found his prices and business practices are always fair. After an undercover investigation that lasted six weeks . . ."

On WSCG, channel 15 news, Stephanie Ward reported: "There's a new record for cars sold in one day here in Albany. Jay Austin Motors sold thirty-two vehicles inside of eight hours. The rush to buy cars came after a news story ran two days ago which highlighted the honest business performed by Jay Austin, who says it was an answer to prayer . . ."

Jay turned off the set. It was too much to relive right now. He needed time to soak in all that God had been doing, from the unexpected arrival of Kevin Cantrell to the recent airing of *NBS Nightly NewsWatch*.

"How'd your call go with your parents?" Judy said.

"Mom cried."

"She's such a doll. I'm sure she's thrilled for us." Judy adjusted herself against the bed's footboard, piling pillows high. "So what'd your dad say?"

"He said we shouldn't be surprised when God is faithful."

"He's right." She paused. "Hey, I tried taping those news

stories, and I keep getting the last half of each interview. I've got the last half of *four* stories. Do you know anyone who could copy these tapes for us to give to your parents?"

"Just take it to church. Don't the church media guys just sit around and copy tapes anyway?"

"I don't know *what* they do. Hey, are you still getting interviewed?"

"I don't know. My whole schedule's a blur. This has been the craziest week of my life."

"Jay, I want to ask you something."

He cringed. Her questions often led to uncomfortable answers.

"God's blessed you because of your faithfulness and obedience in the last couple of months," she said. "But what about all the customers before that?"

"I know. I've been thinking about them." He brought his hands to his face, rubbed his tired eyes. "I was reading about Zacchaeus this morning, who returned money to all those people he took advantage of when he did his tax collecting. That's a painful thought."

"You have something in mind?"

Jay propped himself on his elbows and met the question head-on. Like it or not, God had a way of using Judy's voice to speak to him. "I mean," he said, "not only would that take a lotta money, but I'd have to eat more humble pie than any man alive."

"It's not about you escaping discomfort, Jay. It's about you honoring God with what He's blessed you with."

He laid his head back, closed his eyes. "That's two years of customers. It's probably half of them I cheated."

JUDY

The following Thursday, Judy braved a thunderstorm to meet Jay at the sales office. Todd was in school. The weather had discouraged Judy's plans of a morning stroll with Christina, who'd advised, "If you want the baby to come soon, that's one way to get things moving, Judy." Sam and Max were holed up in the garage, working on another trade-in. The inventory was rebuilding rapidly.

Jay gave her a quick kiss. "Thanks for coming. Let's do this."

"It's the right thing, honey. I'm proud of you."

He took a seat in the copy room. Rolling the chair forward, he faced the first file cabinet. He patted his knees as if to say, "Here goes nothing," and pulled out the lowest drawer.

They had agreed he would start with his oldest transactions and work forward. He would pull the manila folders representing deals that had been ratcheted beyond reasonable profit margins. While he figured the amounts he owed back, she would balance the accounts payable and receivable.

Judy drew her hair back into a ponytail. On the desktop, her framed wedding photo stood as a reminder of the changes that had gone on. Yes, she was here to stand by her husband, in sickness and health—even if the sickness had been spiritual and financial.

She attacked her task with the adding machine and a pencil. Jay did the same at his position in the corner. A few hours later, she set down the last receipt.

"I'm done with the books." She sighed. "You done with your project?"

Jay wore a look of defeat. "Judy, this is going to take a whole lot longer than you think to pay these people back."

"Why?"

"Well, we gotta have enough money for the mortgage and the light bill, but even if we skip a check for me, I still think we oughta pay Sam and Max."

"The good thing is, you're selling cars as fast as you're getting them in. You only have—let's see . . . twelve cars on the lot right now, Jay."

"But our current profits aren't going to cover"—he hefted his sheet of calculations—"the thirty-nine thousand, one hundred twenty-three dollars and fifty cents that I owe previous customers. I think we need to do it in steps."

Judy snapped upright at his words. Had she heard correctly?

Misunderstanding her reaction, Jay said, "Yeah. Pretty ugly, huh?"

"No, hold on." She double-checked the ledger before her, then narrowed her eyes at her husband. "How much did you say?"

"I figure I've made thirty-nine thousand more than I should have, over the past two years."

"No, no, no, no, no." Judy waved off his words. "What was the *exact* amount you said?"

"Thirty-nine thousand, one hundred twenty-three dollars and fifty cents."

As he recited from his paperwork, she tracked along on her own. She dropped her pencil, pushed herself up from her chair, and carried the ledger over to Jay's work area. She plopped it down on the table in front of him. He stared at the balance at the bottom of the page.

Which read: *$39,123.50.*

"Noooo way."

"I don't think it's a coincidence, Jay."

"And this"—his finger stabbed at the figure—"is after all our bills and salaries?"

"Yep. And I checked it twice."

He lifted the ledger and stared at it. "*Noooo* way."

Judy put her hand on her waist. "What do you need? A big neon sign above your head that reads, 'This is a sign from God'?"

"Does God even work in neon?"

"Seriously, honey, don't you see what this means?"

He pushed back in his chair, arms crossed atop his head. "So, I'm supposed to give a hundred percent of our profit away while I'm admitting that I'm a skunk?"

"If God keeps blessing you, that money'll be replaced in a matter of days."

"But what if we stop selling cars like this?"

"*Jay* Austin. You gave this lot to God, and He's going to run it the right way. And it looks like that means repaying all the people you ripped off."

He wore a look of bewilderment. "I can't believe what I'm about to do."

Chapter 29

WALK OF SHAME

JAY

His walk of shame started the next day. Each address on his list was another stepping-stone in his path back to proper relationships with God and people, reordering his finances and righting the wrongs.

The First Step—

Jay eyed the premises from the safety of his car. Overgrown bushes spoke of a tenant with little time for the frivolities of yard work. The single-story brownstone duplex looked quiet, so maybe nobody was home.

"I doubt I'll get that lucky," he muttered.

In the padded binder beside him, on the passenger's seat, large checks in legal envelopes bore the names of those he had cheated. He hated to think of it as stealing, though that was an accurate description of what he had done.

This was crazy. These days, no one expected such extreme measures. What if he just tore up the envelopes and drove away?

"Nope. Time to do this."

Jay turned off the engine and took the first step on his walk. He felt humbled, even frightened. Sure, this was the godly thing to do. But being godly didn't make it easy. Often, in his experience, it was the opposite.

He rang the bell. The door squeaked open, and he had a crazy urge to grab the WD-40 out of his car trunk. Anything, any distraction, to avoid this humiliation—*just going through the area and fixing noisy hinges, ma'am.*

"Yes?" A young black lady stood before him. "May I help you?"

"Ms. Wright?"

She brushed back her hair. "Yes?"

"Um. I'm Jay Austin. I sold a car to you about a year ago."

"Yes, I remember." She seemed pleasant, no repressed anger or bitterness. No shotgun.

Thank God for small favors.

"And, um . . ." He met her eyes. "Well, uh . . . I overcharged you for that car."

She shook her head as though shaking off a fly. "What?"

"And, uh . . . I came to give you a portion of that back. And I wanted to say I'm . . . I'm sorry for doing that, and, um . . . to ask you to forgive me."

Ms. Wright accepted the offered envelope. She pulled out

the check and flinched. She blinked, held it at arm's length, then gave it a second look.

"That's for you."

"This is fif—"—her voice cracked—"fifteen hundred dollars."

"Right. I believe that's what I would've owed you, had I been, uh . . . honest about the sale. I'm sorry about that."

She started to cry, her eyes glued to the paper in her hand. "This is an answer to my prayer. I got laid off my job today. Thank you so much." She embraced Jay, catching him off guard. "Thank you *sooo* much." She looked skyward and lifted a hand. "Thank You, God." Back to Jay. "Thank you."

"You're welcome. Uh . . . thank *you*."

He felt foolish. What was that supposed to mean? Thanks for allowing him to rip her off? Thanks for taking free money from him?

Thank you for letting me put things in order.

Still sniffling, Ms. Wright closed the door and left him standing alone in the mild sun of a February morn. He started to walk off. Stopped. Turned back.

Had he just given away one thousand five hundred greenbacks?

Felt kinda good, actually. He'd expected indignation from her, even anger, and instead he'd been blessed to see the difference one check could make. This was confirmation that he was on the right path.

The Second Step—

He checked the number plate on the house. This was it: *1006*. Having a personal connection made this visit a little more embarrassing. It was the home of Bernie Myers's father.

Oh, well. Had to be done.

Middle-aged Mr. Myers recognized Jay the moment he opened the door. He didn't look too happy about the visit. He said, "What can I do for you, Mr. Austin?"

"Actually, uh . . . I'm here to do something for *you*."

"If you're here to give Bernie his job back, he doesn't want it. 'Fact, you might want to avoid him for the time being."

"No, you don't understand. You're the one I came to talk to, and—"

"The police send you?"

"Police?"

"Bernie's done nothing illegal, you understand? Okay, so he had a little fisticuffs down at the pool hall. Wasn't his fault, I'll tell you that right now."

Jay offered the envelope.

"What's that? I don't want nothing of yours, Mr. Austin."

"It's yours. Not mine."

"Sir?"

"You bought that Cadillac from us, right before Bernie started working for me, and, uh . . . Well, I charged you more than I should've."

Mr. Myers scowled.

"And that's to pay you back. A full nine hundred dollars."

"Nine *hundred*?"

"But if you don't want it—"

"I'll take it." The man showed surprising hand speed.

"And, please," Jay said, "I hope you'll accept my apology."

"I suppose I could do that." They shook on it. "But," Mr.

Myers added, "I'd rather you not mention this to my son. He's not in the best of moods for the time being. He wouldn't understand."

The Third Step—

Scott was wearing a baseball cap when Jay found him. He said that he was still driving the black '88 Accord, that it'd been a good car. Nevertheless, he would gladly take a handout from Jay Austin Motors.

"Got a girlfriend yet?" Jay said, just making conversation.

Scott's smile disappeared.

"Oh, uh . . . well . . ." Jay stuttered. "Hey, we just took in a nice Mustang. White. Convertible. Good condition. Maybe you'd have better luck with that."

The Fourth Step—

Jay had every reason to believe this would be his most difficult encounter. He hung his head and shuffled into the offices of Sherwood Baptist.

Time to face Reverend Michaels.

To his relief, the minister led him beneath a covered walkway, where they could speak out of earshot of the church receptionist. He listened to Jay's account of all that had gone on. He prayed with and encouraged him on his journey, then shook his hand and clapped him on the shoulder.

"Lindsay's still driving the Camry, and she's had nothing but good things to say about it. Jay, I want you to know that we are all saved by grace. Now walk with integrity in it."

"Yes, Reverend."

The Fifth Step—

In the early afternoon, Jay found Miss Marlowe at her office in a social services building downtown. She wore a peach top that highlighted creamy dark skin. Her gravelly voice was in contrast to her gentle mannerisms. He remembered she was a single mother, working two jobs to feed her children—their photos sat on the desk—and he asked himself how he had ever mistreated such a lady.

She took the envelope, then, without opening it, came around and gave him a warm hug. "Mr. Austin, you don't know how much this means. Been eight years, maybe nine, since I had any man tell me that he was sorry. Yes, sir, this means more than I can say."

The Sixth Step—

At a local school, he stopped in just after the last yellow bus had pulled out. He caught the office assistants still tidying things before the weekend, and asked for a Mrs. Shepherd. Frazzled from a long week of dealing with children and parents, she was in for a pleasant surprise.

Except she seemed to misunderstand.

"You're giving me *what*?" She tore the check from the envelope and began screaming with joy. She jumped up and down with the zeal of a pogo-stick champion, hollering for all to hear.

Jay smiled. Passing on joy was its own reward.

An assistant came from the office to see what the commotion was all about.

"I won a *thousand* dollars," Mrs. Shepherd shouted to her friend, hair bouncing on the shoulders of her striped sweater. "I won. I *won*."

Jay's smile faded. Wait. The woman had it all wrong.

"I won a *thousand dollars*!" she yelled, whooping again. Her friend took a look at the check and started jumping up and down along with her.

"No, it's . . ."

Jay gave up. He realized she couldn't hear a thing he was saying. *He* couldn't hear a thing he was saying. He wanted her to understand what was going on here, that he was the good guy, that he'd come to set things right. She was missing the whole point.

Mrs. Shepherd bounded toward Jay. "I've never *won* anything before." She picked up the vocal celebration where she had left off.

"But," he said, "it's not a contest."

"I *won*." She and her friend united their voices in one earsplitting screech and bounced back into the office, leaving him alone in the hallway. "I won a *thousand dollars*. A *thousand dollars*!"

Jay wrinkled his mouth, rolled his eyes, and pivoted toward the exit.

The Seventh Step—

Dinnertime was nearing. Jay's stomach was letting him know it as Benny and Alma Watts led him into the living room of their single-wide trailer, where the smell of nachos and cheese hung in the air.

"Set yourself down," Benny said, pointing to a wooden rocking chair.

"Uh . . ." A pizza delivery box filled the seat.

"Just kick that to the floor."

"Okay." Jay nudged the box over the side with his hand, watched the lid flap open on its way down, releasing a stream of leftover crusts onto the carpet. "Sorry about that."

"Go on and sit. That chair don't bite."

Jay did as he was told. He had grown up in an Atlanta suburb and, aside from Jeff Foxworthy skits, he had little experience with actual—did he dare even think it?—rednecks. He avoided stereotyping, in general.

Speaking of which . . . Was that a General Lee car replica, from *The Dukes of Hazzard*, wedged beneath the left rocker of his seat?

Jay confined his focus to the couple across from him.

Alma Watts had her hair piled high on her head; caked-on makeup and large earrings completed her look. She was smacking her gum—an entire pack, by the looks of it. Benny was barefoot, with his checkered shirt hanging unbuttoned and untucked over a white T-shirt. A stack of laundry sat in a hamper next to him. Behind him, on the sofa back, rested a boot and a stiff sock.

Jay couldn't have made this scene up if he tried.

"I don't wanna take your time," he told them. "Here. This is for you. It's the money I owe you back on that F-150 I sold you."

"What?" Benny accepted the envelope, peeked inside. His eyes narrowed. "You're givin' me a thousand dollars?"

"I am."

"Why? I agreed to buy it at that price."

Alma looked concerned that her husband might not take the money.

"Right," Jay said. "But the information I gave on the truck

wasn't entirely accurate. Uh, you bought the truck on what you *thought* it was worth. I'm . . . I'm here to apologize for that."

"But it don't make *sense* that you just *give* a thousand dollars back. Why would you do that?"

"I guess the best way to explain it is that I want my life to be pleasing to the Lord."

"So you're just *givin'* us a thousand dollars back? No strings attached?"

Jay grinned. "If you'll take it."

Alma snagged the envelope. "Ohhh, *we'll* take it."

Benny snatched it back and angled a finger in her face. "*That* ain't your money. *I* bought the truck."

"Well, then you'd better *take* it. The man's *tryin'* to give it to us."

"Listen. You watch your mouth. This is business."

Jay shifted in the rocker, thought he heard the buckling aluminum of a cheap replica. Should he intervene here? Or escape?

"This *ain't* business." Alma tossed her hair and showed no signs of giving an inch. "He's tryin' to give us *free* money."

"He's givin' *me* free money. You go finish the bean dip."

She leaned forward, talked around her gum. "I swear, Benny—you don't share that money with me, you're gonna be makin' your *own* bean dip."

"Woman."

"Don't you *even* . . ."

He lifted the envelope between them. "I could buy a thousand *dollars'* worth of bean dip."

Jay cleared his throat. "Uh. I probably need to go ahead and go." He extracted himself from the rocker. He had more stops to make.

Benny stood as well, his manner shifting to mellow and courteous. "Man, I appreciate it. And I'm . . . I'm sorry for callin' you a scum-suckin' maggot when I bought that truck."

"I don't remember that."

"Well . . ." Benny Watts realized he had said more than was necessary. He looked off to the side, found no help there, and said, "Well, I'm sorry anyway."

"I appreciate that. You guys have a great night."

"You do the same, okay?"

Jay let himself out. He had to step over the fallen and rusty barbecue grill on the front porch.

Chapter 30

SISTER ACT

JAY

Jay emerged onto the sidewalk outside Jimmie's Hot Dogs. He had his cell phone in one hand, the paper-wrapped meal in the other. Pacing along the large front window, he took bites while washed in the neon glow of the OPEN sign.

"Judy," he spoke into the phone, "you would not believe how easy this has been. I've been to eight or nine houses, a school, an office, the church, and—"

"You really got around."

"Oh, yeah. I've crisscrossed Albany."

"No," she said. "I meant in the past. You got around."

"Ouch."

"But now you're making things right. That's the important thing, Jay. So what's been the response? Pretty good, overall?"

"Yes. People have been blown away when I come to see them. I'll be heading home soon, and I just got one more stop I wanna make."

"Okay. I'm glad it's gone well. And you're being truthful with them, right?"

He swallowed his bite. "Yeah. I mean, it's been incredible. One girl"—he chuckled—"one girl still thinks she won a contest."

"Really?"

"I thought I'd have to eat crow, but this is cake."

"Now, that sounds like the *old* Jay Austin. Just don't become prideful."

"I'm not being prideful."

"Now you sound defensive."

"Judy, I'm . . ." He looked down at the hot-dog dinner, which had tasted so good a minute earlier. His voice lowered. "I'm *not* being prideful."

Jay knew it would take another day or two to complete his walk of shame. Aside from his wife's precision questioning, he'd actually experienced more validation than humiliation, and he found himself looking forward to this last visit for the evening.

The Thirteenth Step—

Miss Katie Harris: widow and schoolteacher.

He was familiar with the type, having grown up with an education-minded mother, and felt confident that a pleasant smile and respectful demeanor would carry him far.

When she invited him inside, he knew he was golden.

She took one end of the couch, and he took the other. Her elderly sister sat at the nearby dining table, munching on some pretzels. A ring that had belonged to Miss Harris's late husband dangled from her necklace, a sobering reminder of her loss. Flowers and framed photos of children and grandchildren adorned the coffee table, a parade of colors and fragrances brought to life by the rays of the setting sun filtering through the window.

Miss Harris peered down through her glasses at the envelope in her hand. "Tell me again why you're here, Mr. Austin?"

He launched into his explanation, awaiting the customary denial and shock that would segue into open-armed forgiveness and gratitude.

Instead, Miss Harris transformed before his eyes from a demure African-American lady into a severe matriarchal figure.

"You *what*?"

"I, uh—"

She planted a hand on her hip. "You cheated *me*?" She pointed at herself.

"Well, I mean, I just wasn't very honest about—"

"So you think you can waltz right in with a twelve-hundred-dollar check and expect me to accept what you've done?"

Jay sat a little straighter. "Well, I'm sorry for what I did."

"You *better* be sorry." She looked at him out of the corner of her eye. "You know how hard it is to make it in this world today?"

Her sister chimed in from the table. "Uh-huh."

"The *last* thing we need is a *dis*honest person taking advantage of old ladies."

"Ma'am," Jay said. "All I'm—"

"Don't you interrupt me. I been workin' forty long years for every penny I got."

"Tha's right," her sister agreed.

"Then a scam artist like *you* tries to take it away."

The sister pointed from the table and said through a bite, "Tell 'im."

"You *better* give me an apology."

"Well," Jay said. "That's why I—"

"Don't you *talk* back to me," Miss Harris said, lifting the envelope like a weapon. "I'm tired of the lies"—she slapped his forehead with the envelope—"the deceit"—*slap*—

"Mmmph." Her sister threw a fist into the air.

Jay winced with each blow, cowering behind his raised hands.

". . . the confections"—*slap*—"and everything else."

Jay sat shell-shocked. "The confections?"

Slap!

"Don't you *sass* me." Miss Harris stared at him. "You keep your mouth shut till I tell you to open it."

From the table: "*Aaaaa*-men."

Miss Harris eyed him, waiting for Jay to slip up, to say one thing or make a move. "Now," she instructed him, "say you're sorry."

"I'm *sorry*."

"Now get outta here and go get right with God . . ."

Jay hustled from the couch to the front door, looking back over his shoulder and feeling like a sullen child sent to his room.

"Before *I* get you right with Him," Miss Harris added.

"Bye," her sister said, then popped in another pretzel.

Fearful of slamming the door and thereby incurring another tirade of righteous wrath, Jay stepped onto the porch and turned to ease it shut. Through the crack between latch and frame, he caught sight of Miss Harris's huge smile.

Unaware of his presence, she wiggled in excitement on the couch. "Ohhh, sweet Jesus!" she exulted. "*Twelve* hundred dollars."

Chapter 31

READY TO DO THIS?

MAX

During Monday morning's coffee break, Max sipped at his hot cider—no coffee, not with his condition—while Jay recounted his adventures along the walk of shame. He ended with the story of Miss Katie Harris.

"So she threw you out?" Max said.

"Oh, she was all over me."

"Probably deserved what you had coming."

Sam was by the fireplace. He tossed his head back, laughing out loud. He pointed. "So you're getting kinda cocky, aren't you, Jay?"

Jay swiveled away in the desk chair.

"That's exactly what it is," Max agreed.

"Hey, whose side are you on anyway?" Jay said. "I've still got another round to go. There's one envelope I'm saving for last."

The main door opened, and in walked a slender blonde woman. She was smartly dressed in a tan sweater over a broad-collared blouse, with cuffs folded back at the wrists. Max recognized her, though he couldn't remember from where.

"Hi, there," Jay said. He walked around the desk. "How are you?"

"Hi. Mr. Austin?"

"Yeah?" He shook her outstretched hand.

"Hillary Vale, WALB News."

Max wagged his chin up and down. Yep, that was it. She was the one who'd covered the story of Bernie Myers's altercation. She was an austere woman, unfazed by the goings-on in this city. Guess that pretty much figured into a newscaster's mentality, or they'd get kicked to the end of the line.

"Of course, Hillary," Jay said. "I've seen you on TV a few times."

"Yes. Well, we caught your story on the national news, and we're wondering if you'd give us an interview as well."

"Uh, sure. But I don't know what I could say that hasn't already been said."

"You just leave that to us. What we would like to do is a live remote from here tomorrow, for our five o'clock newscast. Would that be all right?"

"Okay." Jay slipped his hands into his pants pockets. "That'd be fine."

"All right," she said with earnest excitement. "We'll send the crew over around four o'clock to set up."

"Sure. Look forward to talking with you."

Jay looked at Sam and Max as Miss Vale walked out.

"Well, who needs to advertise," Max said, "when you've got all this free publicity?"

JUDY

Christina had paced Judy through a speedy one-mile walk. With only days to her due date, Judy wanted nothing more than to have this baby. Todd had been just over seven pounds at birth, but this morning her doctor had said this one could be eight pounds, maybe more.

Judy had nearly fainted at the thought.

"Just a few more days of decaf," she said to Christina. "I can't wait."

"But aren't you going to breast-feed? No caffeine till that's over."

"You're no fun."

Christina's infectious laugh said otherwise. She parked outside Starbucks and opened the door for Judy as they headed inside. The rich aromas gave Judy the illusion of caffeine intake. She inhaled twice, eyes closed.

"You have it bad," Christina commented.

"Tell me about it."

They shuffled along in the line. Then, to Judy's consternation, who should arrive but Spindly Blonde and Heavy Rouge. She decided she would speak up this time if they started badmouthing Jay. He was a man—human, yes, and not perfect—but a good man. The man she loved.

Sure enough, Jay Austin became a topic of discussion.

Spindly Blonde: "You *hear* what he's been up to?"

Heavy Rouge rolled her eyes. "'Fraid to ask."

"There ain't no tellin' *what's* got into him. Miss Marlowe, she says he stopped by her office last Friday, just plumb outta nowhere, and gives her back money he says weren't his."

"That so?"

"Heard it right from her own lips. Well, not hers directly, but near 'nuff."

"Doesn't surprise me," said Heavy Rouge. "Not one bit."

"It don't?"

"No, ma'am. He was on the television just the other night, them sayin' how honest he is and whatnot. Ain't we always said he was a decent man?"

"Why, that's *exactly* what we been sayin'."

"Surely is."

Judy cleared her throat and swiveled her swollen belly around, causing both ladies to dodge sideways. "He's not only a decent man," she said, "he's my husband."

Spindly Blonde: "Why, dear, you oughta be thankin' your lucky stars."

"I thank God every day," Judy said.

"So, just between us," Heavy Rouge urged, "tell us what he's like."

"Well, can you keep a secret?"

The ladies edged closer, ready to grab a juicy piece of gossip. "Why, yes we can," said Spindly Blonde.

Judy leaned in and met their eyes. "So can I."

Audible gasps rose from the pair.

"Y'all have a *wonderful* day," Judy said. She turned then to order.

JAY

The WALB truck was parked just outside the lot fence. It was Tuesday evening, and last-minute customers still milled through the vehicle inventory.

Jay would have to trust them to Sam while he was being interviewed by Hillary Vale. Jay thought again of his wife's caution against arrogance, but there was nothing wrong—was there?—with basking, even reveling, in the favor the Lord had given him.

But there was Judy's voice in his conscience again: *"Don't become prideful . . ."* And right behind her voice was Sam's: "Getting kinda cocky . . ."

Jay took his seat as directed on a tall stool in front of the news camera. He lowered his eyes. He asked the Lord to keep him mindful of his place in all this, of his constant need for grace. He repented for his wayward heart, so ready to start collecting glory unto itself.

Beside him, Hillary Vale held a microphone. She wore a dark business suit that highlighted her blonde coiffed hair. She said to her TV crew member with the headphones: "So, we'll stay on the two-shot until we track to the video."

What video? Jay wondered.

Miss Vale turned to him. "Mr. Austin, we need to get a sound check on you. Could you count to five for us, please?"

"Uh . . . One, two, three, four, five."

"We're good?" Miss Vale checked with her cameraman. She

gave a thumbs-up, then took her seat next to Jay. "All right. So, are you ready to do this?"

"I guess so."

"Okay."

The cameraman wheeled a monitor into view on a dolly. Cables and wires slithered across the pavement. For the first time, Jay suspected that something about this interview was going to be different from the others, and worry began to gnaw at his stomach.

In Jay's line of vision behind the camera crew, Max leaned against a car, chewing his gum. The old guy folded his arms, then gave a slight nod of support.

Jay sat up as the cameraman's hand lifted.

"We're on in five, four . . ." Fingers lowered one by one with the count. The man's voiced faded as the last three fingers went down.

They were on.

"Ben," Miss Vale said, looking into the wide eye of the camera, "we are live at Jay Austin Motors in Albany, where things have been very busy ever since that story broke on national news about their honesty policy. Joining us now is the owner, Jay Austin . . ."

BERNIE

So far, Bernie's year had been tough.

There was, of course, the brawl he had been part of at the pool hall. Sure, he'd thrown the first punch. But the part the authorities failed to realize was that grumpy ol' Garrett had shoved a cue stick against his throat. The witnesses seemed to have closed ranks around their buddy, leaving Bernie in the cold.

Not only had the incident smudged Bernie Myers's reputation in this fine city; it had caused further probing into the motorized-vehicle mishap at the Grand Island Golf Course. The course owners seemed intent on recouping some of their losses, even if that meant threatening legal action against the vehicle's operator.

Bernie just hoped Vince Berkley kept his fat mouth shut.

Worst of all, these clouds of suspicion were eating away at his success as a Butch Bowers salesman—one of the most visible around, thanks to the TV spots and . . .

Well, yes, he was just visible all around.

Today, at last, he would strike a blow at the man he held responsible for his recent pitfalls.

Bernie turned up the television's volume in the Butch Bowers AutoWorld break room. He'd roped a few of his new pals into joining him for the show. The news came on. There was that blonde lady, Hillary Vale.

"Oh, yeah." Bernie cackled aloud. "And in all his glory . . . Mr. Jay Austin."

His sales associates wore bland expressions, and one of them even grumbled about this being more airtime for the competition across town.

"Just you watch," Bernie said. "The good part's still coming."

Chapter 32

THE DEFENDER

JUDY

Judy had borrowed a friend's VCR—*video cassette recorder*, she explained to Todd—and hooked it to the TV in her son's room. She had a tape in the machine and the channel set so that she could capture this interview for posterity. Yesterday, her husband had even called a few friends, giving them a heads-up about his next televised appearance.

Everything looked good now. The Record light was on.

Judy found her place on Todd's bed, while he did homework at her feet. She stretched out on her side and nudged him with a toe, letting him know this was the part to watch. "Here's your dad."

Jay's face filled the screen.

"So, Mr. Austin," Miss Vale said, "have things really been that different since this all happened?"

Judy couldn't help but grin. *You go get 'em, honey.*

"Oh, that'd be an understatement," he replied. "You know, one day we're just trying to survive, and the next day they're lined up to buy cars."

Miss Vale: "Now, I know about the power of the press, but it would seem like you already had a good customer base. Have you changed the way you've been doing business at all?"

"Well, um . . ." Jay's brow furrowed.

"You've been in business for over two years now, right?"

"Right."

"And, you've always run your business honestly?"

Judy's frustration paralleled her husband's. She sensed from the reporter's prodding that something was amiss. "What is she doing?"

"Uh . . . ," Jay muttered.

"Well, Mr. Austin, we had the opportunity to speak with a gentleman who claims that he worked with you during your first two years. And his view of the operation is quite different. Let's take a look."

Jay's eyes turned hollow as he followed the woman's gaze.

A video clip took over the screen, and Judy saw Bernie Myers looking smug and relaxed, his arm draped over the back of a couch.

"Honest dealer?" Bernie scoffed. "That's not how I'd describe Jay Austin."

From the bed, Judy groaned.

"I've seen him rip off tons of people—teenagers, young couples, old ladies, even a minister. He even tried to teach *us* how to rip people off. And that's why I left, because of his lack of integrity."

"*What?* You *snake.*" Judy threw a pillow at the screen.

Todd looked up, and Jay squirmed on the screen as the interview went on.

"Mr. Austin," Miss Vale said, "did this man, in fact, work for you?"

"Yes, he did."

"And is he telling the truth? Did you, in fact, *teach* him how to cheat your customers?"

Jay swallowed, then nodded. "I'm ashamed to say this—but, yes, I did."

"So, you're admitting that you were dishonest in your sales?"

"I admit that I, uh . . . used to be dishonest. But I have had a dramatic change in my life."

"Yes, sir." Miss Vale's tone was sad. "But why should the public believe you now?"

Jay's eyes dropped. "I'm not sure how to answer that question."

Miss Vale turned to the camera, her face the picture of abject disappointment: "Well, Ben, last week Jay Austin was being praised for his honesty. Now, though, a former employee says that isn't the whole story. I guess our viewers will just have to decide for themselves. This is Hillary Vale, reporting live from Jay Austin Motors in Albany. Back to you, Ben . . ."

Judy muted the TV. She propped herself against the headboard, lifted her hands over her face, then pulled them down to cover her mouth. She wanted to say unkind things, ungodly things. She wanted to tear out that woman's eyeballs for ambushing her husband. Wanted to tear out Bernie's tongue for speaking accusations.

Wasn't that just the devil's way, to accuse with half-truths?

She could feel her son's eyes on her, and she felt utterly helpless.

BERNIE

"Hey, hey." Bernie jabbed at the break-room TV. "What'd I tell you guys?"

"Yeah, you told us, Bernie. That was pretty slick."

"Slicker than snot on an ice rink."

"Wouldn't go that far," an associate said. "But yeah, you put him in his place, all right. Maybe now we'll get some more customers around here. Heck, if I get a sale outta this, I'll even treat you to a round of golf."

"Uh, thanks. But . . ."

"Not a golfer, huh? That game'll humble the best of them."

"Yeah, I . . ." Bernie didn't like the direction that was going. "You know, why don't you just buy me some biscuits from the Biscuit Barn?"

"The Biscuit Barn? I'll take Pearly's any day."

"Hey. Who's calling the shots here?"

MAX

Jay was staring at the woman, still stunned.

"We're clear," the cameraman said.

"I'm sorry if I caught you off guard, Mr. Austin." Miss Vale rose from her seat and turned to Jay. "But it *is* my job to report all the facts."

Max Kendall shook his head, amazed at the callous attitude of these newscasters. Didn't they realize they were messing with human lives? Stepping over souls while trying to get at their own version of the truth?

Jay rolled his neck and looked at the woman. "I understand, but that . . . that is *not* who I am now."

"Okay," she said, sucking air through her lips. Her look was one of feigned sympathy.

Sam was nearing, and Max went to join him at Jay's side.

"All right," Miss Vale directed, "let's pack up and go. We've got to get back to the studio."

Jay looked up, and Max shook his head again. Already, they'd faced one onslaught that had threatened the lot's survival and their jobs. Why, years ago Max had even stared down the barrel of an M1 Garand and seen men out to kill him. This weren't nothing. No, sir, they'd get through this. They would.

At least, that's what he tried to tell Jay with his eyes.

Jay shuffled toward the reporter. He handed over the lapel mic.

"Thank you," she said, as though she had not just crushed a man's career, his spirit, and his attempt to make things right and choose a higher road.

Jay brushed by Max, heading for the carport on the other side of the garage. This time he wouldn't even meet Max's gaze. Max turned to follow, then decided against it.

Sometimes a man needed his friends at his side.

Other times he needed time alone, just him and the good Lord, trying to hammer things out.

JAY

Jay rounded the garage and found solitude beneath the carport. Behind him, back on the pavement, the TV crew was packing up their equipment and technological weapons of information.

"Lord, I'm *angry*."

He clenched his jaw and paced the concrete slab.

"Where *are* You right now? What's going on?"

He shoved his fists into his pockets and rested his head against a support beam. If it weren't for those lurking cameras, he might be tempted to do something rash. He rocked against the beam, waiting for the pent-up rage to dissipate. Slowly, his own condition impressed itself on him.

"Lord," he said, "I know I deserve this. Would You help me, please? I cannot defend myself."

He heard no response.

He walked over to a chair, pressed fingers against closed eyes, then got down on his knees and decided that he would not move until he sensed some sort of answer, some peace. Something. Anything.

TODD

Todd looked to his mom, whose hands rested on her tummy. She pushed back on the mattress and sat up near the headboard.

"Todd," she said, closing her eyes, "let's pray for Daddy."

He loved his dad. He kneeled on the bed, his hand in his mom's, and listened as she prayed. He watched the intensity in her face and recognized the depth of her love. He'd seen the recent changes around here, and he knew what that TV lady had said was not right.

Yeah, it was the truth. Just not the whole truth.

In Sunday school, they talked about how God was a Father—Mom's Father, Dad's Father, Nana's and Papa's Father.

Even Todd's.

He let go of his mother's hand and slipped to the bench at the foot of his bed. In his jeans and red athletic jersey, he thought about how sometimes on the soccer field he got assigned to play goalie. He liked that position, defending for his team. He would do anything to stop an attempt on goal.

Even throw himself to his knees if he had to.

"Please, God, don't let them take any more cheap shots at my dad."

Chapter 33

BREAKING

MAX

Max stood near the WALB News van, which was warming up to go. He was about to say something to Hillary Vale, but he thought better of it.

First, this wasn't his battle to fight.

Second, Miss Vale was talking with the studio on her cell.

"Yes, we'll be there in thirty minutes. Not a problem. I'll have it packaged for the eleven o'clock." She bent down to write. "Okay, what's the address?"

And there was one more reason . . .

From the lot's far end, a large black lady was advancing as though on a mission. She didn't look mad. Not exactly. On the other hand, she didn't look like she was taking a walk through the tulips either.

"Uh-huh," Miss Vale was saying. "All right, we'll be there. Yes. Thanks."

"Excuse me, Miss Vale?" The large woman was right behind her now, in a red jacket and a long black skirt. She wore sunglasses, and she looked none too happy. "I just saw your report, and I know you're just doing your job, but you need to *know* that ain't the *whole* story."

Max lifted an eyebrow.

"Oh?" To her credit, the reporter lady stopped. "What do you mean?"

"You gonna write this down? You gonna shoot it on the *TV*?"

"That depends. Can I first get your name?"

"Miss Katie Harris."

"All right, Miss Harris, tell me your story."

"Jay Austin, he came to my house and he apologized for the way he misled me. And"—the woman's voice filled with joy—"he paid me back *twelve* hundred dollars."

"He *what*?"

A young couple appeared behind Miss Harris. They were holding hands. The man's checkered shirt was buttoned and tucked in—and were those bean-dip stains on the pocket? As for his wife, she wore a baseball cap that didn't quite go with the necklace over her navy sweatshirt.

"I'm Benny Watts," the man said to Miss Vale. "My wife, Alma, here. And he done the same for us. Jay gave us a thousand dollars back."

"Uh-huh," his wife grunted.

"You've got to be kidding," Miss Vale said.

"No, ma'am."

"This story ain't over"—Miss Harris wagged a finger—"until you report that."

Absorbing every word, Max watched cars begin pulling into empty spaces as more previous buyers arrived. There was Scott. There was the Reverend Michaels.

Max walked around the garage and found Jay in the shadows, shifting his backside into the lawn chair. Max set his hands on his hips. "What're you doing in here, bud?"

His boss looked up. Looked away. "I'm complaining to God."

"Well, while you're in here yapping . . . He's out here working."

Confusion furrowed Jay's brow. He stood and walked around the corner with Max on his tail. People were talking to the reporter, while the cameraman hurried to reposition his equipment. Mary had joined the gathering. From what Max had heard, Jay had signed over her car to her, free and clear.

Jay took a few steps toward Miss Vale.

"No, no, no." Max grabbed his arm. "You stay right here."

Jay shot him a look.

"No, Jay. You let the Lord fight for you."

Miss Vale was surrounded by fifteen to twenty people now, trying to interview them one at a time, while the camera began filming once more.

JUDY

Judy was done praying. She had said all she knew to say. Running a hand back through her hair, she sighed and dared a glance at the television.

"Hey."

The sign for Jay Austin Motors was filling the screen—again.

She hit the remote while Todd hopped up beside her on the bed.

"Good evening," the news anchor said. "I'm Ben Roberts. Our top story tonight is a follow-up to a story we told you about at five. There's another side to the story about used-car dealer, Jay Austin. We go live now to Hillary Vale with the details."

Miss Vale was stationed at the car lot. "Thanks, Ben. After our report on Jay Austin just a half hour ago, these customers showed up at the lot with yet another side of the story." She turned to a red-jacketed black woman. "Miss Harris, you say that Jay Austin came to your house and *returned* money to you?"

"That's right. He said he overcharged me, and he gave me back twelve hundred dollars. He apologized." Miss Harris flashed a wide smile into the camera. "And for that, I commend him."

Judy's eyes brimmed with tears. These people, just everyday folks, were stepping up to defend her husband. She pulled her hands to her mouth and bounced with joy on the mattress. "Oh, Lord, thank You."

Miss Vale turned to another person. "Reverend Michaels, you say that he returned money to you as well?"

"He gave me back two thousand dollars, and apologized, too."

"And what about you, Miss Gardner?"

"He gave me fifteen hundred dollars back, and I'm so grateful for that."

With Todd on his knees beside her, Judy watched the story

unfold. Her excitement grew. "Thank You, Lord." She lifted her chin and clasped her hands to her chest. "Thank You."

Todd was smiling now.

"He gave us back a thousand dollars," said Benny Watts.

"Thank You, Lord," Judy gushed. "Yes."

"Uh-huh." Alma Watts stood beside her husband and spoke in a south Georgia accent. "He said he wanted his life to be pleasin' to the Lord, and I believe him. What you *need* to be doing is talking to that two-faced Bernie Myers joker that used to work here, the one going around accusin' him. Jay met us on the lot that day, but Bernie's the one that sold us that truck."

"That's *right.*" Judy pointed at the screen. "*Yes.*"

Then something twinged inside her.

A flicker of pain.

JAY

Jay could do nothing but watch. Unable to hear what his customers were saying, he knew by their body language they were setting the record straight. Hillary Vale was moving her microphone from one person to the next, giving time for the rest of the truth to be heard.

His bitterness about her earlier ambush melted away.

Where had this additional grace come from? Prayers were even now being answered—despite his stinky attitude.

"Max," he said, "thank you for standing by me."

"Got nowhere else to be."

"Uh-oh."

Miss Katie Harris was marching toward them, shaking a

finger. She settled down on her feet in front of Jay, a woman not to be argued with. "Now, I have *rebuked* you. I have *defended* you. It's time for you to stand up and be a godly man worth defending. Do *you* understand me?"

"Yes, ma'am. I do."

"All right, then. May God bless you."

She left it at that and walked off. Max looked at Jay and raised his eyebrows as if to indicate that it was no joking matter. In the throng of locals, Miss Vale continued her live news update.

BERNIE

The mood at Butch Bowers AutoWorld darkened. Bernie kicked at an orange plastic chair, sent it clattering across the break room. A glass coffee carafe teetered from its perch on a table, then shattered against the tiles.

He could not understand where these fools had come from. For two years, he and Jay Austin had wrung them dry. And now this?

"They're *defending* him. What a buncha losers."

"Seems like you lost on this one," Bernie's associate said.

"Shut up. You don't know."

"He gave them their money back. I mean, how can you—?"

"But we *stole* it from them in the first place."

"We?"

Bernie threw his hands up. "You know what I'm saying. C'mon, who doesn't squeeze a buyer dry when given the chance? I mean—"

In the doorway stood Butch Bowers.

Gulp.

"What *do* you mean, Bernie? Let's hear it. You've already announced your sales techniques to my entire showroom floor out there. Even run off a couple of my customers with those flapping gums."

"Sir, I . . . I . . ."

Butch Bowers stepped up and, with utmost restraint, removed the name tag from Bernie's knitted vest. His fingers wiggled the object at eye level. "Heard you checked yourself out, last time around. Well, Bernie, this time I'm doing that for you. You're done. We don't need the kind of publicity you seem to generate."

Bernie watched his name tag land in the wastebasket.

If there was any symbolism in that, he refused to take note. No, sir. He had money to make and ears to twist with his smooth-talking tongue. He didn't need this place anyway. Good-bye and good riddance.

JUDY

Judy and Todd were jumping with glee and exchanging high fives.

"Oh, yes, Lord. Yes. Yes." Judy rubbed her tummy, which felt ready to burst. She could hardly breathe with this baby pushing up into her rib cage and lungs. "Oh, yes, Lord. Yes." She felt short of breath. She sighed.

And then a slow look of shock came over her. "Oh, no. Oh, *no.*"

"What is it, Mom?"

"Todd, get me the phone."

He slipped off the bed and scurried down the hall.

"Ohhh, no. Ohhh, no." She lifted her eyes to the ceiling, then hefted herself from the bed. "Todd, *hurry*. Get the *phone*. Oh, no, Lord. Ohhh."

She felt something breaking. Water gushed onto the floor. Ready or not, this baby was coming.

Judy Austin was ready.

MAX

Concluding her newscast, Hillary Vale held the mic to the last interviewee and motioned with her free hand for Jay to come join her. Max wasn't sure that was a good idea, but his concerns were cut short by Jay's cell phone.

"It's Judy," Jay told Max. "Probably calling to congratulate us. Hey," he said, gesturing to Miss Vale to hold on a moment. "What? Where are you? No. No, I'm on my way." He clicked the phone shut and gave Max a broad smile. "Judy's in labor."

"Get outta here," Max said. "I'll take care of this."

Jay clapped him on the shoulder and jogged away. Max went to Miss Vale and fed her the latest information.

She grinned and turned toward to the camera. "Well, Ben, we've had quite a turn of events here today. According to these customers behind me, Jay Austin *is* a changed man. And to top it all off . . . his wife just called, she's in labor, and they are now on their way to have their baby at the hospital."

The throng broke into cheers and clapping.

"I'm Hillary Vale, reporting live from Jay Austin Motors in Albany. Back to you."

Chapter 34

BIG STEP FORWARD

JUDY

She was a little daddy's girl. Jay's pride and joy.

Since the moment of Faith Austin's arrival in the world, Jay had been unable to think of anything else, and Judy loved to watch him with her. Was anything more endearing than the sight of a man enraptured with his children? A man willing to look foolish in his displays of fatherly affection?

Judy crept through the dining room's morning light. For the first time in ages, she felt light on her feet and able to move without being noticed. It worked to her advantage as she listened in on the big, manly father talking gibberish to his five-week-old daughter.

"Gaa, gaa. Oooh. Gaa, gaa."

She inched closer.

"Peekaboo. Ohhh, yeah. Open those eyes. Peekaboo."

Judy suppressed a giggle.

"Hey," Jay cooed. He had his baby girl bundled and cozy, cradled in his arms, her little head in his hands. A cloth was laid across his shoulder. "How you doing, Faith? Yeah, you look just like your mother."

Judy moved up behind them. She had no intention of startling Jay. She wanted only to bask in this unguarded display of affection. There was such tenderness in his voice. Such strength.

He said, "You know why we called you Faith? That's what Daddy was learning when you were being born. Yeah, sweetheart. That's right."

Faith's eyes looked up at him, watery and bright and full of wonder.

Judy could stand it no longer. "Hey," she whispered, touching his shoulder from behind the couch.

Jay flinched, but recovered nicely. "Judy. There you are."

"If you're going to go get Todd, you better leave now."

"Shouldn't you be sleeping?"

"No," she said. "I'm fine."

Faith was staring up at her parents as though this was the most wonderful thing in the world, to hear their two voices in the same room.

"Look at her. Just *look* at her." Jay's eyes told Judy he couldn't get enough of this precious bundle of . . . of . . .

Well, yes, she thought . . . *joy*.

But there were also a lot of sleepless nights and soggy diapers and drool and spit rags and heartrending wails to go along with that.

This was a family deal, and they all played their parts. Judy's body was still seeking some sense of normalcy, but thankfully, the men had been hands-on in their help. Todd carted odorous offerings to the hamper. He assisted with dishes and meals. Jay was up most nights, often rocking his baby girl until they fell asleep together. He was no fan of changing-time, yet he accepted his duties with masculine dignity—for the most part.

Only once had Judy heard him scream, and in that particular case she could vouch for a far-worse-than-average digestive disaster.

"Jay, you need to go," she said.

"Is your mom coming over?" He laid Faith against his chest, patting her.

Judy couldn't resist touching that wispy hair. "Yep, she'll be here shortly. We'll be fine, Jay." She moved around and took a seat as the little girl began to fuss. "Faith."

"Okay." Jay handed their daughter over.

"Hey, sweetheart," Judy hushed her. "Hey."

Jay passed the cloth along as well.

"Thank you for watching her so I could rest," Judy said.

"No, I loved it."

"Did you have fun with your daddy, sweetheart?" Judy touched Faith's little chin.

Jay pulled back the sleeve of his sweatshirt, checked the time. "Okay. Well, you know we'll be gone till late tonight."

"Mom's coming over, like I said."

"But what if—?"

"Faith and I'll be just fine, Jay." Judy gave him a reassuring smile. "This'll make Todd's day. You need to go."

"Okay." He reached over and cupped Faith's soft head of hair.

"Go."

He stood. "Okay."

Judy gave all her attention to their newborn, knowing that any sign of weariness, of inattentiveness, would bring her husband swooping back in to the rescue. She'd never seen him so enamored, his heart swollen to such proportions. It was a beautiful thing.

JAY

Jay slipped into the drive-thru line at the Biscuit Barn. He'd spent his waking moments with Faith and neglected breakfast in his sudden dash to get going. His stomach rumbled at the mere hint of bacon and biscuits, orange juice, and a cup of black coffee—none of that froufrou stuff his wife went for.

Through the speaker, the voice was robotic. "Can I take your order?"

"I sure hope so." Jay fired off his wishes, then rolled forward.

As he clawed his wallet from his jeans pocket, he thought about Faith's dedication last weekend at the church. It had been an amazing moment to have Reverend Michaels there, praying over their daughter, asking the Lord's blessing, and sealing the Austins' commitment to be godly parents and to raise Faith into a woman of righteousness and purity.

The car ahead inched to the pickup window. Jay was next.

"C'mon. I'm about to chew through my right arm."

His thoughts returned to the dedication. It had been capped off by the presence of family members. Todd, of course. Judy's mother and stepfather, up from Florida—and her mother was staying in town for a couple of weeks to be of assistance with the newborn. Judy's sister traveled from Chattanooga. Jay's parents made the trip from Atlanta.

And Joey had been there, with his wife, Trish.

Jay was humbled beyond words—to have this kind of support from his older brother, this undeserved favor.

They didn't say a lot. Shook hands. Met eyes.

Afterward, the families went out for Sunday buffet, and Joey bumped into Jay on their way through the line. "You're a stinker," he said. "Always have been."

"I know. Listen, Joey, I'm sorry for—"

"Dad says things've been going well for you here."

"Things've been good. A lot's been changing."

"Well, you look us up the next time you're in Destin. We have a place on the beach, and you're always welcome. I mean it."

That was that. The big apology. The grand forgiveness.

Even more humbling had been a brief dialogue with his father. Jay knew his dad's love was unconditional, yet the unpaid business loan was an invisible obstacle between them, one Jay was determined to tear down. Before the dedication, waiting together in the car for the wives to join them, Jay had turned toward his father.

"Can we talk for a moment?"

"Sure, Son."

"I, uh . . . I don't want anything between us."

"The loan, you mean."

"Yeah."

"Listen, Jay, I know you've been changing the way you do business, and I'm sure you'll be good for it. You just keep doing what you're doing, and we'll extend your deadline." His dad winked. "Of course, I'll have to tack on interest."

"Interest?"

"Don't you think that's fair?"

"Well, I . . ."

"I'm kidding." His dad had a mischievous twinkle in his eye.

"No," Jay said. "Really, I wanna pay you above and beyond."

"How 'bout you send me 10 percent by the end of this month, as a gesture of good faith."

Jay swallowed. "I can do that." And he meant it.

"Good. And you get the rest of it to me by this time next year. As for any interest fees, all I ask is that you invest every penny you can into this beautiful son and daughter of yours. My grandchildren, they're worth more than any money you could ever pay me."

"Yes, sir."

Now, in the drive-thru at the Biscuit Barn, Jay found himself getting misty-eyed at the memory, and he thought this was about the most ridiculous thing ever. You have a baby girl—and suddenly you're a weeping machine? No. C'mon.

"Sir." Robotic voice again. "Please pull ahead."

Jay shifted into first and gunned forward. Sheepishly, he looked up from the low bucket seat. The man standing at the window, *filling* the window, was none other than his former employee, Vince Berkley.

"Vince? That you?"

The big man tried to duck out of sight, but it was too late. He turned back, with his focus aimed off over the car's hood. He was wearing a large paper hat in the shape of a biscuit. "Hi there, Jay."

"Life treating you good, Vince?"

"Yeah, not bad."

"Didn't know you worked here. How you liking it?"

"Good, good."

"Hey, I want you to know there's still an opening for you at Jay Austin Motors, if you feel so inclined."

"I don't."

"Well, if you ever do."

"I won't. I'm, uh, getting into management here. Lotsa perks."

"Really?"

"Oh, yeah. You know, just last month we had the Georgia Bulldogs coach, Mark Richt, come through here."

"Now, there's a man who knows football."

"Got my picture taken with him."

"Impressive. So, uh"—Jay tried to keep the sarcasm out of his voice—"is this a lateral career move, or are you trying to get into management?"

"Oh, it's a big step forward," Vince said.

"You think so?"

"Every move is calculated."

"Ahhh. I see."

"Yeah."

"Yeah."

"That'll be five-eighty-two," Vince said. "You want butter and a free biscuit hat with that?"

MAX

Max unlocked the main office building, hit the alarm, then turned to face the glory of a Friday morning. Tomorrow evening he'd be fishing the Flint River. Maybe later that night, if he felt up to it, he'd go rack 'em up with Garrett—just for fun, for old times' sake.

Right now, though, he and Sam had a car lot to look after.

Fridays could get rough around Jay Austin Motors, but the boss man had a plan to see his son, and there weren't no way Max Kendall was gonna stand in the way of that. He'd never had a father. He'd been left on a garbage heap in the days of the Depression. Not even a blanket around him.

Now, who would do a thing like that?

Max didn't know. Didn't reckon it mattered.

He'd been raised by a foster mother, a broad-shouldered, cuddly woman with powder-softened wrinkles and a smile that showed determination against all odds. That was the kind of example he'd seen, and it worked for him.

Little grace and a lotta love. Yes, sir, those two went a long way.

"'Morning, Sam," he said as his friend rolled up.

"Aww, you beat me here."

"By about forty years—but what's it to you? You ready to sell some cars, or you gonna just stand around jabbering?"

Sam let out a laugh and punched Max in the arm. "Okay, old man, let's show them how it's done."

JAY

Jay parked in the sunshine outside Sherwood Christian Academy, situating the car so that it was clear of other vehicles. No need to risk dinged doors or side panels.

Sure, he was a little paranoid. But this was the car's first full day out.

In jeans, tennis shoes, and a sweatshirt, he headed indoors. He was ready for a casual day, a father-son outing. Todd didn't know he was coming, which made it all the better.

An office assistant led him down a corridor, then directed him toward the third-grade classroom. He nodded and proceeded. The door to the first-grade class was open, and he heard a boy reciting from Psalm 139. Jay stopped, not wanting his squeaky rubber soles to interrupt. He peered around the door and saw a darling dark-haired boy gesturing as he spoke.

". . . and you know me. You know when I sit and when I rise; you perceive my thoughts from afar. You discern my going out and my lying down; you are familiar with all my ways . . ."

The words trailed off as Jay moved to his son's classroom, where the door was also open. He could see kids at their desks and Mrs. Akridge leaned against the wall, near a chalkboard. A girl was giving an oral report before the class.

And there was Todd, eyes turned down.

Jay stepped back out of sight, so as not to be a distraction.

Although he was here to take his son out of school for the day, he would allow the girl to finish.

". . . and she's also bulletproof. I'd be able to help the police fight criminals and robbers. The only thing she can't do is fly, but that's okay. She's still my favorite hero. That's why I would like to be like her."

Jay looked at his watch. They needed to get going.

Mrs. Akridge said, "Thank you, Rachel. You may be seated. Okay, who's next?"

Jay took a step forward, intending to use this interval to his advantage.

"Todd Austin, you're up," the teacher said.

Jay halted. If he barged in now, he would only cause embarrassment. Plus, he was curious to hear what Todd had to say. He detected the *swish-swish* of Todd's jeans as he walked, and the rustling of papers.

"Well, I have many favorite superheroes that I would like to be," Todd said to his class. "But since they're not real, I thought about somebody I *could* be like."

Jay tried to come up with a prediction. A soccer player? A race-car driver? Maybe an artist Todd liked?

"My real-life hero," Todd said, "is my dad."

A knot began to form in Jay's throat.

"He's not perfect, and sometimes he makes mistakes, but he says he's sorry. He's spending more time with me, and sometimes takes me to work with him on Saturdays just so we can talk. He's pretty smart, too. He knows a lot about cars, and even has one that looks like a superhero car. He prays with our family now, and even helps my mom. I like spending time with him."

Jay pushed away from the wall. Swallowed. Stared down at the floor.

"Even though he doesn't have special powers or anything, he is still my favorite hero. So that's who I want to be like."

Jay closed his eyes and took a deep breath. He could feel heat pricking at the corners of his eyes. What was wrong with him? Twice already in one day?

"Very good, Todd," said Mrs. Akridge. "Thank you. You may sit down. Okay, next we'll have Joshua, then Anna, then Catherine. And if time permits, we'll end with Joy and Caleb . . ."

Jay lifted his hands. "Thank You, Lord," he whispered. "Thank You."

TODD

This was so cool. He was getting to sneak out early on a Friday—with his dad. He was wearing his bomber jacket, the one with the shields and patches, and he strutted into the sun feeling snug and mature and ready to take on the world. At Dad's side, he took big steps to keep pace.

"You can get me out of school like this?" he asked.

"Well, I got permission."

"From my teacher?"

"Nah. From your principal."

"You went all the way to the top?"

Dad chuckled. "Well, if your principal's at the top, then yes."

Todd's jaw dropped. Ahead, hunched low and sleek on the

pavement, the white Triumph TR3 awaited. The top was down, and the wire spokes threw spears of sunlight in all directions.

"Whaddya think, Todd?"

"All *right*. Do we get to ride in this car?" He ran to the passenger side.

"Sure do."

"*Yes*."

Todd climbed in beside his father. He liked the way the black seat felt, cupped and leaned back. Chrome and glass glistened.

"Where are we going?"

"Well," Jay said, "I need to test this car on the road, so I figured we'd drive down to Valdosta. You know what's there, right?"

"Wild Adventures. Are we *going* there?"

"Unless you're scared of roller coasters."

"Will you go on the Swamp Thing with me?"

"Anything you want, buddy. But if you ride with me in this car, you've gotta wear these sunglasses and this cap." Jay handed the items over to his son and snugged a red SCA ball cap over his own head.

Todd grinned, realizing there was a plan in place. He put on the gear.

"You ready?" Dad said.

"Okay."

Dad turned the key, and the car whined but didn't turn over.

"Is it the flywheel?" Todd asked.

"You know what a flywheel is?"

"Unless it's working right, you won't go anywhere."

"That's right. Hey, you're pretty smart. But no, we got that fixed."

Dad turned the key again, and the car rumbled to life, with the reliable old engine vibrating throughout the entire chassis.

"Awesome," Todd said.

"We have one stop along the way, just off Newton Road."

"Is it a surprise?"

"For you, no. But look in the glove box. See that envelope in there, with Mr. Herr's name on it? Yeah, for him it's gonna be a surprise. He sold me this car for a lot less than it was worth. I figure it's time to go pay him back and let him hear how this baby sounds. You think that's a good idea?"

Todd ran his hands over the envelope.

"Son?"

"Yeah," Todd said. "It's a *great* idea."

They pulled out onto Old Pretoria Road, passing beneath the dappled shade of pecan trees and live oaks. They wound down toward Mr. Herr's place and found themselves racing along a stretch of straight open road.

Dad raised both hands in the air, and Todd did the same. Jay retook the wheel, then let just one hand ride up and down on the wind currents alongside the TR3. Todd followed suit.

They both looked at each other and smiled.

Dad stepped on the gas.

Epilogue

FIFTEEN YEARS (AND ONE MONTH) LATER

TODD

It's Father's Day. I can't screw this up. Last month, I arrived without a gift for his fiftieth, and although he wouldn't hold that against me, I feel bad.

Where did things go wrong between us?

I don't know.

Sometimes life's not that simple, I guess. I wish it was.

There's a side of me that feels the need to explain everything to Dad, to work it out and understand every nuance of our relationship. I'm an artist. I create. I imagine. It's hard for me to sit by and pretend things don't exist—particularly when every part of my being wants to say otherwise.

My studio in Atlanta's starting to make ends meet, with

growing visibility in the community. Nana and Papa stood by me on my ribbon-cutting day a few years back. Mom made it, too, while Dad tagged along with Faith's basketball squad to a regional tournament in Orlando.

Maybe that was it. The turning point.

These thoughts are churning through my head when I pull into my parents' driveway in my Geo Prism. Not exactly a winner set of wheels from my dad's point of view. But hey, it gets me from here to there.

"Todd, honey." Mom hurries down the steps for a hug.

"Hey, buddy." Dad's waiting at the door, his graying hair even more obvious out here in the June sun.

Papa gets out from the passenger side. He and I came together. Nana went to be with the Lord last year, and neither he nor I have the energy to make the trip alone from Atlanta. We don't say much. We just enjoy being together. I've always felt that way around Papa. As for Nana . . .

Well, I miss her more than I care to think about.

"C'mon, guys, let's get inside. Got the A/C blowing."

We follow my dad's lead. He's got a good point. Things are heating up in Georgia, and soon we'll be sweating buckets between our jaunts from the A/C in the cars to the A/C in restaurants, banks, and offices. How they survived even a couple of decades ago, I have no idea.

In fact, I've done oil canvases on that very theme. My Impressionistic renderings. Imagine Ray Charles sitting on a slab of butter in a pool of emerald foliage and black swamp water. I think you get the idea.

"It's just you two for now," my mom informs Papa and me.

"Where's Faith?"

My kid sister, I find out, is on a youth group outing that's scheduled to return this afternoon. I hope I'll see her later. I'm afraid to see what she's done to my room, which she took over. But it's just a room. I can let it go.

"Happy Father's Day, Dad."

"Thanks," he says back.

"Twenty-four years of fatherhood. How's it feel?"

"How's it feel being twenty-four?"

We both chuckle. I follow him into the living room, where we sit and face his new wide-screen TV. Papa goes to use the restroom.

"I have a present for you."

"You better," he jokes. "I'm not just here for the cake."

"I, uh . . . You remember how on your birthday all I gave you was a card?"

"Hey, what're you supposed to buy dads? It's always tough. You wanna know the truth, Todd—I'm just glad you're here."

"Thanks. I still wanna show you this present before anyone else comes over."

"All right."

Mom walks in with a tray of iced tea and lemonade. "Take your pick."

"Mom, you rock. You always have."

"What's that in your hand, honey?"

"Mom."

"Sit down, Judy. He's about to show us."

We choose our drinks. Mom settles into the armchair across from us. My gaze goes back and forth between my parents, and I feel like a boy again.

This is awkward. Why, though? There's no good reason. Maybe it's that we are such different people. Or that I don't toe all the lines they would like. I'm still feeling my way past college and into the real world, I guess.

"Okay. This is my gift for you, Dad."

He accepts the package, wrapped in brown paper and tied with twine. He pulls at the paper as though peeling the rind from a newly discovered tropical fruit. He believes it could be incredible. Knows it could be fantastic.

He's just not *sure*.

In a moment of revelation, I see how that describes our relationship.

"It's a diary?" he ventures.

I nod. "Pretty close. As close as I could get, anyway."

Mom's eyes are twinkling in that motherly foreknowledge that mystifies men and also scares us just a little. She might not know the details, the concrete facts, but she knows the heart of the matter. She *knows*.

Dad pulls the clothbound book from the wrapping. Though the artwork is upside down from my angle, it doesn't matter much.

"It's a flywheel, isn't it?"

I nod.

"You gave it your own spin with your own colors, but that's a flywheel," he says. "No doubt about it. Hey, it even says *Flywheel*."

He lifts the book for Mom to see and traces the letters with his finger. They are silver, lost amid a fog of swirling blue and the hinted angles of meshing gears.

"Beautiful," Mom says.

Dad and I frown.

"In a masculine sort of way," she amends.

"Dad, at your fiftieth you were saying how you wanted me to write down our memories. Well, I thought about that. You remember our ride in the Triumph, that very first time?"

"Could never forget it."

"Me either. So I figured it was time to fulfill your wish, now that I can't use college term papers as an excuse."

"You've always been able to put words on paper," Mom says.

"I called around. Talked to some of the old gang. Max, he's slowing down but still sharp. Even got Bernie Myers to chat with me."

"Good ol' Bernie."

"I collected their thoughts, some of their quotes and anecdotes, then tried to write it all down the way I saw it. And the way you've told me it was for you."

The way what was?

Dad doesn't have to ask. Faith's too young to remember, of course, but we all know that period was huge in our lives, a crossroads for our family.

He opens the front cover. He pans his eyes down the title page, flips to the table of contents, then to the first line of the story. He nods his head and brings one hand to his mouth. He looks up at me.

"This is incredible, Todd. I, uh . . . I don't even know what to say."

His expression is enough.

"Thank you," he mouths.

"No, Dad, thank *you*. It was a very good thing for me," I tell him. "I needed to remember—you know, everything we've done together, the things you taught me. You've been a great father to me, and I'm sorry I get so wrapped up in my own world sometimes. Doing this, it's reminded me how important it is to get my priorities right, to walk with integrity, and not just live for myself. I've known Christ, but more recently I haven't really been living for Him like I should. Like you showed me. He hasn't been my Everything, and I want Him to be. I really want Him to be."

Dad puts his hand on my shoulder. With tears forming in his eyes, he looks at me and bows his head. He's prayed for me before, but this is different.

I shift uneasily, then decide not to fight this. Not this time.

His other hand comes up and rests on my head. I feel his warmth, his strength. He says, "Dear Lord, You alone know my son's heart. You know his desires, his talents. I commit him and his work to You this day. I pray that You'd bless him as he learns to honor You in everything he sets his hand to. Now, Lord, in Your name, I bless him with faith, creativity, and integrity. I call him a man of love and grace. This is my son."

I feel something breaking inside. I can't describe it.

Maybe there's no reason to.

I grip his hand on my shoulder and nod and give him a hug and tell him thank you—and that's that.

Mom's feet patter away, then come pattering back. She has that homemade laminated bookmark in her hand. It's a cutout from the old drawing I did when I was nine. It's so crude in style. Almost embarrassing. But the number 71 revealed my thoughts of her, and she's as sentimental about it as Dad.

"Here, Jay," she says. "You've got a bookmark for your reading."

He smiles.

Later that afternoon, after dinner and cake, Papa and I get ready to make the trip back to Atlanta. We step out into the wavering heat. We say farewells in the shade beneath the long porch. Mom, Dad, Faith . . .

"Happy Father's Day," I say one more time.

"Enjoy the weather on the way back," Dad says.

It sounds odd, but I think nothing of it until I reach my hand into my jeans pocket. My keys are gone.

"Looking for these?" Papa says. "I get to drive."

"Okay . . ."

"Here's *your* keys," Dad tells me. He holds up a set I haven't seen in years. "I'll help you with the garage door, but you'll have to do the steering part on your own."

"What?"

"It's yours, Todd. What better time to pass it on to my son than today."

"You're giving me the Triumph?"

Dad begins to laugh, reaching out his hand and pointing at my heart. "Let it constantly remind you that if you keep this part right, everything else falls into place."

Caught off guard, I stand in stunned silence.

He smiles and eggs me on. "I can just see it now. The local artist puttering down Peachtree Street in a classic car. You do know how to drive a stick, don't you?"

"Of course."

"So what's the problem?" He winks.

"No problem here."

"Just know, I'll be expecting a call one day from *your* son. The day you pick him from school and take *him* for a ride."

As I take hold of the keys, I can't help but smile.

If anyone is in Christ, he is a new creation;
the old has gone, the new has come!

—2 CORINTHIANS 5:17

Everyone who calls on the name
of the Lord will be saved.

—ROMANS 10:13

ACKNOWLEDGMENTS

From Alex Kendrick and Stephen Kendrick to:

Eric Wilson (writer)—You are a skilled writer and have made these stories leap off the page. We're grateful the Lord crossed our paths.

Christina and Jill (our wives)—Your patience and support for us have been wind in our sails! We love you dearly!

Joshua, Anna, Catherine, Joy, Caleb, Grant, Cohen, and Karis (our kids)—May you grow to know and follow God and His plan for you. He loves you, and so do we. Jesus is Lord!

Larry and Rhonwyn Kendrick (Dad and Mom)—Your encouragement and prayers are a reminder of God's love for us. We cherish you.

Michael Catt and Jim McBride (pastors)—We've learned from you and been blessed by you. This journey has been sweeter because you've walked with us.

Allen Arnold and Amanda Bostic (editors)—Thanks for believing in us! May God bless you for your investment.

Sherwood Baptist Church (home church)—If everyone had a church that lived what they believed, this world would be a different place! You're making a huge impact. Keep walking with Jesus!

ACKNOWLEDGMENTS

From Eric Wilson to:

Alex and Stephen Kendrick (screenwriters)—Getting to know you guys has been one of my most unexpected, recent blessings.

Allen Arnold and Amanda Bostic (editors)—If you keep opening doors, I'll keep walking through them. Thank you, thank you.

Carolyn, Cassie, and Jackie Wilson (wife and daughters)—Thanks for the new chair, constant love, and big smiles. I can't wait to see the braces come off.

For those who've blessed my family with cars over the years (you know who you are)—Without your generosity, we would've been walking.

Matt Bronleewe, River Jordan, Chris Well, and Steven Womack (Nashville-based novelists)—You understand. You get it. Thanks for the encouragement.

Matthew Champion, Rick Moore, and Sean Savacool (Nashville crew)—Our get-togethers are like water and oxygen to me. Thanks for your friendship.

Guaranty RV Centers (Junction City, OR)—The three years I worked there provided eye-opening experiences and great fodder for this story.

Bless the Fall, DecembeRadio, Plumb, Skillet, and Switchfoot (recording artists)—Your music rocked, soothed, and inspired me as I wrote. Keep it comin'.

Readers everywhere (yeah, you!)—You're the reason I keep doing this. I pray this book will help you come to recognize God as your Father. He is good.

A PERSONAL MESSAGE FROM THE KENDRICK BROTHERS

Thank you for reading *Flywheel*! We hope you thoroughly enjoyed Jay Austin's exciting journey. When *Flywheel* the movie was released in theaters and on DVD, the response was overwhelming to us. It was our first movie, and we did not know what to expect. Countless emails from all across the world poured in to tell us how the story influenced viewers personally. Used car salesmen said they were changing their manipulative ways. Men were recommitting to their marriages and families. A U.S. Senator shared how it influenced the ethics of his campaign positively. Prisoners wrote us letters about how they wept and made needed life-changing decisions. This was our blessed hope and reward!

With this in mind, we also want to boldly challenge you in your own spiritual journey. How will the story of *Flywheel* influence you? Will you allow the message of the story penetrate beyond the pages of this book?

If you do not have a relationship with Jesus Christ, we want you to know that He is the Real Deal. We're not talking about religion . . . but a *relationship* with Jesus. He alone has proven to be the missing Link to God that people are longing for . . . and desperately need. That *you* need.

His entire life demonstrates His uniqueness as God in flesh. His virgin birth, sinless life, powerful teachings, amazing miracles, unconditional love, sacrificial death, miraculous resurrection, and impact on the world all are unique to Jesus Christ alone. Try reading Matthew, Mark, Luke, and John in the Bible and see for yourself what those who were with Him witnessed firsthand. He not only is qualified to forgive your sin, but He can also change your heart and make it pleasing towards a holy God. It is foolish to trust in your own goodness to get into Heaven. Only God through Christ can make us clean.

The scriptures say that all of us have fallen short of God's righteousness (Romans 3). That's why He lovingly sent Jesus. His death on the cross was necessary to make things right between sinful people and a holy God. He didn't have to do that. That's just love in action . . . personified.

Regardless of where you are, let us encourage and challenge you, on behalf of Christ, to do what Jay Austin did, and surrender your heart afresh to God. Romans 10:9 says that if you confess with your mouth—Jesus as your Lord (Master or Boss), and you believe in your heart that God has raised Him from the dead, then you will be saved.

If you are already an obedient follower of Christ, then we want to encourage you further in your spiritual journey. We challenge you to let the faith and integrity that Christ brings influence your relationships, children, daily habits, and work environments. Do you model honesty and the golden rule in how you treat others? Have you dedicated your personal ethics and work environment to God? Are there people you need to get right with that you have wronged in the past? Don't wait any longer. Do it!

We encourage you to refocus your passions toward the higher purpose of glorifying God and not living for your own temporary fulfillment in this life. Start your days in the Word of God and in prayer. Pray that people will be "wowed" by the changes that Christ has made in you. And let your commitment be independent of others. People will fail you, reject you, and let you down. But don't be derailed or discouraged. Don't let anything or anyone cause you to stop loving Him. Find a group of believers at a local church that share this passion and that will join you in this great adventure! Then let's plan to rejoice together as we watch God glorify Himself through our lives and do more than we can ask or imagine!

May God bless you!

Alex Kendrick and Stephen Kendrick

FLYWHEEL BOOK DISCUSSION QUESTIONS

1. What did the flywheel represent in the story?

Answer: *Throughout the story, the TR3 convertible car paralleled the condition of Jay Austin's life. The flywheel specifically represented the CENTRAL part of Jay's life that affected all the others and desperately needed to be fixed. That area was LORDSHIP. When Jay Austin got the area of Lordship right and surrendered his life to Jesus Christ, the other areas of his life were then affected and were properly functioning. (Romans 10:9-10, Matthew 16:33)*

2. Was it enough in the beginning of the story that Jay Austin acknowledged that there was a God and attended church on occasion? Read: John 3:1–6, 16–18

Answer: *No. Jesus told Nicodemus, who was a very religious leader, that his religion was not enough, and he still "must be born again" to enter the* *kingdom of Heaven (John 3:1–16). James 2:19 says that the demons believe and tremble . . . but this is not enough. True fellowship and salvation goes beyond a religious belief or public action and leads us to full repentance and surrender in our hearts to Jesus Christ resulting in a living relationship with God. (John 17:3, 1 John 5:11,12, Romans 10:9)*

3. Could you relate to Jay Austin in the first half of the story? In what ways?

4. Why was Jay caught off guard during the minister's prayer after Jay had cheated him?

Answer: *He was afraid of God mistreating Jay the same way Jay had mistreated the minister. Jay's conscience and Galatians 6:7—Whatever a man sows, he will reap.*

5. At the beginning of *Flywheel*, what was Jay's attitude toward himself, his wife, his son, his parents, and his employees? How did each of his relationships change after he surrendered his heart to Christ?

Read: Matthew 22:36-40, 1 John 4:19–21

6. What was holding Jay back from surrendering his life to God in the first half of the story?

Answer: *His pride. He even admitted his problem with pride when he vented to Max. Read: Psalm 10:4, Proverbs 16:18*

7. What factors did God use to humble Jay Austin and cause him to surrender his life over to God?

Answers: *Multiple factors around Jay influenced him.*

- *The prayers of others: the minister, Jay's parents*
- *The influence of believers: his pastor, Max the mechanic*
- *The Word of God: from the sermons he heard in church and on TV*
- *The consequences of his sin:*

DEBT: "I owe money to the bank that I don't have."

CONFLICT: "I have conflict with almost every person in my life."

MISTRUST: "I don't want to be like my dad."—Todd's comment.

"So now you are ripping off ministers." —Judy's comment.

GUILT: Jay—"You grossly manipulated her." Bernie—"You taught me how!"

DEPRESSION: "I don't even like myself, Max"

ANGER: "You are going to shut up now. The next time you open your mouth it better be to eat."

What is God using in your life presently to cause you to seek Him?

8. How do you think Jay's visit from his dad impacted Jay? What motivated Jay to talk to his son Todd about being a better father?

Answer: *He received love and a blessing from his own earthly father and was ready to pass it on. How does this demonstrate John 15:9? In the Old Testament, God blessed Abraham and then Abraham went on to bless his children. This was passed from generation to generation. Ephesians 1:3 says that God blesses Christians with spiritual blessings. How can we pass on those blessings to others?*

9. How did Jay's perspective on his possessions and his money change after he surrendered his life to Christ?

Answer: *He gave his life to God, and then he gave ownership of his lot to God. He and Judy agreed that their money then belonged to the Lord and they were just stewards of it. It was because of this that they were liberated to give or tithe rather than hoard their resources.*

10. How did Jay pursue and guard having a clear conscience?

Answer: *By paying back those he had cheated. (Luke 19:1–9) By apologizing to God first and then to those he had wronged. By refusing to further lie or compromise when encouraged to do so.*

11. In what ways did Jay's life cause others to be in wonder of his commitment to God?

Answer: *After he apologized, Judy responded with, "Is something wrong with you?" "You are serious!"*

The undercover reporter said, "It was a lot different than I thought working here. I thought you would be more devious."

The truck driver remarked, "So you are just giving me a thousand dollars, no questions asked? Why would you do that?"

The banker's questions, "Where are the cars? You sold them? How?"

When Katie Harris said, "Jay Austin came to my house and paid me back $1200 dollars," the reporter responded with, "He what?"

Is your faith lived out in such a way that the world is in wonder of your commitment to God?

12. How did you see the hand of God working to fight for Jay at the end of the strory? Why do you think God did answer his prayers and fight for him?

How was 2 Corinthians 5:17 demonstrated in the life of Jay Austin? It says, "Therefore, if anyone is in Christ, he is a new creation; old things have passed away, behold, all things have become new."

How was Matthew 6:33 demonstrated in Jay's business? "Seek first the kingdom of God and His righteousness and all these things will be added unto you."

13. What areas of Jay's life were affected after he surrendered to Jesus Christ?

Answer: *Every area: his personal relationship with God, his relationship with his wife, his son, his father, his employees, and how he was viewed in the community.*

14. When Jay said, "You're the Boss. You're in charge now." What do you think he meant?

How does this demonstrate what LORDSHIP is all about? (Romans 10:9)

15. Has there ever been a time when you came to a point of total surrender to God?

What is holding you back from completely surrendering yourself to Christ right now?

16. What do you think God wants you to do as a response to reading *Flywheel*? What new commitments or decisions do you need to make? Will you, like Jay Austin, humble yourself and surrender all that you are and all that you have to Jesus Christ?

THE MAKING OF *FLYWHEEL* THE MOVIE

BY ALEX KENDRICK

After reading a national survey in 2002 that said movies were among the most influential factors in our culture today, I asked God for a plot and an opportunity to make a feature film to reach our community. Our pastor, Michael Catt, said that he was open to the idea if we would "pray the money in" since our church budget could not support the venture. Several members of Sherwood Baptist Church in Albany, Georgia, joined the prayer, and soon donations poured in to reach our $20,000 budget.

We purchased one camera and a few lights from Home Depot. Our technical volunteers built a boom mic, track dolly, and camera crane from scratch, then we asked our members who were interested in drama to fill the roles.

My brother, Stephen, helped me write the script for *Flywheel*, and we bathed it in prayer as we began shooting the movie at locations owned by church members. Sunday School classes provided the meals, and after thirty days of shooting, we had the footage to assemble the story.

After two months of editing, scoring, and a number of technical mistakes, we finished the movie the morning of its premiere at our local theater (who agreed to show it for one week and split the proceeds). We rushed the DVD over to the theater, and were astounded when the evening show sold out. The local media covered the event as a news story, and soon thousands of locals bought tickets to see this hometown feature.

What was supposed to be a one week stay, ended up as a six week run, becoming the theater's second highest grossing movie of their sixteen screens. Two more theaters were added in nearby cities as hundreds of emails and phone calls poured in from viewers who were impacted by the story.

Although our initial vision had become reality, God had only begun His work. We were once again shocked when Blockbuster Video added the DVD to their 4,200 stores, and seven different Christian television networks agreed to show it. DVD sales went through the roof, and soon over 100,000 units were sold.

Testimonies came in from men who had rededicated their businesses, returned money to those they had cheated, and given up addictions that had crippled their walks with God. Numerous viewers had accepted Christ as Lord and Savior, and many had renewed their marriage vows.

God took our small production and used it far more than we ever intended or dreamed. We were humbled and stunned at what He could do when a body of believers unify in prayer and work for God's glory.

The following year, our second movie was produced called *Facing the Giants*. That movie has an amazing story all its own, and once again God amazed us with doors that only He could have opened.

Today, our third movie, *Fireproof*, has been produced. And we look forward with anticipation at what the Lord will do. He is still in the business of doing the impossible and changing lives. May He get all the glory!

1. Makeup—Associate Producer and actress Lisa Arnold helps Alex Kendrick with makeup.

2. Christopher Rudolph operates a homemade boom mic.

3. First Shot—Director/ Writer/ Actor Alex Kendrick plays Jay Austin in the first shot of the movie.

1. Tracy and Alex Set a Shot—Alex Kendrick and Tracy Goode prepare to shoot a scene in the office.

2. Directing the Boys—Alex directs Richie Hunnewell and Janzen Barnes.

3. Shooting the Boys—The small Sherwood crew shoots a living room scene.

5. At the Office—Tracy shoots Alex at his desk.

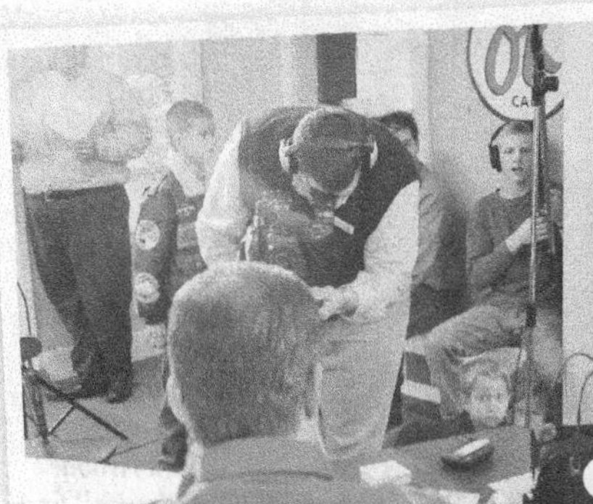

4. Shooting from the Tub—Associate Producer/ Actor Tracy Goode shoots a scene from the bathtub.

6. Kendrick Brothers—Associate Producer/ Writer Stephen Kendrick makes a call between shots as Alex preps a scene.

1. Alex Kendrick Directs—Alex works with Tracy on a shot.

2. Tracy Shoots Alex—Tracy Goode operates the camera as Alex plays Jay Austin.

3. Walter Burnett plays Max Kendall the mechanic.

4. Walter Burnett and Alex Kendrick next to the Triumph TR3—the classic car used in Flywheel *the movie.*

5. Flywheel *Crew—the hardworking crew of Sherwood Pictures' first movie.*

ALSO AVAILABLE

ABOUT THE AUTHORS

ALEX KENDRICK and STEPHEN KENDRICK helped Sherwood Baptist establish Sherwood Pictures in 2003. They have co-written *Flywheel*, *Facing the Giants*, *Fireproof*, and the upcoming film *Courageous*. Both live in Albany, Georgia, and serve in leadership positions at the Sherwood Baptist Church; Alex is associate minister, and Stephen is associate teaching pastor.

ERIC WILSON is the *New York Times* best-selling writer of *Fireproof*, the novelization, as well as the novelizations of *Flywheel* and *Facing the Giants*. He lives in Nashville, Tennessee, with his wife and two daughters.